Prai
Happily Never After

"A giggle-inducing romp that readers won't be able to object to."
—Lana Ferguson, *USA Today* bestselling author of
The Fake Mate

"*Happily Never After* takes an irresistibly fun concept and expertly delivers on its promise, brimming with hilariously cheeky banter and so-red-hot-it'll-make-you-sweat chemistry between its lovable lead characters. Lynn Painter has a true gift for crafting wildly entertaining rom-coms, and this is her best one yet."
—Nicolas DiDomizio, author of *Nearlywed*

"Lynn Painter writes the rom-com banter of my dreams! *Happily Never After* is a sparkling, hilarious, sexy romance that leaps off the page and is just begging to be made into a movie."
—Sarah Adams, *New York Times* bestselling author of
The Rule Book

"Well crafted and filled to the brim with sexual tension, *Happily Never After* is rom-com gold! We fell head over heels for the romance and the undeniably swoony chemistry. Max and Sophie are two characters so perfect for each other that you can't help but want to smoosh them together."
—*New York Times* bestselling authors Krista & Becca Ritchie

"A rom-com for the cynics. . . . The supporting cast is equally funny and helps to round out an entertaining yarn that doesn't take itself too seriously." —*Library Journal*

Praise for

The Love Wager

"Painter follows up *Mr. Wrong Number* with an equally cute friends to lovers romance. . . . Their equally filthy sense of humor makes their connection feel real and their game of constant one-upmanship is a lot of fun. Painter's fans won't be disappointed." —*Publishers Weekly*

"A fun, flirty, and timely read from Painter . . . with likable characters to boot." —*Library Journal*

"Honestly, this book was so much fun and I can't believe it took me this long to finally pick Lynn Painter. Her books are a hoot." —Culturess

"Lynn Painter . . . provides the perfect rom-com escape in *The Love Wager*, a trope-driven romance that will remind readers, as they laugh themselves to tears, why they love the genre." —Shelf Awareness

Praise for

Mr. Wrong Number

"Smart, sexy, and downright hilarious. *Mr. Wrong Number* is an absolutely pitch-perfect romantic comedy."
—Christina Lauren, *New York Times* bestselling author of
Tangled Up in You

"This book is an absolute blast, a classic rom-com setup with a modern twist. Lynn Painter's clever, charming voice sparkles on every page."
—Rachel Lynn Solomon, *USA Today* bestselling author of
Business or Pleasure

"The most sidesplittingly funny, shenanigan-packed, sexual tension–filled book I've read in a long, long time. I dare you not to fall in love with Olivia and Colin, but most of all I dare you not to fall in love with Lynn Painter's writing!"
—Ali Hazelwood, #1 *New York Times* bestselling author of
Bride

"If you like your romances steamy, then *Mr. Wrong Number* by Lynn Painter is sure to leave you hot and bothered in a good way."
—PopSugar

Accidentally

Amy

Lynn Painter

Berkley Romance
New York

BERKLEY ROMANCE
Published by Berkley
An imprint of Penguin Random House LLC
penguinrandomhouse.com

Book design by Ashley Tucker
Title page art by Vikivector/Shutterstock

Library of Congress Cataloging-in-Publication Data

Names: Painter, Lynn, author.
Title: Accidentally Amy / Lynn Painter.
Description: First edition. | New York: Berkley Romance, 2025.
Identifiers: LCCN 2024017693 (print) | LCCN 2024017694 (ebook) |
ISBN 9780593817087 (trade paperback) | ISBN 9780593817094 (ebook)
Subjects: LCGFT: Romance fiction. | Novels.
Classification: LCC PS3616.A337846 A64 2025 (print) |
LCC PS3616.A337846 (ebook) | DDC 813/.6—dc23/eng/20240422
LC record available at https://lccn.loc.gov/2024017693
LC ebook record available at https://lccn.loc.gov/2024017694

Accidentally Amy was originally self-published, in different form, in 2022.

First Berkley Romance Edition: January 2025

Printed in the United States of America
1st Printing

For Kevin:
In addition to the lifetime of
things I need to thank you for,
thank you for this book idea

Author's Note

This book was never meant to be a book.

Accidentally Amy began as a serial, as my way of trying to give newsletter subscribers *something* for being kind enough to allow me to drop into their inboxes. Every month(ish), I sent out a new chapter of Izzy and Blake's rom-com. It was the most fun I've ever had writing because it was like a choose-your-own adventure (for me). When I sat down to write new sections, I had no idea where the characters were headed or what they were going to do; I simply snuck along on their shenanigans and enjoyed the ride.

Once the serial concluded, I self-published the "manuscript" to make it available in book form for the subscribers who'd requested it. But, friend—it has *nagged* at me. I've always wanted to go back to those speedily drafted chapters and change up a few things, so when Berkley offered to publish it, I was OVER-JOYED to finally have that chance!

Please enjoy this updated version of my former serial, now with ten thousand(ish) new words, a different POV, new characters, no typos (hopefully), and a lot more Blake and Izzy.

Happy reading!

Accidentally Amy

Chapter One

Izzy

"Amy?"

I sighed impatiently and watched as the barista yelled out the name (not mine), then set down the cup. I could see it was a large pumpkin spice latte, the same drink I'd ordered, and I found myself wildly jealous of Amy, whoever she might be.

Because I wanted—no, needed—to get my drink and get the hell out of there.

Please yell Izzy next. Please yell Izzy next.

If I were a responsible adult, I would've seen the long line at Scooter's Coffee and opted not to get a coffee that morning. But it was the first day of the pumpkin spice latte, so my annual vice refused to be denied, regardless of the fact that I was starting a new job in T minus thirty minutes.

Yes, I was taking quite the moronic risk.

My new employer, Ellis Enterprises, was a big tech company with a reputation for being environmentally conscious and employee-friendly. They had workout facilities, a childcare center, a free cafeteria, and a 4:00 p.m. daily happy hour; Ellis was renowned for being a great place to work.

Which meant that I was definitely going to punch myself in the face if my lack of self-discipline made me late on the very first day.

"Amy?" The barista said it again, and I looked around the busy coffee shop. There was a group of women at a big table on the other side of the café, all dressed in athletic clothes and looking like barre fitness models; perhaps one of *them* was Amy.

I felt like Amy was quickly becoming my nemesis.

Come get your coffee, Amy, you lucky son of a bitch.

I glanced down at my watch and stifled a groan. *Shit, shit, shit.* If they didn't call my name in the next three minutes—and they probably wouldn't, because there were a *lot* of empty cups sitting in front of the espresso machine—I was going to have to kiss that overpriced drink goodbye and abort the mission.

"Amy!" The barista said it again, sounding agitated this time, and before I had time to think, I heard myself mutter—

"I'm Amy."

And . . . I reached out and grabbed the cup.

I knew it was wrong, I really did, but I needed to go and I needed that drink and I'd already paid, so it wasn't really stealing, right? And obviously *Amy* was in no hurry whatsoever. She'd probably changed her mind and had already left the building. Surely that was a possibility.

Right?

I put my palm over the name Amy, closed my fingers around the cup, and turned, ready to sprint out of the shop before some

Scooter's security officer tackled me to the ground for my egregious latte thievery, or Amy herself appeared before me.

But then I rammed right into a wall.

"Gah!" *Oh, my God.* It wasn't a wall at all, but a rock-hard chest, encased in a starched white dress shirt and a charcoal tie. I stared in horror as my cup crushed on impact, the lid popped off, and hot pumpkin coffee splurted all over the chest. "I'm so sorry!"

I looked up and—*whoa.*

You know how in movies everything can freeze when a character sees the Big Thing? Well, that was happening to me as I made eye contact with Mr. Chest. He was looking down at me with dark eyes, really intense dark eyes that weren't so much brown as they were the richest shade of burnt amber. His eyebrows were black, his hair was black, his perfectly maintained scruff was black, and even his suit was black, which all worked together to form some sort of contrasting frame for his face's gorgeous bone structure and perfectly shaped mouth.

He was like Roy Kent's taller American brother or something, and I didn't think I was physically capable of closing my mouth at that moment.

Until I felt the hot coffee seeping into my own shirt.

That made the moment unfreeze itself. I muttered another charming, "*Gahhhh,*" tossed my crumpled cup (RIP latte) into the trash can, and grabbed a stack of napkins from the end of the counter.

"I can't believe I ran right into you," I babbled, rubbing the clump of napkins over his shirt with one hand while I dabbed at my own (thank God it was black) with the other. I was kind of

mashing the napkins against the man's chest, patting and dab-
bing and trying to do anything to make the huge splotch of coffee disappear. "One minute I was grabbing my drink, the next I
was ramming your chest with boiling latte. I'm not even sure—"

"It's fine." His voice was dark, too, rich and baritone and a
little bit raspy. I glanced up, and he was giving me a half smile,
like he was entertained by the impromptu pectoral rubdown,
and something about that look hit me square in the gut. He
said, "I hated this shirt anyway."

I dropped my hands and said, "I did, too, but I didn't know
how to tell you. Hence the pumpkin spice latte."

He gave a little laugh. "Subtle, but effective."

I set the napkins on the bar top beside us and bit down on
my lower lip to stop myself from grinning. *Because I should feel
bad about scalding the man, right? Smiling is not the appropriate
reaction here, correct?* I cleared my throat and said, "I really *am*
sorry. I'd be happy to get it dry-cleaned for you or something . . . ?
A better person would offer to replace it, but I have a feeling it's
out of my price range."

He did the half-bark, half-laugh sound again that I could
feel in my toes, and he said, "What makes you say that?"

"It's soaking wet and I still can't see through it. That has to
mean it's quality."

"Were you trying to?" he asked.

"What—see through your shirt?"

He gave a nod.

I shrugged. "I wasn't trying, per se, but I *am* a curious girl.
I'd be lying if I said I wasn't checking for a third nipple."

He didn't say anything for a minute, still sort of smiling but now with a tiny wrinkle between his brows, and I knew my cheeks were turning red. *Did you really just say* third nipple, *you dumbass?* Sometimes I wondered why it was so difficult for me to just keep my mouth shut.

He cleared his throat and said, "I promise there isn't one, not that there's anything wrong with having three."

I *did* grin then. "I mean, the more the merrier, right?"

His mouth split into a slow, wide smile that was oddly powerful. It was almost like I *felt* it pass over me, like hot summer sun warming cool skin. "Are we sure that applies here?"

"Definitely not, but I couldn't let a moment pass without speaking," I said.

"I can see that about you."

"Hey," I said with a dose of fake offense, "just because I scalded your chest doesn't mean you can insult me."

"I feel like it actually *does* mean that."

"Fair." I nodded in agreement and said, "I'll even give you one more. Go."

"This seems like a trap."

"Do it," I said, crossing my arms and wondering if he felt it, too, this delicious bit of chemistry. "Go. Slam me, bro."

His eyes crinkled at the edges when he looked at me, like he was amused by the fact that someone would dare to call him *bro*, and he said, "Fine. I'm shocked you can see out of those glasses—they're very dirty."

"Oh, my God," I said around a laugh, "you *actually* insulted me."

"You told me to," he said, then he gestured with his hand— very big, not that I noticed—for me to give him my glasses.

"No." I knew my eyebrows were all screwed together as I shook my head. "*No*. Seriously?"

"Come on."

"Okay," I relented, laughing at the ridiculousness as I removed my glasses and handed them to the guy. "Here you go."

He reached into the inside pocket of his suit jacket—*very nice suit, by the way*—and pulled out a microfiber cloth. He looked down at my glasses (which were always dirty) as he buffed the lenses, and I wondered what in God's name was actually happening.

Was this *GQ* model seriously cleaning the filth off my spectacles? I said, "They're usually not—"

"Yes, I think they probably are," he teased, without looking up.

"Yeah, they usually are," I agreed as he handed them back. I slid them up the bridge of my nose, tilted my head, and said, "Oh, wow, you're a man."

For a split second he blessed me with a grin that acknowledged my stupid joke, but then . . . *then*. The grin was gone, and all that was left behind was this wildly potent, one-hundred-proof, undiluted expression of interest as he gave me full-on eye contact. *With a jaw flex*. The moment held, and I felt like I was being physically pulled closer to the guy. The entire world went quiet as an invisible string tugged me toward him.

"Blake!"

Both our heads whipped toward the barista, and I might've audibly gasped at the interruption, but I couldn't be sure.

"Um, that's me," he said, his eyes narrowing on me for a split second—like he was thinking something *about me*—before he pointed and leaned forward to reach around me for his cup. The faint smell of cologne hit me as he grabbed his coffee, a subtle scent that was crisp and somehow woodsy, and I had the inexplicable urge to nuzzle his throat.

Get it together, dipshit. Be cool.

He leaned down so I could hear him over the noise of the crowded coffee shop, and his deep voice found my ear with, "Do you want to grab a table—"

"Oh, no—what time is it?" The word *table* jolted me into real life and damn it, I was screwing up. *Damn it, damn it, damn it.* He might've said the time, I don't know, but I was too busy pulling my phone out of my pocket to hear him. I looked at the display, panic surging through me, and I muttered, "Oh, my God, I'm late, I have to go."

He was still watching me with that look on his face as I fished my keys out of my pocket, and I knew I needed to say *something* before sprinting to my car like a lunatic.

"I come here every morning around seven forty-five, so if you want to be reimbursed for the dry cleaning or say hello and eat a cake bite or, um, anything else," I rambled, "I'll be here tomorrow."

"Okay—"

"Gotta run—nice meeting you!" I bolted for the exit, literally jogging around tables in my three-inch patent leather pumps. And as I pulled open the door, I heard that butterfly-inducing voice say from behind me—

"I guess I'll see you tomorrow, then, Amy."

Amy?

Oh, no.

Chapter Two

Izzy

I hitched the tote bag over my shoulder and headed for the elevators, feeling downright giddy over the way my first day was going so far. I'd spent all morning with my team, shadowing the HR generalist whose position I was filling, and it'd been—no joke—fun.

Seriously.

Everyone in the department seemed to get along, the work appeared to be challenging but not too stressful, and I actually had an (incredibly small) office with my name on the door.

And yes, I had already taken multiple photos.

In addition to that little nugget of fantasticality, Incite Fitness—the city's hottest health club—was located on the twelfth floor of the building next door, and Ellis employees were able to use it for free. *For. Free.* So I'd just run three miles on the treadmill, showered, and brushed my teeth, which left me more than ready for part two of my amazing day.

As I walked down the hall, the elevator doors started to close.

"Wait!" I yelled, just in case someone was listening and wanted to be nice. I expected nothing, so when a hand reached out and stopped the doors, I very nearly squealed with delight.

Could the day *get* any better?

"Thank you," I sang as I ran over and hopped into the elevator.

"No problem," the person inside said. "What fl—"

"Oh. My. God." I stared at the guy and couldn't believe my eyes. It was Mr. Chest from Scooter's. In *my* elevator. I think my mouth was once again hanging open in his presence as I breathlessly managed to form the words "It's *you*."

He was still wearing his fancy suit, but the tips of his hair were wet, like he'd just showered, and I could smell his soap. He looked just as surprised to see me as I was to see him, but then his mouth turned up into one of those toe-curling, genuinely happy smiles that always bumped an exceptionally handsome man right up to a work of art. He said in that ridiculously deep voice, "Talk about your small world."

The elevator doors slid closed, and he gestured with his thumb to the floor buttons.

"Oh. Yeah. Lobby, please," I said, even though I was so shocked I could barely remember how to language. All morning, I'd been forcing myself *not* to think about Mr. Chest, because not only did I need to focus on the new job, but also there was no way in hell a Scooter's meet-cute would ever pan out into something real.

But now, here he was.

Dun-dun-duuuun.

"So, um," he said. "Do you work around here, or do you belong to this gym?"

"I was working out because—" I started, but then he nodded and cut me off.

"Okay, I don't normally do this sort of thing, but someone's going to get on this elevator any minute now, so I have to talk fast."

His expression was purposeful and intense, but his mouth was relaxed, like he was enjoying our encounter. I watched the numbers light up on the display over the doors as we descended.

Eleven, ten, nine . . .

Please don't stop, please don't stop.

"I know we're strangers," he said, his eyes so focused on me that I fought the urge to fix my hair or fidget with my lip gloss. "But—"

Eight, seven, six . . .

Talk faster before someone gets on!

"I can't stop thinking about—"

Five, four, three . . .

I reached out and hit the emergency button behind him.

The elevator car jolted to a halt, which made Mr. Chest stop talking as I stumbled closer to him. *Did I really just do that?* I watched his eyes narrow a fraction, and a wrinkle appeared between his brows.

"No, no—I'm not stopping for creepy reasons," I said quickly, shaking my head and putting up my hands. "This isn't a bunny-boiling, *Silence of the Lambs* situation, where I'm trying to have my way with you in an elevator or something. It's just that I—"

"*Fatal Attraction*," he interrupted.

"What?"

"The bunny boiling was in *Fatal Attraction*," he repeated, and the wrinkle of concern disappeared as his mouth twitched.

"Oh, right," I agreed with a nod. "Well, this isn't that situation, either. I just really want to hear what you have to say without reaching the ground floor first. That's all this little stoppage is about, I promise."

"What I have to say . . ." He stepped a little closer, but not in an intimidating way. It was more . . . intimate. It reminded me of the way Darcy said, *Mr. Wickham?* and stepped closer to Elizabeth during his rain proposal in the hand-flex version of *Pride and Prejudice*. I kind of wondered if I was going to faint dead away for the first time in my life as he put his hands in the pockets of his suit pants and said, "Is— I have meetings all afternoon, but can I please call you later?"

Yes, yes, a thousand times yes.

"On the telephone?" I said. "Like a psycho?"

"Well, I'm shit with emojis," he said, looking half-serious and a little boyish.

"Send a lot of accidental eggplants?"

"No," he said with a laugh.

"Use the same tired cry-laughing smiley for everything, like a total wank?"

"Is that a wank thing to do?"

"Absolutely, it is."

"Well, then, um, yes." His eyes were on mine as he said, "But honestly, all wankiness aside—"

"Wankitude," I corrected. "Or is it wankery? Wanktasticality?"

"Wankiness," he repeated, shutting down my babbles. "All wankiness aside, I rather like hearing the voice of the person I'm talking to."

I felt like I needed garlic or some type of dagger I could plunge into Mr. Chest's chest as protection, because statements like that were a straight-up assault on my ovaries. He *rather liked* hearing the person's voice?

Just take my heart now, you gorgeous wanker.

"I'll give you my number," I said, trying not to seem too eager. "But I make no promises on the whole phone call thing. I fear I may start mashing the numerical keypad and shouting emoji names at random out of confusion."

"Eggplant, eggplant?" he said with an absolute straight face.

"Our conversation will have to take a pretty wild turn for that to be my emoji-shout of choice, but you never know." I looked down at his shirt. "Do you have a closet full of fresh shirts at your office, or did you have to go home after I drizzled your Calvin Klein?"

"I ran home."

I still felt bad about that. "Please tell me you live close to Scooter's."

"You seem pretty interested in my personal information," he said, his eyes getting a teasing glint that made me want to ruffle his hair. "You sure you're not a bunny boiler?"

I tilted my head and wondered if he had pets. "Do you *have* a bunny?"

An eyebrow went up. "Why do you want to know?"

"I'm fascinated by the pets people keep," I admitted, my eyes wandering all over his face. "And if you told me you had a bunny, I think I'd find you to be the most interesting man in this elevator."

He smiled a little more, and his dimples popped.

Fucking dimples.

I'm going to need that dagger stat.

He said, "Words cannot express how much I regret to inform you that I am not one in possession of a rabbit."

I bit down on my lower lip to hold in the laugh, worried my interest in him was as subtle as a neon Times Square billboard. "It *is* tragic, but perhaps you might consider adopting one . . . ?"

He leaned a little closer, and just like that, there was white-hot electricity in the elevator. Our faces were close, and I was very aware all of a sudden that we were alone in a stopped elevator car. My oxygen was now his freshly showered scent, and I wanted to breathe it in until I hyperventilated. His voice was quieter and seemed a bit huskier when he said, "If I didn't already have a cat, I'd be begging you to go with me to the shelter and pick out a bunny this very minute."

"You have . . . a cat?" I asked in a near whisper, defeated with the realization that even a dagger through the heart couldn't protect me if Mr. Chest was a cat guy.

"I have two," he said, and then he grinned.

A dirty grin.

He *knew.* Somehow he knew he was killing me and my lady parts with his feline affiliations.

"You're the worst," I said, no longer able to hold in the smile.

"I'm gonna need that number," he replied, pulling out his phone. "Stat."

"Well, stat *is* very serious business." I'd barely gotten out all ten of my digits when the call button in the elevator car started ringing.

"We should probably turn this thing back on before the authorities arrive," he said, his jaw clenching and unclenching in a way that made me want to watch for hours.

"Yeah," I agreed, taking a step away from him and touching my lips. "I don't want to have to answer that call."

"Afraid of panicking and screaming, *evil smile*?" he asked as he depressed the emergency stop button.

"Among other things, yes." The elevator car lurched and started moving, and as I watched the number display start counting down again, I wondered what he'd do if I reached around him and pressed it yet again.

I mean, I would *never*, but it was definitely a tempting fantasy.

Chapter Three

Blake

I hit send on an email and glanced at my watch for the tenth time that hour. It was five fifteen, I'd just finished my last meeting, and I still needed to wrap up a few things before I could take off for the night. I usually worked later than this, because I accomplished a great deal more when I was the only one in the office, but I hadn't been able to focus since running into the Scooter's girl in the elevator during lunch.

What were the odds?

The last thing in the world that I was looking for was a relationship, even a casual one. Skye and I called off our engagement months ago, yet the residual ick had me determined to stay single for a long-ass time.

Forever sounded pretty fucking awesome to me at that point.

But there was just something about the Scooter's girl. *Amy.* After so much dishonesty with Skye, so many little white lies that piled up as teasers to her Big-Ass Lie, it was refreshing to be

around someone who seemed so open. I'd only met her for a total of five minutes, so technically I didn't know dick about her,
but compared to my just-let-me-explain former fiancée, she
felt . . . real.

I hated small talk—and most people—in general, yet talking to her had been *fun*. After we'd gone our separate ways in
front of the Incite building, I'd sent her a quick text, just so she
had my number.

Testing 1-2-3.

She'd responded immediately. NOW who's the bunny boiler?
I JUST left the building and you're already texting. Obsessed
much, Joe Goldberg?

I'd stopped walking to send: Did I mention that one of my
cats is blind?

Because the look that had crossed her face in the elevator
when I said I had a cat was fucking golden.

She replied, You are a menace, Mr. Chest, and I should probably block you for that sort of filth. Also, on a random side note,
when you call tonight, make sure you have the kitties nearby so
I can hear their little meows.

Damn it if I wasn't really looking forward to calling her.

Fucking lunacy, that.

"Knock, knock."

I looked up and Pam Carson, the HR manager, was leaning
into my office.

"Hey, Pam," I said, giving her a smile even though all I
wanted was for her to go away.

"Hey." She smiled back and said, "Listen, Isabella Shay, our new generalist, started today, and I just wanted to introduce you before she goes home. If you have a second."

"Sure," I said, even though I had no interest in meeting her new employee.

It wasn't that I was uncaring, but Pam—and the entire HR department—ran like a well-oiled machine. Technically, on the org chart, they were part of my team, but unless something unusual was going on, the HR director handled everything and I had very little contact with the group.

Except when Pam showed up at my door every few months to introduce me to a new hire.

"Isabella, this is Blake Phillips."

Pam stepped sideways in the doorway, and a brunette smiled and raised her hand in a casual wave. I opened my mouth to say, *Nice to meet you*, but the girl standing just outside my office looked exactly like—*no, holy shit, it was*—Scooter's Amy.

What in the actual hell?

Izzy

"You have *got* to be kidding." I knew I was beaming like a toddler looking at an ice-cream cone, but what else could I do except grin? Fate was literally throwing this man at me. This big, gorgeous, charming man. I said, "You *again*?"

"This is getting ridiculous." Mr. Chest looked super important, sitting behind the huge desk in the huge office. He was smiling at me, but that wrinkle was back between his eyebrows.

"Do you two know each other?" Pam asked, swinging her

gaze back and forth between us like nothing had ever been more interesting.

"I spilled coffee all over this guy at Scooter's this morning." *And also gave him my number.* "It's a shockingly small world."

Mr. Chest leaned back a little in his chair and crossed his arms, looking every inch the executive. A very expensive-looking watch peeked out from under his right cuff, and I think I was distracted by it because I didn't quite get it when he said, "Pam called you Isabella."

"Yes . . . ?" *Is it an actual Rolex?*

"So I thought you said your name was Amy."

"Oh." *Oh, noooo.* I'd been so locked in on the prettiness of his face and the shine of his watch that I'd forgotten all about the stolen coffee. My face was instantly hot as I stammered, "Oh, uh, yeah. Um."

He asked, "Is Amy your middle name?"

I suddenly felt like I was on trial. He looked like a stern prosecutor—*hot thought to be revisited later*—and Pam was like a juror, quietly watching the cross-examination. I opened my mouth and was about to snatch up his middle name excuse like the liar I'd apparently become, when Pam said, "No, her middle name is Clarence. Right, Izzy? Isn't that what you told me when you filled out the I-9 form?"

God, why? Why did I ramble nervously to my new boss about my stupid middle name?

Pam laughed and said to Blake, "I think she said it was her grandfather's name. Isabella Clarence—can you imagine?"

I rubbed my lips together for a second—*shit, shit, shit*—

before confessing, "Amy isn't actually my name at all. It's, uh, kind of a funny story."

Blake's head tilted just the tiniest bit.

I said, "Let me explain."

Pam kept smiling, looking at me like she was waiting for a hilarious tale, but Blake was doing that jaw-clench thing and absolutely not smiling anymore.

He kind of looked pissed.

He kind of looked like the twin brother of the charming man I'd flirted with in the elevator. He was now Bloke, Hot Blake's grumpy twin brother.

"Okay, so, I was running a little behind and didn't want to be late for my first day at Ellis. I paid for my drink, but the line was super long. Like, so long that I was going to have to bail before I even got my coffee, right?"

Pam was still into it, listening in amused anticipation, but Blake just looked impatient, like he wanted me to shut the hell up.

Hard same, Bloke.

I looked down at my feet and just let the admission fly. "So after they called for Amy three times and no one came for the drink, I, um, I might've said that I was Amy."

"You did *not*," Pam said, full on laughing.

I tried giving Blake an adorably playful smile. "It didn't pay off, though, because I ended up spilling the drink all over Blake here."

"Um." He cleared his throat, clearly unmoved by my attempt at adorability. "Are you saying that you took someone else's drink?"

That reminded me of the *you took someone's reservation?* bit in the movie *Date Night*, but I needed to keep that thought to myself and focus on the task at hand.

The task that was apparently . . . well, not looking like a thief at my new job.

"I mean," I started, trying to make him understand. "I *paid* and we ordered the same thing, so—"

"So does that make it *not* her drink, then?" He looked at me like I'd just confessed to beheading a puppy. "Amy's drink is fair game for anyone who prepaid for the same order, is that what you're saying?"

I glanced at Pam, who looked suddenly uncomfortable with the exchange, and said, "It was a very uncool thing to do, I know."

"I don't know about uncool," Bloke said, his eyes pinning me in place like he was the hawk and I was the mouse he found too annoying to eat, so he just wanted to play with me until I was dead. "But it was definitely dishonest."

"So very, very dishonest." I gritted my teeth and tried to stay calm, because I wanted this job more than I wanted to tell off the ultrahot, über-judgmental asshole. But what a *jerk*. I crossed my arms over my chest, breathed in through my nose, and said, "You have no idea, at this moment, how much I regret every single thing that transpired today in relation to that dishonest cup of coffee. If I could go back and undo all of it, every single moment, I absolutely would."

His eyes stayed on me, unwavering, and his expression was unreadable.

But I knew that he knew what I was saying.

"I'm going to take off and let you get back to work," I said, lifting my lips so the baring of my teeth looked like a smile. "It was very nice meeting you."

He raised an eyebrow. "Was it?"

"Of course," I said, coughing out a little laugh and smiling at Pam to make sure she knew that everything was fine. But the second Pam looked away from me, I couldn't stop myself. I was so disappointed in the lost possibilities of Mr. Chest that I gave Blake a tiny headshake and mouthed the word *nope*.

Which made his jaw clench and his eyes narrow.

Which made me feel like I'd scored some sort of point.

"We'll get out of your hair now, Blake," Pam tittered, and I let her lead me away from the office and out to the elevators. My heart was racing and my brain was scrambling as I tried to determine how screwed I was in regard to my new job.

I mean, I worked on a different floor from Bloke, so that was good. And he didn't seem like someone prone to office gossip (mostly because he came across as an arrogant jackass who didn't have time for other people), so hopefully no one else in the company would ever learn of my latte pilferage.

Technically, all that had happened was I earned the disapproval of some random Ellis employee who worked upstairs. As long as Pam didn't have an issue with my atrocities, I'd probably be okay.

But as we waited for the elevator, she said the very worst thing possible.

"I know Blake can seem a little intimidating," she said, smiling as she looked up at the number display above the elevators. "But that's just because he's very focused. He's actually a really nice guy once you get to know him."

"Could've fooled me," I muttered, relieved she didn't seem upset about the awkward interaction with Bloke.

That made her smile. "He takes his job very seriously, that's all."

I tried, but I couldn't recall what exactly his job *was*. Had she told me? She'd introduced me to like ten people in a row, so I'd been on autopilot, but then the minute I'd seen him sitting behind the desk, I'd stopped hearing her voice altogether. "What is his title again?"

"He's an administrative vice president," she said as the elevator bell dinged.

"An *AVP*?" I said, as calmly as I could when my brain was exploding and yelling, *Noooooooooo!* all at the same time. "So that would make him . . . ?"

"Our boss." The elevator doors opened, and Pam smiled at the two women inside as she said, "Blake is technically the boss of everyone in administration at Ellis."

Chapter Four

Blake

"You think I won't throw you out of the game?"

"It's fucking rec league," my brother Jason yelled at the ref, stepping a little too close to the guy (who was about a foot shorter than him). "Swallow the whistle and the power trip, and let us play basketball. Christ."

"Jace," AJ said, grabbing Jason's arm and pulling him back. "Will you shut the hell up so we can finish the game?"

AJ was a year younger than Jason and only *slightly* less confrontational. I loved my brothers, but they were overcompetitive hotheads when it came to sports.

"I'll shut up if Chrome Dome here will stop pretending he's an NBA official."

Spoiler: We didn't get to finish the game.

Because when the ref threw Jason out, that made *AJ* get in the ref's face, which got *his* stupid ass tossed, too. And since there were only seven guys on our team, and one of them wasn't there because his wife just had a baby, we had to forfeit because we didn't have enough players.

Which was how it came to pass that we were eating wings at Oscar's before it was even dark outside.

"I'm not sad about *this*," AJ said, picking up his bottle of Heineken. "I was fucking starving."

"You're always starving," Chloe said, grabbing a french fry from his plate. She usually met us for postgame wings but avoided our games because they were ugly. Her words—which meant she'd fit right into this family. "The scariest part of marrying you is the fear that I'll never have enough food to keep you happy."

"Well, there's that and the fact that you're gonna have to live with that piece of shit," Jason said while licking the wing sauce off his fingers. "Did you know that he used to talk to himself, like, all the time? And I don't mean a little bit, I mean all the fucking time. Our next-door neighbors must've thought—"

"It was my coping mechanism for living with *you*," AJ said around a laugh. "A guy can only take so many hours of armpit jail before he cracks."

"Do I want to know what armpit jail is?" Chloe asked me quietly.

"No, you don't, and it's exactly what it sounds like," I told her, picking up my pint glass. "If AJ was bugging us, Jason would subject him to punishment in the form of his nose being held against Jason's armpit."

"It was so much worse than it sounds," AJ said. "He'd yell, 'Armpit jail!' as loud as he could, over and over again, and I swear to God I could *taste* the smell of those pits."

"That is so disgusting," Chloe said, shaking her head. "Yet absolutely unsurprising. How did you live with these two animals, Blake?"

"Mommy always saved him," Jason said matter-of-factly while tearing into a wing.

"Every time," I agreed, shrugging. "I was her favorite."

"Only because you're the baby," AJ said. "Fucking Blakey."

That sent my brothers into a loud argument about who was the second favorite, but I lost interest because I caught a glimpse of a dark-haired woman at the bar. It wasn't *her*, but it reminded me of her.

Amy slash Isabella.

Talk about a disappointment. Not that I was looking for anything relationship-shaped with some stranger I met at Scooter's, but she'd seemed *interesting* to me when I hadn't been *interested* in a very long time.

Until she'd revealed herself to be an adorably interesting liar.

I still couldn't believe she'd looked me in the face and mouthed the word *nope*. Like, who did that?

"Who's that?" I heard from behind me, and when I turned around, I saw Kylie, Jason's wife, approaching the table. She nodded toward the dark-haired woman I'd been unknowingly staring at while thinking of Amy—*no*, Isabella. "You like her?"

Kylie was . . . *Kylie*. Perfect for my brother. Strong, independent, hilarious, and very much like she'd been born into our noisy family.

"Nope," I said, reaching for my beer. "She just reminded me of someone."

"Yeah, well, I want to know who." Kylie sat down beside

me, not even pausing to engage with my brothers as she reached over and snagged one of my fries. "Because you haven't even looked at a woman since Skye."

"I have, too," I said. "I'm looking at *you*, aren't I?"

"Gross," she replied, rolling her eyes as she popped the french fry into her mouth. "You know what I mean."

"Yeah," I agreed, appreciating that she was always looking out for me, even if I didn't want her to be. "But I'm good, Ky."

I'd been officially single for six months, and it was absolutely true that I hadn't noticed a woman since the breakup with Skye.

Honestly, it was like she'd killed off my ability to care.

"I saw her at the gym last week," Kylie said, her eyes on my face like she was searching for my reaction. "And she asked about you."

"Yeah?" I said, genuinely unaffected. My love for Skye had died the minute she lied to my face, and I wished her nothing but the best.

"Who, Skye?" Jason drained his beer before saying, "You didn't tell me that."

"That's because you're obnoxious about her," Kylie said, picking up a napkin and handing it to him. "Your chin."

"Thanks," he said, wiping his beard. "And she was a lying asshole to my brother—she doesn't deserve to know how he's doing. She *deserves* my obnoxiousness."

"I don't like her, either," Kylie said, pointing to the spot he was missing with the napkin. "But when you hear her name, you act like we're discussing an ax murderer. She might be a liar, but she didn't kill anyone, Jason."

That made me snort, because it was true.

Jason and Skye had gotten along great until I told him what happened, and the minute he heard about her dishonesty, she became enemy number one.

Instantly dead to him.

"If *I* saw her at the gym," AJ said, grinning, "I'd be super insanely nice to her, like, 'Heyyyy, Skye, how are you,' with the smile of a horror movie clown, just to make her paranoid."

"Your man is terrifying." Kylie pointed at him and said to Chloe, "Sociopathic."

"Yeah, but it's kind of hot." Chloe reached out a hand to squeeze AJ's face like he was a toddler. "See?"

"I do *not*."

The night devolved into watching football and playing sports trivia, which meant that (as always) our table got *loud*. AJ and I ganged up on Jason for his stupid answers even though our team managed to dominate the competition, while Kylie and Chloe found another table to root for and yelled their asses off when we got beat.

So kind of a typical Monday night.

I'd managed to completely forget about the whole Amy/Isabella thing until I got home and fed the cats.

When you call tonight, make sure you have the kitties nearby so I can hear their little meows.

The minute I opened the cabinet and reached for the cat food, my brain reminded me that in another universe, one where she wasn't a liar and on the Ellis payroll, I might be calling her at that very moment.

Chapter Five

Izzy

"Iz, your cat's in my apartment," Josh yelled from upstairs as I checked my mailbox.

"Seriously?" I sighed and wondered who'd been in my apartment since I left that morning. I looked over at my door and yep—it was ajar.

Thank God the general entrance to the building required a key.

My grandparents owned the building as their investment property. An older building, it sat in the middle of a midcentury middle-class neighborhood, offering four one-bedroom units. But instead of their leasing the apartments to college students and young professionals to make a pretty penny on premium rent, all four units in the building were leased at a discounted rate to Millie and Burt's grandchildren.

I was grateful for the sweet deal on rent, as well as the landlords who adored me, but it came with a few less-than-ideal caveats. First, I'd lost count of the number of times I'd come home to find my grandpa tinkering in my apartment or my grandma "tidying things up a bit."

Also, to make things "easier for everyone," my grandparents had given each of us a copy of the master key so they didn't have to mess around with individual locks.

Sometimes it felt like I lived in a big house with my cousins instead of my own private apartment.

My younger cousin, Emily, beautiful and funny and right across the hall, could often be found letting herself into my apartment, borrowing my clothes and leaving notes that said things like "I have your black shoes—will return later."

Daphne, my other cousin, lived upstairs and was generally a quiet person aside from the occasional cosplay party she hosted for her fellow LARPers. Did she sometimes let herself into my place when she was out of food and didn't feel like going to the store?

Yes, yes she did.

But did she replace the food she borrowed?

No, no she did not.

Josh was the best building-mate cousin out of the trio. He was an IT workaholic, so I rarely saw him at all aside from the occasional laundry room run-in, and he only got into my stuff when he ran out of beer and didn't want to go to the store.

I ran up the stairs and retrieved the Darkling, apologizing to Josh for the black fur deposits my cat had left on his fancy white sofa.

"It's cool," he said in a huge cloud of smoke, because my favorite cousin was also a total vape hound.

By the time I finally got inside my apartment and kicked off my shoes, I was ready for a *lot* of inactivity.

Because my day, in and of itself, had been a LOT.

I changed into my pajamas (yes, at 6:10 p.m.), grabbed a Diet Coke, and went into the living room, where the McDonald's bag I'd snagged on the way home was now soggy and grease-stained in the bottom of my purse.

I grabbed the remote and turned on the TV, needing escape as I pulled out my dinner. The Darkling walked back and forth on the back of the couch, stepping on my neck and being his usual dickish self, and I couldn't help but sigh yet again.

What was I going to do?

I unwrapped my hamburger and kind of wanted to cry. I'd finally found what seemed like the perfect job, with a company that was considered to be the best place to work in the entire freaking world, and I'd totally blown myself up. I'd somehow managed to lie to and insult a vice president on my very first day.

As if that weren't enough of an aww-shit sandwich, I was so profoundly disappointed in AVP Blake's awful character arc that I could cry. He'd started off the day like some dashing hero in a rom-com, attractive and charming and filled with promise, but then, in an instant, he'd shown himself to be a pompous, arrogant, judgmental jerk.

A jerk who would most likely be firing me the following day.

Is it possible to salvage this? I wanted to believe there was a chance, but he'd looked disgusted with me *before* I'd behaved like a child. There was no way in hell he was going to be okay with me working for him after the lie and the "nope."

No way.

A knot formed in my stomach at the thought of job hunting; I *hated* job hunting. It was the worst in *good* times, but in this tough market, where even the overqualified were struggling to get hired, it was a nightmare.

And how was I going to explain this to a potential employer? As someone whose career tasks often included interviewing candidates, I was incredibly aware of the question mark that would now be on my employment record.

Because by leaving Ellis off my résumé (which I would *have* to do since explaining away a one-day stint wasn't an option), it was going to look as if I'd left my former job of two years without having anything else lined up.

Which was a total red flag in my book.

It suggested things like forced resignation, impulsiveness, or *at best*, a person who navigated her life without any sort of a plan.

And damn it—I was none of those things.

I was a planner, a rule follower, a freaking model employee who worked her ass off in whatever role she was given, for God's sake.

Yet suddenly it didn't matter.

Congratulations, you latte-stealing loser.

I shoved a fistful of fries into my mouth before grabbing my phone and checking for messages. *Nothing.* Because I was a homebody who didn't have much of a social life, it wasn't uncommon for me to be messageless on a Monday evening.

But tonight it stung more than usual.

Because after a day full of promise that had slowly reduced itself to merely a new job that I would probably be losing, the lack of messages felt like a pathetic exclamation point on my life.

Blake

Seriously?

I couldn't believe it was her.

I'd purposely avoided Scooter's in order to avoid running into *her*, yet here she was, Scooter's Amy, standing in front of me in the 6:30 a.m. line at Peet's Coffee.

Wonderful.

She hadn't noticed me yet, thank God, so I kept my eyes on my phone in hopes of keeping that whole invisibility thing going. I'd just finished my run and wanted to take a coffee home with me while I showered and got ready for work, but she looked ready for work already.

High heels, sleek ponytail, black laptop bag.

On a side note, why would she be going in so early on her second day? I knew Pam rarely showed up before nine, so the only thing she could be doing with a two-hour head start was shopping for shoes while attempting to appear hardworking.

Which was on-brand for the person I thought she probably was.

She *did* smell really fucking good, though; I'd give her that. Whatever scent she wore wasn't too flowery, wasn't too sweet, yet smelled like something I wanted to hyperventilate on.

I kept my eyes trained on my inbox until she ordered.

"Can I please get a large mocha?" she asked.

No latte today, Amy?

"Sure," the barista said. "What's the name on the order?"

I don't know what came over me, but I couldn't stop myself from saying, "It's Amy, isn't it?"

That ponytail whipped around so quickly I nearly lost an eye. She blinked in surprise, looked down at my crappy running clothes, and then returned her gaze to the smiling woman behind the counter. "It's Izzy, actually."

I instantly regretted saying anything, because I had zero desire to talk to her, but apparently my petty side had a mind of its own.

"And he will have . . ." She turned and looked at me with raised eyebrows.

"What?"

She pointed her wallet at me and gave me a fake smile. "I'm buying you a coffee—what do you want?"

I glanced past her, and the barista was watching me with her eyebrows up, as well, waiting for my order.

"No, thank you," I said, a little thrown by the offer.

"Aren't you here for coffee?" Izzy asked, her eyebrows dropping and scrunching together in confusion.

"Well, yes, but I can get it." I cleared my throat and said, "Thanks, though."

She tilted her head and looked at me like I was the world's biggest asshole. "You won't accept a coffee from me?"

"It's not like that," I said defensively, mostly because she was watching me like I'd just delivered the world's nastiest insult.

"You just enjoy paying, is that it?" she said, and I think she was being funny but I couldn't quite tell. "You *prefer* to part with your money instead of just politely taking coffee from someone who wants to apologize to you?"

I couldn't let someone on my team spend money on me, so I said, "You can't apologize by buying me coffee—"

"So that's a no, then?" she interrupted, her smart-ass smile disappearing as she glanced at the line behind me.

"It's not appropriate for me to accept a coffee from you," I corrected quietly, gritting my teeth to hold back the irritation in my voice. "But I appreciate the thought."

"Sure you do," she muttered under her breath, turning away from me. Her voice was rich with sarcasm when she said, "I guess it's just the one coffee, then."

She paid and moved to the other end of the counter to wait for her drink, and it occurred to me that I was going to have to do the same. I was going to have to stand beside her while we both waited for our coffees.

"What can I get for *you*?" the barista said, looking at me like I'd just done something atrocious.

I glanced over at my newest employee, who was staring at the ground with pink cheeks, and I decided to save us both.

"Uh, I think I'm going to hold off," I said. "Thanks, though."

I turned and headed for the exit, moving as fast as my legs would take me.

I was going to Scooter's, damn it.

Izzy

Well, that went well, I thought as I watched him exit the coffee shop.

I'd gone through the five stages of mortification as soon as he'd walked into Peet's, I swear to God.

Stage 1: Oh, God, please don't see me.

Stage 2: Oh, he's mocking me to the barista. How fantastic.

Stage 3: Be the bigger person and apologize.

Stage 4: He's refusing my apology, holy shitballs.

Stage 5: Be defensive and awkward as hell.

I was glad he left, because I wouldn't have been capable of *not* acting like an absolute sketch ball while we waited for our drinks together, but now I was more nervous than ever about going to work.

Because that man was definitely going to fire me.

I mean, when I offered to buy him a coffee, he looked at me like he was a father staring at his most disappointing child, like my mere existence was taxing to his Zen or something.

I wanted to scream, *All I did was snag a drink, you dick*, but that definitely wasn't going to help my situation. But it was hard to believe that the coffee was it, the only thing that'd changed him from a flirtatious, charming stranger to the glaring executive who seemed to hate me on sight.

I mean, aside from my snarkiness after the fact, but that'd been after the fact, so I didn't think it counted.

I walked to the Ellis building and went straight to my office, because I had a lot of work I wanted to tackle before Pam got there. I wanted to read the employee handbook, log in to the HR software to get my bearings, and memorize the building layout so I didn't get off on an incorrect floor and look like a noob.

My employment at Ellis might be precarious, but until Blake Phillips fired me, I was going to give it my all.

"This isn't something you'll normally be involved in, but since you're shadowing me, it's your lucky day."

I grabbed a notepad and my coffee before following Pam toward the conference room. "Boring?"

"If you make it to lunch without nodding off," she said, giving me a look, "I'll be surprised."

I wasn't looking forward to sitting through a boring meeting, but I *was* a little interested in the process. It was the annual benefit renewal strategy session, where our current insurance provider would be pitching its plan for the upcoming year, which Pam would in turn pitch to Ellis's board of directors, who would ultimately make all the decisions.

Exciting? No. Interesting? I kind of thought yes, but I'd always been into administrative red tape; as a kid, Businesswoman with Many Files was my absolute favorite game of pretend.

Pam introduced me to the broker, Kelli, before we took our

seats around the huge conference table. We were early, so Pam chatted with people as they filtered in while I doodled on my notepad.

Just before the meeting was about to begin, I heard *his* voice. He was talking quietly, but my ears definitely picked up the Blake in the room, and it took every bit of discipline I had not to turn and look toward the doorway.

Kelli launched into her presentation, projecting slide after slide of cost analysis and comparisons of what the plan had cost the year before. I took copious notes at first, but after a couple hours, I lost my verve and switched to mere listening.

Just when my eyes were getting heavy, a question came from the other end of the conference table.

"Do those numbers reflect the midyear change to the 505? I didn't see that in the data."

Since everyone looked at the speaker, I allowed my eyes to seek him out. I turned my head toward Blake's voice, and my stomach dropped when I looked at him.

What was he, the freaking king? He was sitting in a conference chair, just like everyone else, but there was something about him that just screamed LEADER. Maybe it was his posture, the superhero-esque girth of his stupendous chest, or the arrogant hawklike intelligence in his stare; I didn't know what "it" was, exactly, but the man had an aura of power.

He was dressed impeccably, like yesterday—perfect suit (charcoal this time), pressed shirt, tie—but he was wearing glasses today. A pair of stylish frames sat atop his strong nose, making him look like the most intelligent human hottie in the cosmos. He looked smart and so attractive that I wondered how many women in that room were fantasizing about him that very minute.

I would guess all of them.

As if hearing my thoughts, he locked his eyes on mine. Kelli answered his question, and he appeared to be listening, but his eyes were just a *little* to the left of Kelli's location, wholly focused on me while his jaw did that little flex-unflex thing.

Yes, I know you hate me—no need to give me the flex.

I rolled in my lips and met his gaze, lifting my chin a little just to make sure he didn't think he intimidated me. It was mind-blowing that this man had seemed kind of into me twenty-four hours ago when all I got from him today was supreme irritation.

"Does that answer your question, Blake?" Kelli asked.

He gave a nod. "Yes. Thank you, Kelli."

When the meeting finally ended, I followed Pam out the door, wondering how many people were exiting between Blake and me. Was he still lingering in the back of the conference room, discussing data with the people who cared about data, or was he exiting right behind me, his big body mere inches from mine?

A tiny shiver slithered down my spine at the thought, which was ludicrous. *Get a grip, Iz*, I thought as I headed back toward my office. Unfortunately, the tie on the back of my straitjacket sweater caught on the door hinge, jerking me backward.

"Gah!" I looked down at where I was connected to the door just as Blake was approaching the doorway, talking to two other executives. *No, no, no.* I looked over my shoulder, reaching a hand around to untether myself as quickly as humanly possible.

"Izzy?" Pam said, stopping and turning around.

Blake and his cohorts reached the doorway at that moment, and I watched his eyes absorb my situation in a split second. *Please kill me. Just let me die of embarrassment this very minute.*

He almost looked like he was going to smile—almost—before he said, "Hang on."

He stepped closer, his cologne swirling around my sensibilities like some kind of olfactory roofie, before he said, "Looks like you're stuck."

Does it? Gee, thanks for the summation, Bloke.

"Little bit," I said, feeling like the world's biggest idiot.

"Here." He unhooked my tie from the hinge in a half second, freeing me.

But I felt all of his fingertips like they were burning my skin through the sweater. The awareness of him that'd existed in the elevator ride yesterday was instantly back.

And it almost felt like his left hand—just the tippiest tips of his fingers—had rested on my lower back for the millisecond it'd taken for him to disengage me from the door.

"Thanks," I said, my cheeks on fire as I met his gaze.

It feels like he's reading my mind somehow, I thought as his dark eyes moved over my face.

I gave him what I hoped looked like a smile before taking off in the closest thing to a sprint I could manage while wearing three-inch pumps.

The rest of the day was blessedly uneventful, with nary a Blake sighting, and I breathed a sigh of relief. Pam had intimated yesterday that he wasn't often seen in our department, and I was damn glad to hear it.

Because men like Blake turned women like me into bumbling idiots, and I had no interest in playing that part. Ellis could be a career launchpad for me, a place where I could figure it all out, and I wasn't about to let AVP Blake screw it up for me.

Chapter Seven

Blake

"Here is my concern." I set down my cup of coffee and glanced at my notes. "I really like the product, I think it'd be a great fit for warehouse and transportation personnel, but I don't see how our front office employees would benefit from this."

"Do they have to?" Pam asked, crossing her arms over her chest as she stood beside the spot where her slides were being projected onto the wall of the meeting room. "If we can improve workplace safety by requiring all employees to watch a daily ninety-second video, does it really matter if there are days where it doesn't apply to everyone?"

Pam was great at her job and fantastic at finding ways to make the business run more efficiently, from a human capital standpoint.

What she *wasn't* great at was considering feedback.

"Hear me out, I think it might," I said, smiling because I didn't want her to feel defensive. "Because if we create a culture where more than half of our employees think it's okay to ignore the safety videos because they aren't applicable, then we risk lessening the value of safety overall as a company. On the other hand, if we were to require *only* warehouse and transportation workers to watch the videos, then it feels unfair to them, like they're being singled out, and safety engagement goes down. So though I agree with the idea of 'greater good' here, I'm still not sure it's the right move."

Brad, my boss, nodded in agreement.

Which made Pam frown.

"Push back, though," I added, "if you disagree."

"What if we customize?" I heard from the other end of the table.

I turned to look in the direction I'd purposely avoided looking since Scooter's Amy had walked in. I'd done a spectacular job of pretending she didn't exist, but since she was now talking directly to me, I couldn't really ignore her any longer.

I'd seen her a few times over the past couple of weeks, but we'd both done our best to avoid each other.

When she was stepping into the elevator last Friday, I hung back and waited for the next one. When we both ended up in the break room at the same time yesterday, I ditched my desire for coffee and hightailed it back to my office.

"Our rep assured us they can customize the content, so perhaps we can create separate videos for the front office," she said. "Videos that speak to their specific roles."

Jeff, the director of safety, looked at her and said, "What, like, how to avoid paper cuts?"

That immediately made me think of Darryl's "Nerf life" bit

from *The Office*, but I cleared my throat and inquired, "What exactly are you picturing?"

"How to avoid repetitive motion injuries," Pam interjected, nodding enthusiastically. "The importance of ergonomics, parking lot safety—"

Nerf life, I thought, and I could tell she was losing Brad with this take. The program had way too big a price tag to justify carpal tunnel warnings. Its primary benefit was prioritizing safety culture within the organization, but this wasn't *that*.

"Forgive me for being presumptuous," Scooter's Amy said, looking directly at Brad. Her eyes were bright, like she knew she had a good hand, when she added, "But we can also customize the videos to cover more than just physical safety. We can use them for cybersecurity, to train employees on how better to spot phishing attacks. Or for recruiting—how to refer a friend for a job opportunity. It's even a great way to spread wellness updates and innovations."

Brad tilted his head and got the look on his face that meant he was interested. Eyebrows down, mouth puckered, fingers stroking chin.

But something about it bugged the shit out of me.

Maybe it was the knowing expression on *her* face, the way she looked victorious. It rubbed me the wrong way, especially when Scooter's Amy was probably lying about the system's capabilities just to get the approval to cross the finish line.

"It can do that?" he asked.

"Oh, absolutely," she said, nodding and smiling. "We could even roll out the ethics touchpoints via this platform if we wanted to."

Brad had been all hot and bothered for a while now about launching an ethics module, where the training team would create entertaining videos that served to remind employees of the company's core values.

"Ethics touchpoints," I said, looking directly at her. *Time to make you squirm, Amy.* "Now I'm intrigued. Tell me about ethics, *Isabella.*"

Izzy

I opened my mouth but had no idea what to say.

"Um." I cleared my throat and did my best not to glare at him, but it was difficult. I felt all eyes on me as my cheeks burned. "I mean—"

"I know you're new, so let me give you an example of the concept, and you can tell me if the platform can handle it," he said, and I really hated the smugness in his tone. There was a ghost of a smirk on his lips. "Let's say we wanted to create a video on workplace integrity. The training team might come up with some sort of anecdote showing an employee as they decide whether or not to take something that isn't theirs, or perhaps make a choice whether or not to tell a lie."

"Okay . . . ?" I said, looking at Pam, who didn't appear to be aware of what he was doing. I felt like I was getting stabbed in front of an entire conference room full of people who had no idea it was happening as Blake looked at me like he was enjoying himself.

Why won't he let this go? Does he seriously equate my latte pilferage with employee theft?

"Obviously the point of the video would be to show that integrity means doing the right thing, even when no one is watching," he said, and his annoyingly chiseled jaw did that clench-unclench thing again. "Do you think a ninety-second piece could achieve that?"

"I, um, I think it'd actually be perfect," I said, trying to focus on the question and not his accusing undertones. My face was burning and my forehead felt hot, but I managed to answer, "A quick hit could be far more impactful than something longer."

"Go on," Brad said, and I appreciated the fact that he didn't look like he wanted to squash me. *He* actually looked interested, which immediately gave me the spark I needed.

I met Blake's judgmental stare and felt my own almost smirk forming when I said, "Well, Brad, the video Blake described could come off as *sanctimonious* or perhaps a little *overblown* in a longer format."

This time I felt supremely satisfied when I saw the telltale jaw flex, like I'd achieved a goal I hadn't known I'd been striving for. I tilted my head, kept my eyes on Blake's, and said, "But I really think the brevity of this delivery system can soften the judgmental preachiness of what Blake described and produce something relatable."

"Absolutely," Pam said, giving me a grin as she nodded. "We have complete control over the content, so the sky's the limit."

I smiled back at her, feeling great about my contribution to what was basically a sales pitch. We needed Blake and Brad to okay the expenditure, so even though we weren't salespeople, we were working our asses off to sell it to them in order to use the package for safety support.

By the time the meeting wrapped up, Pam was laughing with Brad, and we had the green light to move forward. I was absolutely energized as I trailed behind them, feeling so engaged already in this new job that I wanted to skip down the hallway.

"Isabella," I heard from behind me, and I gritted my teeth. "Can you hang back for a sec?"

I slowly turned around, and Blake was the only other person still in the meeting room.

And he didn't look happy.

He was wearing another nice suit—navy, this time—and today's glasses were tortoiseshell, but all of that attractive stylishness didn't change the fact that he was glaring at me like I'd just carved my name into the side of his car with a rock.

"Sure," I bit out, looking over my shoulder as the other meeting attendees left the room, hearing Rose's voice in *Titanic* when the lifeboats were leaving. *Come back! Come back!* I turned back to him and said, "What's up?"

I don't know what I expected, but it wasn't for him to walk across the room, closing the distance between us so he was standing *right* in front of me. He was tall, so he towered over me in his *GQ* style while glowering down at me.

Towering *and* glowering *sound ridiculous together.*

He was ridiculous.

He glanced over my head, toward the door, before lowering his voice and saying, "You do know that the expectation of honesty is *not* sanctimonious, correct? I guess I'd just like to clarify this, because it was a little alarming to hear a new employee casually disregard ethics as something *overblown*."

He was too close, and it was messing with my ability to think.

I hated his attitude and everything he was saying, yet my eyes were stuck on his mouth and my nose was stuck on his subtle cologne and my ears were getting lost in the low timbre of his deep voice.

He was looking down at me, and it felt like the air between us was thick and volatile, like the space between a magnet and steel as the two were being pulled closer together.

A wrinkle formed between his eyebrows as he watched me, and his Adam's apple moved around a swallow, just above his tie.

Man, that is a muscular neck.

"Um," I said, flustered all of a sudden.

"Um?" His voice was even quieter now, and I swear I saw his eyes dip down to my mouth.

"Um," I repeated, clearing my throat, and somehow that noise cleared away the fog.

Instantly I was back, staring up into the glowering, towering face of the jerk who treated me like a criminal because of a tiny little latte crime. I lifted my chin and said, "I'm sorry to have alarmed you, *Mr.* Phillips, but please know that my disregard was not for ethics at all, but for a sanctimonious video that might potentially be *perceived* as overblown."

He didn't say anything, just glared—glowered—down at me.

"I have to go now," I said, stepping around him to walk toward the door. "Have a nice day."

I was so happy to have the last word as I strode out of the conference room, feeling like a final-word-delivering badass, but then he ruined it by saying, "Watch out for that rug."

The *instant* I tripped over the puckered rug that lay in the hallway, just outside the room.

And you know how sometimes you say things on autopilot in a physical situation, like muttering *damn it* when you stub your toe on the coffee table? Yeah, well, that was the only explanation for how I could've possibly said through clenched teeth, to my *boss's boss*, the words "Thanks a lot, jackass."

Just as I face-planted in the hallway.

Chapter Eight

Izzy

"That did *not* happen, holy shit."

"Swear to God," I said as I came out of the kitchen with two bottles of Heineken in my hands, shaking my head because I still couldn't believe it.

"Did the jackass at least help you up?" Josh asked, taking a beer while grinning like my shame was the funniest thing he'd ever heard.

"He didn't have to, because my loud *oof* brought everyone out of their offices," I said, plopping down on the couch, still mortified by my klutziness. "The entire floor collectively stepped into the hallway with offers of aid."

"I'm sorry, but that is hilarious." He laughed, shaking his head. "You're a legend already."

"Fantastic."

My cousin had been in my apartment when I got home, watching some soccer match that wasn't on any of his streaming services but was apparently included in mine, so at least I had someone to vent to about my nightmarish afternoon.

"Do you think he heard you?" Josh asked before taking a long drink.

"Oh, there is no way he didn't," I said. "But the second it was out of my mouth, the commotion exploded, with everyone gathering to witness my legendary sprawl, so there wasn't a chance to connect. By the time I was back on my feet and *not* surrounded by colleagues gawking at my bloody knees, he was gone."

He glanced over at me from underneath his ridiculously bushy eyebrows. "You know you're getting fired, right?"

I sighed and plopped down onto the sofa beside him. "Yeah, I know."

I watched the rest of the match with him, knocking back a few more beers, but I wasn't really watching as everything kept replaying in my mind.

Because I couldn't understand how it'd all gone so wrong at Ellis.

On the one hand, I'd settled into a job that I knew I'd be good at. That I already *was* good at. I killed it during the meeting that afternoon, and after the great tumble, Pam had stopped by my office to tell me how much she appreciated my quick thinking and ingenuity.

Yet I was about to get fired.

How is this possible?

Unbelievably, and absolutely ridiculously, it all pointed back to that ill-fated latte. If I hadn't snagged Amy's drink, none of this would've happened.

It was absurd, but factual.

My thievery had driven the nauseatingly scrupulous *Mr.* Phillips to treat me like a criminal, which had driven me to behave like a defensive, angry teenager.

Damn you and your delicious beverages, Scooter's.

It was tough to swallow, because I'd never been the type of person to take someone else's coffee (what kind of person did that, right?), and I *definitely* wasn't the type of person to call my boss a name, even if they deserved it.

Yet I'd somehow managed to do both.

And as I sat there after Josh left, mildly tipsy and contemplative, it occurred to me that I hadn't *technically* apologized to Blake for the lie. I mean, for the record, I hadn't lied to him, but since I hadn't corrected his assumption about my name, it stood to reason that he might consider it untruthful.

I grabbed my phone from the coffee table and clicked into my messages. I knew it was a bad idea, but I felt like I had nothing to lose.

I found the text Blake had sent me after that elevator ride a couple weeks ago, before everything went south, and wrote:

Hi. I will lose your number after this, so don't get freaked out that an employee is texting you. But I have a question.

I waited for a response, but after about two minutes, I texted:

Okay—obviously you're ignoring me, which I get. Because AVP. Still . . . can I talk to you for a sec?

I waited a few more minutes.

I counted to ten, and then wrote:

Okay, well, I'M going to talk, even if you choose to ignore me.

I
Am
Sorry
About
The
Latte Misunderstanding
I
Am
A
Very
Honest
Person
Who
Simply
Lost
Her
Head
For
A
Second
When
Panicking
About
Possibly
Being
Late
On
Her
First

Day

I've never stolen anything or lied about my identity.

*Well actually I had a fake ID my freshman year of college that said I was Connie Brockman, but it was so bad that I only used it once because when the bouncer looked at it for more than five seconds, I confessed and went home.

Right as I hit send, *again*, my phone started ringing, which made me scream. I looked at the display, and it was Blake.

AAAAAAAAAAHHHH.

I raised the phone to my ear and said, as calmly as possible, "Hello?"

"I seriously didn't know someone could be *that* textually irritating."

The man had the deepest, sexiest voice, reminding me of when he'd looked down at me in the conference room and spoken in that quiet, rumbling voice. Such a shame. I said, "What can I say—I'm an overachiever."

"As much as I enjoy hearing my phone ping every five seconds, I feel I must inform you that I will not be responding to your messages."

I rolled my eyes and reached for the Cheetos that Josh had left on my coffee table. "Because you have fat thumbs and can't keep up?"

"Because it would be unprofessional for me to be texting an employee."

I said, "What if I was texting that I was too sick to work?"

"A call to the office would be the best course of action," he replied.

"What if I was texting to tell you the office phones weren't working?"

I heard him clear his throat and wondered what he was wearing. His deep voice sounded polite and businesslike when he said, "Miss Shay, is there something I can help you with?"

"*Miss Shay*? Oof." I sat back on the couch, glad I was a little buzzed, and said exactly what I was thinking. "Listen, I just want to say that if you're going to fire me for the lie and for when I was kind of a jerk to you, can you please just do it now? It's been hard enough the past two weeks, just waiting for it, and I can't deal with it hanging over my head."

"*I* have no plans whatsoever regarding your employment." He sounded like he thought I was absurd when he said, "Pam is your manager, so she's the only one who makes those decisions. And that lie happened outside of work, so it doesn't really fall under any Ellis policies."

"But you're her boss."

"Yep," he said.

"And I called you a jackass."

"Wait, when did you call me a jackass?"

Shit. I said in a slow, apologetic tone, cursing my big mouth, "When I was face-planting this afternoon . . . ?"

He made a sound, a deep noise of surprise like he hadn't expected to be amused by me, and said, "I missed that."

"I'm very quick with obscenities. My special gift, really."

"So it would seem."

"Okay. So, to summarize," I said, unable to wrap my head around it, "you're telling me that you're going to do *nothing* about my unprofessional behavior."

"Correct."

"I still have my job."

"Yes."

"Wow." I couldn't believe it. Was this man for real? I knew the best course of action would be an abrupt subject change, but still I said, "I feel like I should thank you."

"So . . . ?"

"So thank you, I guess."

"Wow, so heartfelt."

I ignored that, because something about the off-duty sound of his voice made me miss the guy I'd met on my first day. *Weird, right?* Still, I heard myself say, "Now, um, can I talk to you as Izzy from the coffee shop for a second, not Izzy from work?"

"The girl I met in the coffee shop wasn't named Izzy," he said, sounding terse, "so I don't actually know how that game would work."

I thought about it for a second, got an idea, then pressed the end call button.

Blake

Did she just hang up on me?

Before I could even process that, the phone started ringing.

"Hello?" I answered.

"Hi, is this Mr. Chest?" she asked, and I was annoyed that I liked the sound of her voice when she was clearly a flake.

Which is why I asked, "What are you doing?"

"Hi, um, this is Amy—we met at the coffee shop and then in the elevator a couple weeks ago . . . ?"

"Yeah." I picked up the bottle of Dos Equis that was sitting beside my laptop and took a long drink, irritated by the ridiculous situation I suddenly found myself in. Not only was Amy a liar who wasn't actually Amy at all, but she was underneath me on the Ellis org chart.

Talk about a lose-lose scenario.

Even if I was cool with casual dishonesty, which I so fucking wasn't, Scooter's Girl was on my payroll now, so she was simply an employee. Nothing more, nothing less.

She said, "I know nothing about your career and you know nothing about mine, this is just a call between two people who met in a coffee shop and in an elevator. Nothing we say is connected to any two people who might work at the same company. Are we clear?"

I sighed. "What's this about, *Amy*?"

"Okay, well, I'm certain you think I'm a horrible person because of the coffee lie, but in my life, I'm usually honest to a fault. So to prove myself, I'm going to tell you five embarrassingly honest things about myself."

"Okay," I said, knowing I should stop her but too interested in hearing the five things to actually do it. Goodyear walked up to the desk, bumped into it, and then started meowing and walking in circles until I picked him up and set him on my lap.

"First of all, I think you should know that even though I'm an adult, I still sleep with my baby pillow. It's nothing freaky— I'm not into wearing onesies and pretending I'm a baby—but my mother never pried the pillow out of my sticky hands like she should have, so I still need that lumpy little rectangle in order to get a good night's sleep."

I was smiling, damn her. "Um, noted."

"The second thing—I have a large pizza delivered to my apartment at least once a week, even though I live alone."

"Tell me what you watch while you eat it," I said, wondering what kind of apartment she lived in.

"I'm very much a creature of habit, so it's one of two things. I either turn on *Gilmore Girls* and rewatch episodes I've already seen, or I watch *Little House on the Prairie*."

"You're shitting me." My grandma loved that show, and sadly, I'd seen nearly every episode.

"I'm not," she said. "My grandma loves that show, so I grew up watching it every time I went over to her house. I swear to God that Charles Ingalls has ruined men for me by being so damn perfect."

"That *is* a high man bar, isn't it?"

She said, "The Mount Kilimanjaro of man bars, for sure."

I heard something rustling, and I wasn't sure how, but I knew. "What is that—potato chips?"

"Charles Ingalls would never put me on the spot like that, for the record," she said, laughing. "But you are close. Cheetos."

"Lucky." I couldn't think of the last time I'd had Cheetos. "I had a Clif bar for dinner."

"That's because you're Mr. Chest," she said, reminding me of the way she'd called me that via text. "No way would your pecs be that spectacular if you filled them with trans fats and french fries."

"Did you just compliment my pecs?"

"Settle down, Chest, it's just an observation. No different than 'there's a book, that is a car, those are spectacular pectorals.'"

I wasn't sure how she was making me laugh when I'd wanted to shake her a few hours earlier, but I scratched Goodyear's head and said, "I'm taking it as a compliment, no matter what you say."

"Suit yourself. Honest question—can you do a one-handed push-up?"

"Probably . . . ?"

"Fascinating. I will file that little morsel away to revisit later." She made a noise in her throat and said, "Okay, third fact about me. Also, I hope you're preparing yours."

"My what?"

"Your five facts, dumbass. This is important."

"I never said that I would—"

"*Number three*," she said, using the same tone a teacher would use if a student were interrupting, "I'm a little obsessed with sports fanfic."

I said, "I'll be honest—I don't know what those words mean."

"You don't know what fanfic is?" she asked.

"I mean, sort of," I said. "It's just, like, people making up new stories about existing works, right?"

"Yes." She sounded a little impressed. "And these are fictional stories about real athletes and teams."

"Like *actual* NFL players?"

"Yes."

"Ah. Okay," I said, even though I didn't really understand it.

"Obviously you don't understand, and that's fine. I'll be sure to say, 'Ah, okay,' about your number three when your turn comes around."

"I'm not—"

"*Number four*," she barked out, a smile in her voice, "I grew up here, have a brother—Alex—in Phoenix, and I was briefly famous in eighth grade when a video of me falling down my school's stairs went viral."

"I will need a link or it isn't true," I said, turning my head so I didn't get a mouthful of tail as Goodyear started walking in circles on my chest, trying to get comfortable.

"Sending right now," she said, laughing. My phone buzzed with a text notification. "But if you make fun of my hair, I swear to God I will shank you with an ice pick."

"Do you *have* an ice pick?" I asked.

"Of course not. Does anyone? Has anyone in the history of life ever needed an ice pick, other than, um, ice harvesters?"

"I don't think ice harvester is a thing," I said.

"Agree to disagree. Okay. Are you ready for number five?"

"I don't know, am I?"

"You can't be."

"Then I'm not."

"All right." It sounded like she let out a huge breath before she said, "Number five. I totaled my car on the interstate last year when I sneezed."

I couldn't *not* smile. Again, even as Goodyear's claws dug into my thigh. "Yeah, I'm gonna need more information. Also, I'm assuming you were okay . . . ?"

"I was fine. My foot involuntarily slammed on the brakes when I sneezed," she explained, "which sent a Honda CRV slamming into my backside, which pushed me into the side of a Ford Expedition."

"Is it weird that I'm impressed by your recollection of the makes and models of the vehicles involved?" I asked, laughing against my will.

"Not at all—I am incredibly impressive."

"Not what I said," I countered.

"I know it's what you meant," she replied. "Okay, now you."

"No, thank you."

"Then I'll ask you five."

"Do I have a choice here?" I asked, knowing I needed to end the conversation and get off the phone. But—*damn it*—there was just something about her that made me want to linger.

"Okay, number one. Where did you grow up, and where did you go to college?"

"I grew up in Omaha," I said, "and went to college in Minnesota."

"Were you in a frat?" she asked.

"I played basketball."

"Shut up—so did I!"

"Really?" She hadn't struck me as looking particularly athletic, but maybe that was because I'd been obsessed with her legs in those high heels and had been a little blind to pretty much everything else. "Where?"

"La Vista Middle School."

I was smiling again, damn it. "Tell me everything."

She told me about how she only went out for basketball in ninth grade because her friend Lindy wanted to, and how she scored a whopping two points over the course of the season. She rambled about running hundreds of laps because of missed free throws, and finished the story with "Yes, the coaches hated me, but I feel like I might've taught them a little something, too."

"I think they probably just hated you."

"Can it, Chest." I thought I heard the *Little House* theme song in the background just before she said, "Okay, number two. Were you mad when I spilled coffee on you a couple weeks ago? Honest answers only."

Honest answer. I reached for my beer and said, "The honest answer—and I'm only copping to this because we will *not* be talking after tonight and this conversation is unrelated to the two people who work at the same company—is that you spilling coffee on me was a fucking lovely surprise."

Her voice was quiet when she said, "It was?"

"Sure. It's not often that a funny, charming, beautiful girl appears out of nowhere and starts rubbing your chest in the middle of a coffee shop."

Her breathless laugh made me wish I could see her face, especially when she said, "I felt the same way, to be honest."

"I *am* a charming girl, thank you for noticing," I said. "And I did *not* rub your chest, for the record."

"You know what I mean."

"Yeah," I agreed.

"Okay, um, number three," she said. "What is your—"

"Number three—when you stepped into the elevator at Incite, I had an instant daydream about hitting the stop button and seeing what transpired. So when you actually did it . . . hell, it felt like a Big Fate kind of moment."

She didn't laugh, didn't say anything, and I let my head fall backward so I could stare at the ceiling and regret actually saying those fucking words out loud.

After a moment, I said, "You there?"

I heard her clear her throat. "So is there any way to go back—"

"No." I looked out the window over my desk, out at the city lights, and felt a heavy load of disappointment settle over me as I said, "There are rules, and I have ethics. Regardless of the Amy thing, Isabella Shay is on my team, therefore off-limits."

"But I—"

"Actually, I should probably go now." I grabbed Goodyear, stood, and walked toward the kitchen. I needed to feed the cats and get on with life sans Scooter's Girl. "You know we can't text and call anymore, right?"

"Um," she said, and something about her tone made me stop walking. I listened like she was about to tell me a secret, gripping the phone and standing frozen. "Isabella Shay is your employee, so you definitely shouldn't be communicating with her after hours. But if, from time to time, you were to get a random text from Amy, a girl you met at Scooter's, would that be such a bad thing?"

Shit, shit, shit, shit, I thought, knowing the right answer. There were no gray areas regarding ethics in the workplace—I wholeheartedly believed that. So I didn't know what the fuck was wrong with me when I heard myself say, "I suppose not."

"Okay, I have to go now. Bye."

Before I could say a word, the call ended.

Which didn't surprise me this time, because Isabella Shay was a giant question mark.

I went into the kitchen and grabbed a can of tuna from the cupboard, holding Goodyear against my chest as I wondered who the girl really was.

And just as I was setting the bowl on the floor and putting down Goodyear, my phone buzzed.

Hi, it's Amy from Scooter's.

Chapter Nine

Izzy

There he is.

I paused in the break room doorway, suddenly nervous as I watched him press the button on the Keurig. I hadn't seen Blake at work since last week, when I'd fallen in the hallway, and I wasn't sure how he was going to act in a face-to-face scenario.

Because we'd been texting every day.

Nothing major, just a few random conversations here and there.

But *never* between Blake and Izzy.

No, those conversations belonged to Mr. Chest and Scooter's Amy, two free-spirited people who happened to now be textual friends. AVP Blake and HR Izzy were definitely not those people.

"In or out?" Ben from IT said, pausing beside me. "Don't get stuck between me and my caffeine, HR. It won't go well."

I smiled and went into the break room, forcing myself to

only look at Ben and not the executive who was wearing a gorgeous blue suit with a stunning striped tie. "I wouldn't dream of it."

"I didn't peg you to be a coffee drinker," he said as he wandered toward the side of the room where the bank of Keurig machines were lined up. "You seem like a tea person."

"I feel insulted by that assumption, for some reason." I was talking to Ben, and looking at Ben, but somehow hyperaware of the fact that Blake had noticed us. I don't know how I knew, but I just *felt* it. "I'm all about the Red Bull, to be honest."

I went over to the vending machine that had Red Bull in the third row, and held my debit card against the reader, my back to the side of the room where the coffee machines lived.

"What's up, Blake?" I heard Ben say.

"Just getting my fix, you know," Blake's deep voice said, and I bit down on my bottom lip, refusing to turn around.

"Same, same," Ben replied. "I'm surprised I made it this long."

"It's all up from here, right?" I heard Blake say, and I could hear that he was walking toward the door. I still didn't turn around, and I let out my breath when I heard his footsteps exit the break room and head down the hallway.

Thank God.

Because I didn't want to see Blake Phillips, AVP, and I definitely didn't want to interact with him. I knew it was a little delusional, thinking I could keep this going without catching feelings, but I wasn't ready to be realistic.

I just wanted to lean into the workaround for now, which meant the farther I stayed away from that VP, the better things would be with me and my texting buddy, Mr. Chest.

I knew we'd have to occasionally engage, but I didn't want to do that anytime soon.

Blake

What a little prick.

I sat down behind my desk, irritated as hell by the way Ben had been looking at Izzy. She'd been focused on buying her energy drink, as she should, while that little prick had leered at her ass like it existed simply so he could stare at it.

What a prick.

I mean, was she ridiculously attractive and hard to look away from? *Yes.* Did the sound of her voice make you want to lean in and listen to everything she had to say? *Absolutely.*

But she wasn't a piece of meat, for God's sake.

And I was pretty sure he was married.

Not my problem, I told myself, opening the spreadsheet that needed my all-day attention. Work did its thing and sucked me in, and I managed not to think about her for the rest of the day.

But as soon as I got home, I found myself checking for messages from Scooter's Amy.

And when I didn't get any after thirty minutes, I sent one.

I just finished cleaning up cat vomit, in case you're wondering how my night is going.

I felt restless after sending the text and sat down on the couch. I wasn't sure if it had to do with seeing Izzy at work, not hearing from her since I'd gotten home, or the real-life reality that I'd just cleaned up four separate spots of disgusting cat vomit, but I felt like I needed to *do* something.

My phone buzzed.

Amy: Take solace in the fact that I am wildly jealous that you're in your warm abode right now, cleaning up yack. That sounds heavenly.

I texted, Where are you right now?

Amy: Let's just say I'm taking a walk.

I glanced at the wall of windows on the other side of my living room. In the rain?? In the dark??

Amy: It wasn't my number one choice, but I'll be home soon and will probably drown to death in the hot shower that I will refuse to ever leave.

Thunder rumbled, and I watched lightning flash through the sky. What the hell? She couldn't be serious, could she? I messaged: Are you serious right now?

Amy: My car died, but I'm almost home.

Shit. Not only was it pouring, but it was kind of a violent electrical storm.

I texted, Why didn't you call someone? Or an Uber??

I tried wrapping my mind around the idea that she was walking in the loud storm at that very minute.

Amy: I called an Uber, but the first one cxld and the second one was going to take too long. I thought walking would be faster.

I stared at the phone in my hand, unable to even understand what she'd been thinking. I texted, How close are you?

Amy: I'll be home in twenty.

Twenty minutes? I grabbed my keys off the coffee table and stood.

I texted, Drop me your location.

Amy: I'm fine.

I went into the hall and grabbed some towels from the linen closet and a hoodie from the dryer. I'm headed that way already so it's NBD. Just drop me your location.

Amy: AVP Blake cannot give me a ride. I'm almost there so no worries. Thanks, tho.

I don't know why, but my stress was through the roof as I pictured her out in the storm, all alone. I texted, Mr. Chest is going for a drive, not Blake. Tell me where you are.

After the longest thirty seconds of my life, she texted back.

Amy: You know that Burger King that's right off the interstate on Dodge?

Me: You're at the BK?

Amy: I should be there in ten minutes.

Me: Where are you this second?

Amy: Walking on the side of the interstate, somewhere between the Dinker's exit and Dodge.

I wasn't sure where she lived, but that BK wasn't too far from my place.

As soon as I pulled out of my parking garage, it was impossible to see through the deluge, even with my wipers on high. I couldn't believe she was walking in that. Why hadn't she called someone? I squinted when I got close to where she said she was, slowing and trying to see a person through the rain and the darkness.

And then I saw her.

It was exactly like she'd said.

She was walking on the side of the interstate, a dark, huddled figure barely visible on the freeway shoulder. I threw on my hazards and slowed, rolling down my window so she could see it was me and not some creeper as I stopped beside her.

"It's me—get in!" I yelled.

I couldn't see her face through the rain, but she must've seen all she needed, because she ran to my car. She threw open the passenger door and looked ready to jump inside, when she stopped short. She looked down at the seat and said, "I'm soaked. I don't want to ruin your leather seats."

"Get in," I bit out, wanting to grab her arm and jerk her into the dry car. "They'll be fine."

She got in and slammed the door, and as she sat, I saw just how drenched she was. Her hair was dripping and her clothes were saturated and her face was wet as she wiped it with wet hands. She was shaking—her body was literally racked with tremors—and I reached between the seats and grabbed a towel.

"Oh, my God, I love you so much," she breathed, taking the towel and rubbing it over her head before just wrapping it around her like it was a blanket. "Thank you."

"No problem," I said, wishing she'd stop shivering so violently. "I brought a dry hoodie, too."

"I'm fine," she said around chattering teeth. "My apartment is on Fiftieth and Sullivan."

I put the car in gear and pulled onto the road, distracted by the way she was shivering. So much so that I said, "You're soaked to the bone. You should take off your wet shirt and put on the hoodie."

I expected a smart-ass comment, but she was clearly in the throes of hypothermia, because all she said was "Keep your eyes on the road or I'll kick your ass, Chest."

"You got it," I said, merging into the other lane. I cranked up the heat, ignoring the shirt removal that was going on in my periphery. Obviously she was so cold she no longer cared about privacy, because she wasn't even trying to duck down or hide herself from other vehicles' lines of sight. Not that anyone could see anything, between the darkness and the downpour.

"Turn at the light," she said, pulling the hoodie over her head. "And then take your first right, onto Price Avenue."

"Got it," I said, hitting my turn signal as I slowed for the turn.

"My building is the redbrick fourplex, way down on the corner; it's about a block." She pulled her hair out of the hoodie and leaned forward to hold her hands up to the dashboard vent. "I didn't want you to come, but I'm so incredibly happy that you did."

"Why didn't you call someone?" I asked. "I can't believe you didn't just sit in your dry car and wait for help."

"I tried my cousin and he didn't answer," she said, putting her face scant centimeters from the vent. "And I wasn't that far from home."

"Not that far?" It was unfathomable that she'd been strolling alongside the interstate, where anyone could've run her down. "It would've taken you forty-five more minutes to get home, if you didn't get hit or struck by lightning first."

"Hey. You're not allowed to scold me unless you know my middle name." There was a teasing in her voice. "Since you don't, Mr. Chest from Scooter's, you should—"

"Clarence."

I heard her gasp, and she was smiling with her mouth wide open when I glanced over. "I forgot that you know that."

"This it?" I asked, pulling to a stop in front of an apartment building. It looked old but well maintained, surrounded by a lot of tall trees, and for some reason, I could picture her living there.

"Yes." She reached for the car door with shaking hands. "Thank you so much for coming to get me."

"No problem."

"Do you want to come in for a slice of the hot pizza I will be ordering the minute my fingers thaw?"

No. NO. Of course no, the only answer was no. I put the car in first and yanked up the parking brake. "I'll order while you drown in the hot shower. Deal?"

"Deal so hard," she replied, sounding pleased with my idiotic answer.

What am I doing, what am I doing, what am I doing?

We ran for the door, which was probably a moot point since she was already drenched, but it didn't seem to matter to us. And when we got to her stoop, I took the keys from her shaking fingers and unlocked the building door for her.

"Okay," she said, the dim light of the entryway seeming ridiculously bright after so much darkness. She looked up at me, her wet face streaked with mascara, and said, "Don't judge me for my furnishings."

"I would never."

"You say that now," she said, opening the door to her unit, which was clearly unlocked, "but wait until you see it."

When she pushed in the door, it was like walking into someone's grandmother's apartment. She had a pink sofa, two matching pink-and-gold-velvet side chairs, and a huge painting of a garden scene hung on the wall behind the couch. Crochet doilies sat on both end tables, and I was surprised to see a normal

TV on the other side of the room, as opposed to some huge con-
sole with old-school rabbit ears.

"You're into retro," I said, looking around at the *interesting*
turn-of-the-century decor.

"You're kidding, right?" She dropped the towel on one of
the chairs and turned on a floor lamp. "When I moved in here,
my grandma surprised me by furnishing the entire place for me;
it was her gift."

"Oh, God."

"Right?" She crossed her arms, looking tiny in my XL Bears
hoodie, and said, "I'll tell you the whole story after I shower.
Remote's on the coffee table, beer is in the fridge, and my credit
card is in my purse if you want to order the pizza."

"I've got it." Did she usually make a habit of keeping her
front door unlocked and letting strangers rifle through her
purse? "Go shower."

"God bless you," she said, and then she disappeared down
the hallway and into the back of the apartment.

"What toppings?" I yelled.

"Anything but pineapple."

"Combo?"

"Yes, please, but no mushrooms."

What am I doing?

I placed the pizza order while I turned on a football game,
and I heard the shower start as I walked into her kitchen and
grabbed a beer from the fridge.

*How can someone function with only condiments, choc-
olate milk, diet soda, and beer in their refrigerator?*

I was about to sit back down on the sofa, when a guy walked through the front door. A guy with a bushy beard, Adidas joggers, no shirt, and no shoes.

He stopped short, looking surprised to see me.

Same, bro.

Then his eyes went down to my beer, and he said, "You drinkin' my beer?"

I opened my mouth to respond, but the guy laughed and said, "Just messin'. Where's Iz?"

"Shower," I said slowly, having no idea how to respond, because I didn't know who this guy was to her and what he was doing there.

"Good—I need to steal a few things. Don't tell."

I watched as the guy went into the kitchen, grabbed three beers and an unopened bag of Cool Ranch Doritos, and then turned and headed for the door.

"Is she okay with this?" I asked, feeling like I should step in or something.

"Yeah, she owes me," the guy said, smiling like it was no big deal. "Tell her the Darkling puked on my bed today, so I'm collecting."

"And you are . . . ?"

"Oh, my God, clearly an asshole," he said, and shifted the stolen items to his left hand. He extended his right and said, "I'm Josh, her cousin. I live upstairs."

"Blake," I said, hating the relief I felt that the guy who was clearly very familiar with Izzy was family and not something more complicated. "Her car broke down on the interstate—"

"That explains the missed calls." Josh shook his head. "And I told her, after her starter caught on fire, that she needed to get a new car before she got stranded. But you know how she is."

I actually had no idea.

"Maybe now she'll listen," he said.

And I just said, "Maybe," in agreement, because what else could I possibly say?

"Well, it was nice meeting you," Josh said, then added, "Hey, will you come grab the cat?"

Am I in an episode of The Twilight Zone? I got up and followed the guy out of her apartment and up the stairs, moving out of pure curiosity. And even though he'd asked me to "grab the cat," I almost laughed when the guy shoved an asshole cat at me (the asshole scaled my chest with all of his claws) because the entire situation was so . . . unusual.

By the time she (I still couldn't think of her as Izzy *or* Amy, so she was simply "she" at that point) returned to the living room, the cat was purring on my lap.

She stopped, looking at me with her eyebrows crinkled together. "The Darkling is sitting on your lap."

"Why does that conjure the unfortunate image of Ben Barnes reclining on my thighs?"

She smiled. "But he hates everyone—even me, half the time."

I wasn't sure how she managed to look hot with wet hair while wearing sweats and fuzzy socks, but she just did. Maybe it was because she just looked so . . . at home, like she was freshly showered and ready to settle in for the night.

What the hell is wrong with me, thinking idiotic thoughts like that?

"Josh said you owe him because this guy puked on his couch."

"That mooching dick." She shook her head and said, "If Josh didn't feed him sushi all the time, he wouldn't puke. Did he take my beer?"

"Only a couple. Does he babysit the cat for you or something?" I asked.

The door buzzer sounded, and she held up a finger. "I'll tell you the whole story of this building after I get that."

"The tip's already been charged to my card, so we're good, by the way."

"Okay, thanks." She opened the apartment door and went out to the stoop to meet the pizza guy. I heard her say, "Hey, Austin," and I was somehow unsurprised when the delivery driver launched into conversation like they were lifelong friends.

I had no idea why her unorthodox *everything* was charming the hell out of me. Shouldn't I have been annoyed, or at least marginally put off, by half-dressed wandering cousins and antique store apartments? Why did those things just make me want to learn every little thing about her?

It didn't matter.

I needed to knock that shit off and get out of there. I'd given her a ride to be nice, but nothing good could come from hanging out at Isabella Shay's apartment. I was going to get in my car and forget that I even knew where she lived.

Just as soon as we finished the pizza.

Chapter Ten

Izzy

I carried in the pizza, my stomach empty of food but also filled with butterflies. Because—*holy crap*—Mr. Chest was sitting on my couch with the Darkling in his lap.

He looked like the centerfold of a hot-guys-who-like-cats calendar.

He had on jeans and a black sweater that just *hugged* those impressive pectorals, and I had to clear my throat and focus on shutting the door behind me, because my cheeks were suddenly burning.

Be cool, you loser.

But being cool was difficult when the universe was messing with me. This man, this incredibly charming and attractive man, kept getting thrown in my path. It was bad enough when we were just randomly running into each other in public places, but when he'd shown up on the side of the freeway in the midst of my meltdown, I almost hadn't believed my eyes.

Because at first, when my car died, I'd been calm. I tried calling my cousins, and when none of them answered, I decided to just wait it out. Surely a cop would pass by eventually, see my flashers, and rescue me.

But then my flashers quit working and my phone battery dropped down to 2 percent. That changed everything. Suddenly I was imagining all the things that could happen: a car slamming into my car, a serial killer happening upon me, lightning striking, water rising enough in the ditch beside the shoulder to submerge my car. I'd started to panic, ultimately deciding to get out and walk.

And after five minutes of stumbling through the down-pour, I knew I'd made a huge mistake. I'd been bawling and panicking when Blake literally rescued me from the thunder and lightning. So if I believed in fate and that sort of meant-to-be nonsense—and I *so* did not—I'd be freaking out right about now.

I had no idea what to say as I set the pizza box on the coffee table. His unwavering gaze all but penetrated my soul, so like the coward I was, I went into the kitchen to grab the plates. I felt like I needed to address the whole *what are we doing?* elephant in the room, but I wasn't sure exactly how to do it.

But by the time I pulled myself together and walked out of the kitchen, Josh was there. He was sitting next to Chest, shoving half a slice of pizza in his mouth while he told Blake about Billboard Assholes.

"Oh, look—it's you. Quit taking my beer and also put on a shirt." I set down the plates and rolled my eyes as Josh ignored me and kept talking. Blake was grinning as he listened to my idiot cousin expound upon the rules of his ridiculous game, so I helped myself to a slice.

I was too hungry to wait.

"Okay, that sounds hilarious," Blake said to Josh, and I was surprised he could look so fun. He'd been so hard-core businessy in the conference room, and flirtatiously hot at Scooter's and in the elevator, but I never would've guessed he'd be laughing like he thought the made-up game was genuinely funny.

"Good, because you're playing," Josh said.

"Dude, no," I said, shooting Blake an apologetic look before telling Josh, "he just came by to save me from drowning. He's not really a Billboard Assholes kind of guy."

"How would *you* know?" Blake asked, giving me a questioning look.

"Because I know. Stakes are high, and you won't win."

"Whoa," he said, scowling. "What makes you think I'd lose?"

I pulled a piece of pepperoni off my pizza and said, "You've never played—just trust me. You'd lose."

"I think you could totally win," Josh said, rolling his eyes like I was absurd.

"Will you stop," I said as I popped the pepperoni in my mouth. Then I said to Blake, "Come here."

I went into the kitchen, and he followed without question, thank God. Once we were out of Josh's earshot, I told him, "You're right. I don't know you. And I'm sure you win at nearly everything you do. But not this game."

He was so tall that he towered over me—I guess I forgot. I suddenly felt fidgety and frazzled, but surely it had nothing to do with his attractiveness, and everything to do with human survival instincts.

Riiiiiight.

An amused look crossed his face, a slow smile, and it looked ridiculously good on him. "I'm sure I can—"

"You're not listening." I cut him off because he needed to understand. "You're an AVP who wears suits that probably cost more than our rent every month. Billboard Assholes is not for you."

"Well, I'm in," Blake pronounced, giving me bossy eye contact that made me a tiny bit more flustered. *Is it hot in here?* He was standing close enough for me to smell his cologne and stare directly at his throat, which was, for a throat, remarkably appealing. "And you're going to be my partner."

"You guys were talking about team-play Billboard Assholes?" I shook my head and said, "No way, that's even worse. I can't let you play."

"What are you—"

"Shhh." I cut him off again. He had no idea what he was dealing with. "These guys live by the motto that it's not fun unless someone loses, so they play for high stakes. If you lose, there's no getting out of paying the price."

"Are you trying to *protect* me?" he asked, his eyes narrowed marginally.

"Kind of." I cleared my throat and said, "See, Josh and his friends bought a few billboards around town as an investment package a few years ago. But there's one billboard that's in a terrible location so they can never lease the space."

"So . . . ?" he said, his eyebrows cocked together.

"So they use it for their own entertainment." I tucked my wet hair behind my ears and said, "The loser of Billboard Assholes gets their face put on the billboard for an entire month."

"No shit?" he said, his mouth slowly sliding into another grin. Wow, there really *was* a mischievous side to him that I wouldn't hate exploring if he weren't my boss and I weren't a corporate minion. He asked, "What does the winner get?"

"To write the caption."

He started laughing, which made me smile, but he still didn't get it. "No, no—it's hilarious. But now you can see why someone like you can't play."

His smile flatlined. "Someone like me."

"My face was up on the billboard in August 2021 with the caption 'The face of herpes can take any form—get tested.'"

He looked horrified for a moment before he laughed. "Dear God."

"Very *not* vice presidential, right?"

Blake seemed to consider that for a moment before saying, "Well, I'm not going to lose."

He wasn't going to listen, but I repeated, "No, you totally will."

"How could you know that?"

"It's a very complex game," I said. "You should trust me."

"Hey." Josh came into the kitchen and said, "In or out? We want to get started."

I looked at Blake, who winked at me—*dear Lord*—before saying, "We are *so* in."

"Wrong." Kyle, Josh's best friend, smiled from across the kitchen table and said to Blake, "Haribo eventually found success with gummy bears, but Hans Riegel's first product was actually hard, colorless candies."

"Damn it," I muttered, impressed by Blake's knowledge of trivia but irritated by his unwillingness to consult his teammate before just blurting out an answer.

"That means the point goes to us," Kyle said, looking smug as he put the card back into the box. "Unless you want a physical challenge."

"We'll take the physical challenge," Blake said, looking unfazed. He probably assumed it was something easy, a random athletic task that someone fit like him could do in his sleep.

"No, we won't," I corrected. "We're only down by one, no need to panic."

"Too late—he said it," Kyle said, reaching into the red box for a card. "Physical challenge it is."

I groaned.

"I've got this, no worries," Blake said.

I just shook my head and sighed. *Typical man, assuming he knows something about something he knows nothing about.*

Kyle said, "Your challenge is as follows. The two of you must crab walk *down* the stairs, side by side, without falling. You must have hands and feet on the same steps at the same time. For example, four hands must be on the same stair at all times, as well as four feet on the same respective step. Also, you may not speak to each other during the challenge; nonverbal is the only acceptable form of communication."

Blake asked, "Did you say crab walk *down* the—"

"Also," Kyle continued, ignoring Blake, "you must sing 'Someone like You' by Adele throughout the entire challenge. Any questions?"

Blake looked speechless, which made me want to scream, *I told you!*

Blake asked, "What if I don't know that song?"

"Only one team member has to sing. But how do you not know that song?"

Blake looked at me and asked, "Do *you* know it?"

"Of course I do. How do you not?"

Josh started singing the song at the top of his lungs, and everyone else who wasn't Blake or me joined in. There were a total of ten people playing—I knew four of them—and they'd definitely all hit the booze harder than Blake or I.

"Can we have a one-minute conference before timer?" I asked.

"Forty-five seconds," Kyle said.

"Can you show us the crab walk?" I knew what a crab walk was, but hopefully this was some sort of forward-facing derivative I was unfamiliar with.

Josh dropped to the floor, propped himself up on his arms, and started moving backward. He looked ridiculous, pale and shirtless and crab walking around the living room, and if I weren't so tense at the idea of Blake's consequences, I'd be cracking up.

"You're going to die," Ella said, shaking her head. She was Kyle's girlfriend, and usually stayed home on game night. "There's no way you can do it backward down the stairs."

"Her legs are so much shorter than mine," Blake said, as if

that would matter to any of them. No one even responded, be-cause the game was all about having to do the impossible.

"Okay," Kyle said. "Ready for your forty-five?"

I said to Blake, "We have to talk fast, all strategy. Got it?"

He gave a nod, looking as serious as he had in the boardroom.

"Okay, we're ready," I said.

Josh set a timer on his phone, and Kyle said, "Forty-five-second strategy starts . . . now!"

"We go slow," I said quietly to Blake. "I'll nod every time we should move down a step."

"*I'll* nod," Blake corrected, and for some reason, I trusted that it was the right call. "And we rest our asses on each step—that's the only way not to fall."

I verified, "So hands down, ass rest, feet down, and so on?"

"Bingo." Blake flexed his jaw before adding, "And total eye contact—only look at me—so we don't get dizzy."

Like looking at you doesn't already make me feel a little dizzy.

"Okay," I said. "And I'll sing super slow to set the tempo."

"If you start to fall," Blake said, "forget about the game."

"Ditto."

"Time's up," Kyle said.

The entire party left the apartment, leaving the door wide open, and stood on the landing to watch the event.

"It's only one point," Josh said to us, looking serious for a second. "You sure it's worth it?"

"Every point counts," I said, focused and ready. I couldn't let Blake end up on the billboard, even if he deserved it for being overly ambitious.

"Agreed," said Blake, giving another quick nod.

We looked at each other, and I wanted to laugh because it was obvious that he was just as stupidly competitive as I was. For someone wildly unathletic, I had a hard time ever saying no to a challenge.

Hence the herpes billboard.

We sat down at the top of the stairs.

"The challenge starts . . . NOW!" Kyle yelled.

"*I heard*," I sang, looking at Blake. He gave the nod, and we each propped ourselves into position before moving our hands down to the first step. "*That you're settled down.*"

He gave another nod, and we both slowly moved our hands down yet another step. I felt like I was going to topple ass over feet down the stairs, but I kept my eyes on Blake's and focused on our synchronized movements.

He was so much bigger than me that I barely had any room on the step. I had like an eighth of the space, and my entire right side was glued to his left side.

I continued singing, and the group at the top of the stairs started singing along with me, which wasn't surprising because Josh and his friends went to karaoke nearly every weekend.

Blake nodded again, and we slowly moved our backsides to rest on the next step. Another nod, and we slowly moved our feet.

"*Old friend,*" I belted out, "*why are you so shy?*"

I looked at Blake, but instead of nodding, he grinned at my song, a full-on smile that showed all of his teeth and those gorgeous dimples.

Dimples so gorgeous, in fact, that my cheeks warmed and I laughed, which made my hand slip, and then in a split second, I was falling rapidly backward down the stairs.

"Izzy!" I heard Blake yell my name—*has he ever said my actual name before?*—just as I fell to a stop against the door at the building's entrance.

Thankfully, Blake was *good* at trivia. After losing that point—and stopping the game for ten minutes so the entire group could tend to the cut by my eyebrow—we got back into it. Blake sat next to me at the kitchen table, and we proceeded to win the next eight points.

Team Bliz—my brilliant name choice—was surprisingly in sync. Every time we got a question, we put our heads together and quietly conferred for our full fifteen seconds. Of course, the more I drank, the more aware I became of the size of him, the smell of him, and the deep, rumbly sound of his voice.

And more of that shockingly playful side.

I was having *fun* with my sort of boss—who I didn't *really* know, like, *at all*, and it felt like we were actual friends.

Weird, right?

When we landed on Ted & Wally's ice-cream flavors as a topic, I told Blake, "I've got this one—step off."

To which he replied, "Your knowledge of junk food is truly staggering. I defer to your genius."

I flipped him off, he reached out and lowered my finger, and then I dissolved into laughter.

We weren't friends, right?

Yeah, no. Far from it, actually.

Just after midnight, the game reached an epic climax where there was a three-way tie.

"Physical challenge decides all," Josh said, grinning at his friends. "The way the game was intended."

Applause broke out, though most of it came from the people *not* in the game.

"I won't let you down this time," I quietly said to Blake, leaning close enough to breathe in his cologne.

His eyes were teasing when he leaned in even closer. "See that you don't."

Um, damn.

After everyone drew numbers, Josh and Kyle were first up. Their physical challenge was for one person to run down to the stop sign at the corner in under ten seconds—while piggybacking their teammate.

"Impossible," Blake said, looking out the big bay window. "That's impossible."

"Nothing is impossible if you want it badly enough," Kyle replied, looking like he truly believed that.

Blake looked at me then, in a way that made my stomach flip over.

But the moment disappeared when everyone got up and headed for the door. Blake went with them, and I followed close behind.

The rain had let up and it was only sprinkling now, and the whole group cheered as Kyle climbed onto Josh's back. Their strategy was for Josh to focus only on sprinting, not on holding Kyle, and Kyle was going to focus on doing his best to hang on.

"It's a decent strategy," Blake said while he watched the contestants.

"For sure," I said, allowing myself to drink him in while he watched my idiot cousin get ready to race down the block. I'd realized while we'd been playing trivia that it wasn't just his good looks that made me a little swoony around him. No, it was the one-two-three punch of intelligence, confidence, and charm. I was certain if someone screamed, *Help, it's the zombie apocalypse*, Blake would know exactly what to do to keep everyone safe and would delegate appropriately.

While being polite.

Of course, in my mind, he'd also have to do a lot of shirtless wood chopping. There was no end to the amount of wood we'd need if zombies were afoot.

"GO!"

Josh took off running, looking hilarious as he swung his arms as hard as he could. Kyle struggled to find purchase, choking Josh for a brief moment before grasping at his back and then slowly falling off. He tackled Josh as he fell, with the endgame being both of them face-planting on the pavement *hard*.

After a solid minute of groaning, they sat up and checked to see just how badly they'd scraped their knees.

"Are you ready?"

I looked away from them and at Blake, who was watching me from his spot to my right. His voice was quiet and deep, and it had to be the beer that made it sound suggestive to me.

Had to be.

I took a deep breath and said, "Oh, yeah—I am *beyond* ready."

Then I looked at a spot somewhere over his shoulder and added, "As ready as I can be. Um, when faced with a Billboard Assholes physical challenge, that is."

It felt like his gaze sharpened when I said that, like my words showed him exactly what was happening in my perverted little mind. He gave a terse nod and muttered something that sounded like "Fucking A right," but I couldn't be sure, because he turned and walked toward the building the minute the words had left his mouth.

Oh-kay.

"So what happens if we all lose the physical challenge?" Ella asked as the group went back to the apartment.

"Rock, paper, scissors," Josh replied.

"You're kidding me," I said, touching my tender forehead with my index finger. "After all the madness, it boils down to a playground game of rock, paper, scissors?"

He laughed and looked pleased with himself. "Well, our version includes an actual rock, a sharp pair of scissors, and a wall-size sheet of flypaper."

Of course it did. "God help us all."

When we made it inside, the next physical challenge was floor lava. Ella and her friend Claire had to make it to every room of the apartment without their feet touching the hardwood. It *sounded* simple, but alas, it was not. They each fell hard enough to make even Blake laugh-cry as they leapt from the couch to the kitchen table like incredibly clumsy flying squirrels.

"This is it," Blake said to me as Josh reached for our challenge card. "The other teams failed, so we just have to complete this one tiny challenge and we win."

I wanted to mock him, but I found it somehow sweet that he thought winning a physical challenge was even a possibility for me. It was so optimistic.

"Okay, Team Bliz." Josh read the card and smiled. "Super simple. One competitor does fifty push-ups with the other competitor on their back. The ride-along competitor has to bounce a tennis ball—one bounce per push-up. Push-ups must be continuous, as must the bouncing of the ball. You lose if you stop or if you lose control of the ball."

Shit. I was terrible with balls. I'd never been sporty, or even remotely coordinated. Me bouncing a ball usually resulted in me chasing said ball.

"Also, the spectators will be shooting Nerf foam bullets at you the entire time."

"C'mere," Blake said, grabbing my sleeve and pulling me off to the side. That intense look was back as he said, "It might feel weird, but I think the best way to do this is if you lie on me face down. That way your balance won't hinder my push-ups, since you'll be glued to my body—you know, even weight distribution and everything—and you can bounce the ball in front of us fairly easily."

I said skeptically, "Do you think you can do fifty push-ups with me on your back?"

He shrugged and seemed chill about it. "Maybe. Let's go."

"How do I, um," I said, feeling awkward as hell. "Embark?"

His smirk returned, only this one was a little bit filthy. His dark eyes were all over me when he said, "I'm going to lie down, and then you can climb on top of me. Cool?"

I couldn't manage words, so I just nodded.

Blake dropped to the floor, lying on his stomach with his arms out to his sides. I got down on my knees beside him, and it was hard not to laugh at the ridiculousness. Six people stood around us, Nerf guns aimed at our faces, while I tried to figure out the best way to mount my boss's boss.

"We can do this, Iz," Blake said, giving me a face full of confidence.

"That's twice," I said, quietly so no one else could hear, "that you've said my real name."

"Well, hop on and make me say it again when we win."

He didn't mean that suggestively, did he? I knew the answer, but he just made me so fucking aware of him. I managed, "Okay, boarding."

I climbed onto him, my legs on his legs, my chest on his back. Josh handed me the tennis ball, and I lowered my face to Blake's ear. "Are you good?"

"Fine," he said, his voice tight. "Let's do it already."

"Okay," Josh said gleefully, the little prick. "Three, two, one—go!"

Blake pushed against the floor with ease, and I gave the ball a tiny bounce as Josh's friends unloaded their guns. Blake did push-ups faster than I would've imagined, and I carefully gave the ball another bounce, glad he'd had a solid plan. The ball was right there, in front of me, so as long as I kept the bounces small and controlled, I might actually pull it off.

The Nerf bullets were annoying, but light enough where they just kind of bounced around. I asked, "You doing okay, Blake?"

"Never better," he said, and it almost felt like he meant it. His push-ups were so smooth, fast, and flawless that I stopped feeling guilty about my weight on him; obviously he could handle it.

"It's totally unfair," Josh said to his friends as they reloaded their Nerf guns, "that this particular challenge was drawn when Izzy brought the fucking Witcher to our party."

I kept my concentration on the tennis ball, but I was impressed as hell as he pounded out the push-ups. When he reached forty, I started getting excited. *Holy shit—we're going to win a physical challenge!* The group started counting loudly, shooting faster and directing their aim at my face once it became clear that Blake wasn't going to make a mistake.

I was the weakest link.

When we hit fifty, Blake collapsed face down on the floor with me lying on top of him. I started laughing and said into his ear, "You're a damn hero, Mr. Chest. Now say my name."

He started laughing, still face down, and groaned, "*Izzy!*" at the top of his lungs.

I smiled and nodded. "That's right, baby. You say it."

Chapter Eleven

Blake

"It seems like a different night than when you rescued me."

"Yeah." I pulled the keys out of my front pocket as Izzy walked me to my car. The party had just broken up after a very painful-looking battle of rock, paper, scissors, and the residential street was incredibly quiet. "It's been a surreal few hours."

"I warned you," she said with a laugh, and I just looked straight ahead, didn't look at her whatsoever. I couldn't. Because what I'd learned while playing the world's most ridiculous game was that the way she wrinkled her nose when she laughed made me . . . *distracted*. I'd found myself staring, watching her, just waiting for the charming little crinkle.

Like a fucking idiot.

"Yes, you did," I agreed. "I have no regrets, but now that I know, I appreciate what you tried to do."

I cleared my throat and stopped beside my car.

"Listen. Blake." She set her hand on my arm, a wordless request for eye contact. I looked at her—*damn, she is short*—and she grinned in a way that made me want to tousle her hair. "Thank you for saving me from the storm. You have no idea how badly I was freaking out before you arrived."

"No problem," I said, my eyes getting caught on the bow of her upper lip.

"It's probably my buzz talking," she said, and I felt a rush of satisfaction when her nose crinkled. "But even after cracking my head open, I had a great time tonight."

"I didn't mean to, but same."

"I know everything with us is all tied up in work restrictions—and that's fine," she said. "But since we're both a little tipsy, there's something I want to say."

I wasn't the slightest bit tipsy. At all. I'd had one beer at her apartment while she showered, and that was it, but I also wasn't about to correct her when I was dying to hear what she had to say. "Okay."

Was her upper lip different than everyone else's upper lip? What was it about that tiny little valley that made me marginally obsessed? I couldn't keep my eyes off it.

"I absolutely know that we cannot, um, have any sort of romantic relationship." Her mouth fell a little open and she blinked fast, awkwardly adding, "I mean, not relationship, I don't mean relationship, like I want a relationship, I just mean—"

"I get it."

She sighed and nodded. Popped a nervous little grin and said, "So I guess I just wanted to tell you that, um, I think we should behave as if tonight never happened, like we never hung out outside of work."

"Agreed," I said, my nose finding her soft, soapy scent among the smell of the rain.

"You were just being a Good Samaritan." She took a step closer, close enough that I could see by the glow of the streetlight the tiniest freckle on the bridge of her nose. Her voice was soft and breathy when she said, "But if this night never happened, would it be that bad to maybe, just once, see what it would've been like to—"

"Are you suggesting we kiss?" I couldn't believe how calm I sounded when I was actually torn between screaming, *Fuck yes holy shit*, and *I gotta go*.

She gnawed on her bottom lip and nodded.

It was a terrible idea. It was a terrible idea and I needed to shut it all down. But I looked at her upturned face, her blue eyes that were a little heavy-lidded, and I said, "Fuck. Yes. Holy shit."

Izzy

His mouth was just as confident and sure as every other thing about him. His big hands cradled my face, and his teeth nipped at my bottom lip before he angled his head and went deep.

As he opened his mouth wide over mine, his tongue slid inside, and I raised my hands to his chest, flexing my fingers against his pecs. He made a growling sound that I could feel under my palms as he fed me unbridled kisses, the kind that felt more like he was trying to consume me than kiss me, which I was SO there for. Our breathing was loud and labored, and I wanted every little thing his mouth was giving me.

Dear God, we were on fire.

His hands moved down to my waist and he pulled me closer, leaving me no choice but to fall into it. I wrapped my arms around his neck as he nipped at my lip again, sending a shiver down my spine, and I heard myself make a noise when he traced my upper lip with his tongue.

More. I just wanted more as his mouth moved over mine as if we were alone, in the dark, all stretched out on a bed. His kiss was all sex—really good sex—and I curled my fingernails into the back of his neck as I pressed my body into his, into his hard wall of a chest.

My knees almost buckled when his hands slid down to the curve of my ass and pulled me flush against him.

Holy shit.

"Damn it," he said, lifting his head just enough to give me a white-hot look. He looked like a fantasy villain, all dark eyes and crackling intensity, and I wanted to inhale every bit of that darkness. "Why the hell is it so good with us?"

"No idea," I breathed, not wanting to stop for conversation or a freight train bearing down on us or even a world war. All I wanted was Blake Phillips all over me.

But my eyes caught his tortured gaze again, and I realized I was an idiot. Nothing good could come from dipping my toes in the pool of how good we might've been. It would only take another minute of mouth sex and we'd be back in my apartment; I could totally feel that. And even if the night was fire—*and yes, it SO will be because holy shit if he can do push-ups with me on his back what else can he do dear* Lord—it would only delay the inevitable.

Blake Phillips had principles, and they were way more important to him than chemistry.

I inhaled a shaky breath, dropped my hands to my sides, stepped out of his embrace, and said, "Okay. Well. Now we know, right?"

His expression changed, going from intense to confused, and then he swallowed. Gave a nod of agreement as he put his hands in his front pockets. His voice was gravelly when he said, "Yes, we do."

"Thanks again for the ride, and I swear this night never happened."

"Um, you're welcome," he said, his face unreadable. "Yeah."

I turned and went back into the building, not daring to glance at him over my shoulder. I felt ridiculously, foolishly emotional, and I just wanted to climb into bed and fall asleep for the whole weekend. I locked the door and disposed of the pizza box, and I'd just climbed into bed and turned off the light when I got a text notification.

I fumbled for my glasses before grabbing the phone from the nightstand. I read it in the dark, then read it again.

Mr. Chest: I had the WEIRDEST evening, Scooter's Amy.

Do you have time for a bonkers story, or are you busy?

I sat up in bed and texted, First of all, don't be an idiot—I ALWAYS have time for bonkers stories. Second of all, does this mean we can be friends, even though our counterparts have decided to go their separate ways?

Three seconds later, my phone started ringing. Blake was calling, and I didn't know if I should answer or not.

Chapter Twelve

Blake

My phone buzzed, and I pulled it out of my pocket.

Izzy: Running late—SO SORRY!

I wanted to laugh as I responded with Yes, I'm aware. We were supposed to meet fifteen minutes ago.

When I'd arrived at Scooter's, I briefly considered ordering a latte for her but thought better of it. The whole point of this meeting was to discuss whether or not we could be friends outside of work, so buying her things probably wasn't a good idea.

Izzy: I thought I could ride a bike faster than I actually can. be there in five.

I set my phone on the table and took a few swallows of coffee. In the short time I'd known her, Izzy had consistently surprised me.

And that was putting it mildly.

Less than twelve hours before, when I'd called her after our batshit-crazy night, she'd ignored my call and sent me a text instead.

I picked up my phone again and scrolled through the exchange as I waited for her.

Izzy: I'm not answering because I need to think.

Blake: Um . . . ?

Izzy: Imma b honest w/u. I like u and want 2 b ur friend.

Blake: What happened to your texting? Are you a middle schooler now?

Izzy: I'm trying to jot down some ideas before I lose them so that was my attempt at quick texting.

Blake: So I repeat my original Um . . . ?

Izzy: I'm preparing some notes on how we can be friends without jeopardizing our careers. Would you be interested in meeting at Scooter's tomorrow morning to review?

Blake: 8am?

Izzy: Perfect. Our Scooter's?

I set my phone down again. *Our* Scooter's.

At that moment, I saw her through the front window. She was bent down, locking up a bike that looked to be a child's bike, wearing a black pullover and black leggings with a messenger bag slung across her body.

When she straightened and took off her helmet, the sight of her face made me feel something in my gut.

Holy shit, were those fucking butterflies? They were. They were fucking butterflies.

God help me, I was now the equivalent of a hormonal adolescent.

Izzy

I could barely walk as I entered Scooter's, my legs like jelly. Since my car was currently at a county impound lot because the city towed it before I'd had a chance to remember its roadside existence, I was currently carless.

I'd foolishly thought, *No big deal, I'll borrow Daphne's bike.* I ran five miles every morning, so in theory, leisurely riding a bike to Scooter's would be easier.

Right?

Wrong.

I wasn't sure whether it was the bike, the hills, or my pathetic thighs, but I almost gave up three times during my wayward journey. It was only Blake's villainous eyes and hilarious texting that forced me to power through the wicked leg shakes.

I was excited to see him again.

I ran a hand over my ponytail and ordered a latte, refusing to search for him until I had my drink. I needed to focus on my goal and not be distracted by his ridiculous good looks.

Side note: Blake had been in my dream last night, wearing long, flowing robes and a dangerous vibe that made me wake up empathizing with Bella Swan's vampirious propensities.

That wasn't concerning *at all*, the way he was infiltrating my brain even while I was sleeping.

And my goal that morning, for real, was so lame.

Sad, really.

Because my goal, in a nutshell, was to convince him to be my friend.

That was it: *Please be my friend.*

I was like first-grade Isabella all over again. Some things never changed.

"Izzy?" the barista yelled, reading the label.

"Thank you." I grabbed my drink and immediately saw Blake, sitting at a table in the back.

He was wearing a black hoodie, which should've made him look casual, but something about him just screamed IMPOR-TANT. The watch, the clean haircut, the big hands—well, okay, the big hands didn't make him important, per se, but my eyes sure enjoyed them; the whole package just shouted SUC-CESSFUL.

"Good morning." Blake smiled up at me in a way that made me smile back, and I was glad he wasn't one of those guys who stood up when a woman approached. I knew it came from a tra-ditional, respectful place, but it always made me feel awkward and like I was a little less of an adult than the man rising to his feet.

"I am so sorry I'm late." I pulled off my bag, set it on one of the extra chairs at the table, and sat down. "As it turns out, I'm a terrible cyclist."

"I could've picked you up," he said, his dark eyes warm as he wrapped a hand around his cup.

I really had to force myself to stop thinking about those big hands on my face and on my waist as he'd kissed the ever-loving shit out of me mere hours before.

"Nope," I managed, reaching over to unzip my bag. "Against the rules."

"We have rules," he said with a raised eyebrow.

"The most important part of my plan," I explained as I took out my laptop and turned it on, "are the rules."

"Did you sleep at all last night?" he asked.

I looked up from my computer, shocked by how concerned he sounded. And dear Lord, he *looked* concerned, too. He was watching me like the last thing in the world he wanted was for me to miss out on a good night's sleep, and it was too much.

Questions like that—from him—could totally destroy me.

I returned my focus to my laptop, feeling shaky. "Yeah, I only need four hours, so I'm good."

Blake

She wasn't wearing any makeup.

For some reason, as I watched her clicking into files on her computer, I loved that she wasn't wearing makeup. Not in a sexist she-doesn't-need-it or I-like-the-natural-look way—hell, I didn't care who wore what—but I was glad she didn't feel compelled to put it on in order to meet me at Scooter's.

It felt like she was comfortable with me.

"Okay. So." She turned her laptop so I could see the display, and said, "Scooch closer."

I followed her order, moving my chair closer, and wanted to laugh when she muttered under her breath, "Good boy."

She opened a PowerPoint and immediately started talking. "As we both know, you are above me on the Ellis org chart, which means we cannot have any sort of romantic relationship—or contact—whatsoever."

"Correct," I agreed, even though I didn't like the way it felt in my mouth. It was a thousand percent accurate, but acknowledging the fact out loud was depressing.

However, I *did* like the big red X she'd put over our names on her slide; that was pretty funny shit.

"Since that is nonnegotiable," she said, clicking on another slide, "we can never be alone together."

"That seems a little overdramatic, don't you think?"

I regretted it the instant I said it, because she looked embarrassed. But before I could backtrack, she said, "Would you trust us to finish this meeting in your car? Or at my apartment?"

Our eyes locked, and holy shit, she was right; we could never be alone together. I'd been staring at her mouth since the minute she sat down, remembering the way it'd felt to kiss her.

"Touché," I said casually, as if it didn't matter. "You're right."

She nodded very seriously. "So rule number one: We're never alone."

"Agreed," I said, wondering if that fruity smell was her hair or her perfume.

"I read the entire handbook last night," she continued, rubbing her lips together like she needed Chapstick, "and there is no rule that says an executive cannot be friends with a subordinate outside of work."

I watched her resolute face. *I read the entire handbook.*

"So if you're interested in pursuing a casual friendship—and it's totally fine if you're not—I have some ideas on how we can keep it entirely separate from work."

Her blue gaze moved from her computer to my face, and I wondered if it were possible for me to say no to her. Something about her eye contact, the directness of her pretty gaze, made me want to give her every single thing she needed.

Fucking dangerous, that.

Izzy

I was such a loser.

There I sat, at a table in our Scooter's, essentially begging him to be my friend.

But I knew I'd regret not throwing it out there.

Because the truth of it was, I didn't know how to make friends. Maybe I had at one time, but I had no idea how to do it as an adult. Like, I felt I'd missed a class on this or something.

In high school, I had the friends that I'd always had, since kindergarten. In college, I immediately started hanging out with my dorm-assigned roommate, who'd been my bestie for all four years.

But when I moved to Omaha after graduation to take a grown-up job, things were different. I had a lot of nice coworkers, but I'd never put myself out there to make those relationships anything other than workplace acquaintances. Like, how did that work? *Hi, can I play with you guys?* The idea of doing that made me too anxious, so I'd just said goodbye to those people every day at five and then I'd gone home.

Rinse and repeat until now.

Thank God my cousins were fun. It was pathetic that at the moment they were my only friends, but that was, in fact, my reality.

Which was probably why I was so desperate to hang on to my new friend. I'd connected with Blake in such a natural way, especially when we were texting. I was somehow totally myself with him, and I didn't want to lose that.

His eyes were on my face, intense enough to make me nervous, and then he said, "Keep talking, Iz."

Iz. Oh, God.

I cleared my throat and said, "I come to this Scooter's every morning at seven. So if you ever want a coffee on a weekday and happen to be here, and we run into each other, it's totally acceptable to sit down and have a coffee together, right?"

His mouth twitched, like he wanted to smile, but he gave a nod instead.

"Now," I said, encouraged that he was staying with me. "I go to the Bookworm after work every Tuesday to look at new releases. If I ran into you there and we happened to chat while book shopping, well, that would be absolutely aboveboard."

"Agreed."

Agreed!

I sounded calm and casual when I explained, "This way, nothing is a lie. If we see a coworker, we actually *did* run into each other, so it's completely legit."

Blake did grin then and said, "They have an incredible happy hour at Upstream that I often hit after work on Thursdays. I usually belly up to the bar and have a pizza for dinner, and if you happened to show up on the stool beside me, also eating, that would just be a wild coincidence."

I couldn't be cool—I beamed at him, my gorgeous new friend. "I love Upstream!"

He grinned back in a way that made me need supplemental oxygen. "Same."

We spent the next ten minutes sharing our habitual sched-
ules, tossing out a handful of occasions where we might possibly run into each other. I added them all to the spreadsheet and
emailed a copy of it to Blake (his personal email, of course), just
in case he wished to reference it at a later date.

"So we should probably cover texting next," I said, taking a
drink of my latte.

"You have texting rules. Of course," he said, and his small
smile reminded me of Edward in *Pretty Woman* when he was
negotiating Vivian's payment.

"Well, I think that if we both agree to never discuss work,
never discuss people from work, and never text during working
hours, then texting is probably a feasible form of communication."

"And phone calls?" he asked, his dark eyes twinkling with
amusement.

*Have I mentioned how gorgeous this man is? Like, I want
to take Polaroids of his every expression and catalog them with
perfect adjectives.*

Yes, I am aware I sound like a creeper.

Totally Blake's fault.

I was happy *he* was the one to ask about calls, because I really
liked talking to him on the phone. Which was weird because I
was usually an avid hater of phone talking. "I think the same rules
would apply, don't you?"

"Same rules," he agreed, nodding yet again.

"So," I said, shutting my laptop and resting my chin on my
hand. "Did we just become best friends?"

"Depends," he said, giving me a smart-ass little smile.

"On?"

"On what it means to you." His hands were wrapped around his cup, and I noticed he had nice fingernails. "If you want someone to bail you out of jail or be your blood brother, I'm not the guy."

"I'm not the guy, either," I agreed.

"But if it means I'll come get you when your car breaks down in the rain, then yes, we are."

"Nope, sorry, buddy," I said, shaking my head. "Can't be alone together."

"Come on—there have to be exceptions," he said, his eyebrows furrowing.

"I just don't think that's wise," I reiterated. "We need to keep that Pandora's box closed."

"Are you sure?" he asked, mimicking me by putting *his* chin on *his* hand. "Because a best friend who can give you and your bike a ride home would be pretty handy right about now, wouldn't it?"

Dear Lord, those words were verbal seduction.

Blake

I watched as her eyes got soft, as she smiled a dreamy little smile. "That *would* be nice, but I think we have to keep these lines clear."

"You're telling me that if I called you, stranded on the side of the road, you wouldn't save me?"

She rolled her eyes and said, "You have a very nice car, Blake. You don't need me, because you have roadside assistance."

I tried again. "If I called you because I was too drunk to drive . . . ?"

"I'd get an Uber for my bestie Blake."

"Fine," I said, irritated even though I knew she was right. "You can ride all four miles home on that toddler bike."

"You saw it?" She sat back in her chair and gave me an embarrassed grin. "It's pretty bad, right? I'll probably walk it halfway back, to be honest."

"Izzy—"

"Nope."

I wasn't used to feeling powerless. I wasn't a fan. "There's no convincing you?"

She shook her head and said, "Afraid not."

"Well, what if I drive your bike home and call you an Uber?" The obsessive part of me that always needed to find the solution to a problem was spinning in circles.

She looked like she wanted to say yes. She asked, "Would you mind dropping the bike at my building and I'll just run home?"

"Deal."

"You're such a great best friend," she said, grinning, and I had no idea why I was playing with fire like this. Toying with the line wasn't my thing, yet I found myself utterly incapable of stepping back.

"Oh, I know."

We relaxed a little after that and had another coffee, discussing the NFL matchups slated for later that weekend and our potential fantasy trades. Izzy spewed data and statistics like she was a game-day analyst, and I was genuinely disappointed when it was time to leave.

"Izzy, what if you sit in the back seat?" I asked as I loaded her bike into my trunk.

"What?" She set her messenger bag next to the bike, since she couldn't run with it, and gave me a look. "What do you mean?"

"If you sit in the *back* seat, nothing can accidentally transpire between us."

She furrowed her brows and tilted her head, considering the idea. "Hmm . . . I'm not sure."

"For the love of God, Iz," I said, slamming the trunk closed and looking down at her like she was a child. "Get in the damn back seat."

Her eyes narrowed, and I thought she was going to debate yet again and make me lose my mind, but then her mouth—goddamn, *that mouth*—slid up into a sexy grin. She gave her head a shake, shrugged her shoulders, and said, "My best friend makes me sit in the back seat of his car like I'm a little bitty baby child. Nice."

She walked around me, opened the passenger-side back door, and climbed into my car.

I had only one thought as I got in and buckled my seat belt: I fucking love my new best friend.

Chapter Thirteen

Izzy

I looked at my watch—almost noon.

I ignored the growl in my stomach and wished time would move faster. My breakfast—a can of Rockstar and a chocolate Pop-Tart—was no longer doing the trick, and I needed sustenance. I usually ate lunch at eleven, like a senior citizen, but that day, I was holding out until twelve thirty.

No reason—I just feel like waiting, I thought as I got out my compact and added a little blush and lip gloss to my face.

Thirty minutes later, when the alarm on my wrist buzzed, I stuck my debit card in the pocket of my skirt and stood. Grabbing my black peacoat, I slid my arms into it as I left my office, heading for the exit like my ass was on fire.

Butterflies were going wild in my stomach as I rode the elevator down, which was ridiculous, because I was just grabbing food. *It's what people do at lunchtime, right?* Nothing weird about that at all. Just because I knew that *certain people* enjoyed the Monday specials at Caniglia's food truck, and they usually took their lunch sometime between twelve thirty and one—well, that shouldn't make me nervous. Lots of people did that.

I pulled out my phone as I walked the two blocks to the mobile Italian restaurant. *No texts.* It wasn't a surprise, really, that Blake was radio silent during the workday; he was all-business, after all, and we'd made rules.

But after he'd dropped me and the bike off at my building after coffee, we'd pretty much been in an endless texting conversation for the rest of the day.

I'd texted him while we each watched the same football game, I'd texted him as I'd gone down into the creepy basement to do laundry, and I'd texted him while I'd given the Darkling a bath. For someone so aboveboard and executive-like in person, he was surprisingly fun on the phone.

That morning, when I'd been walking toward the building (I had to take the bus downtown because my car was still impounded), I'd felt my phone buzz in my purse. And when I pulled it out, Blake had texted, I can see you from my window.

The Ellis building was an all-windowed skyscraper, and even though I knew Blake worked on the fifteenth floor, I had no idea where exactly that was on the face of the building. So I'd stopped and responded: You have to be lying.

Blake: Black tights, black boots, black coat, red purse and—is that a piece of toast in your hand?

I'd laughed and texted back: A Pop-Tart. And quit being a creeper.

Blake: I was simply looking out the window, and there you were. Shocked the hell out of me, tbh.

Izzy: Can you tell what I'm doing now?

I'd switched Pop-Tart hands so I could hold up my arm and flip off the building.

Blake: Not very nice.

Izzy: You're interrupting my breakfast stroll; THAT isn't very nice. Can you tell what I'm doing NOW?

I started hopping on one foot.

Blake: Making a spectacle of yourself.

Izzy: No one is watching me but you.

Blake: The man behind you begs to differ.

I'd turned around, but no one was walking behind me.

Blake: Made you look.

His idiotic texting had put me in a great mood as I'd breezed into work, and it hadn't waned all day. But now, for some reason, I was nervous to see him. Even though we'd shared our frequent whereabouts with the sole purpose of possibly running into each other, what if he didn't want me there? What if he'd changed his mind and didn't want to be my sort-of friend?

Really, it was just a little nerve-racking, being the first one to casually happen upon the place that the other one happened to mention they might be visiting. Felt a little stalker-y, if I was being honest.

It's no big deal, I told myself as I turned onto the next block.

He probably wasn't even there anyway.

Blake

I could tell it was her, even though she was still a half block away. I leaned against the front of the building and thought it was the same as when I'd happened to glance out my office window this morning and immediately spotted her down on the street below.

Fucking weird.

It was like Where's Waldo?, only Izzy wasn't wearing stripes, and my superpower was apparently being able to instantly find her in a crowd.

I put my hands in my pockets and allowed myself to watch her, mostly because there was no way she could see me yet. Her hair was down, blowing in the fall breeze, and she reminded me of Meg Ryan in *You've Got Mail* with her dark tights, skirt, wool coat, and scarf.

She should have a damn pumpkin under her arm and a coffee in her hand.

But as I watched her walking in my direction, I felt them again.

Fucking butterflies.

What in the hell was *with* that?

Nope. Fuck that. Not butterflies, no way. If I were interested in her, the way my stomach felt at that moment might possibly be butterfly-related, but I wasn't. In all actuality, what I was feeling was just, shit, uh . . . gladness.

Seriously—gladness?

It was lame as hell, but yes, I was simply glad to see my friend. Lunch with a buddy was better than lunch alone, so I was glad to see her.

That was all.

I straightened and walked over to the food truck, getting in line. I looked at the menu board for a solid ten seconds before I heard, "Blake?"

I turned around, and *shit*. She was smiling up at me with that mouth, those lips, and the soft smell of her perfume was coming at me like some kind of a . . . uh . . . *shit*, something I couldn't ignore. Or something.

What the fuck is wrong with me?

Her cheeks were pink, her eyes bright, and my chest felt a little tight as I looked at her lipstick.

"I thought that was you," she said with a teasing glint in her eyes.

"It *is* me," I replied, unable to stop myself from grinning back. "Are you out trolling for calzone, too?"

She leaned in a little closer and said, "To be honest, I've never been a fan of the dough-dome pizza that they call calzone. I like my slices big, open, and melty. Just like my men."

"Did you seriously just say that?"

"I know, ew. I was trying something." She crinkled her nose, narrowed her eyes, and said, "I don't think it hit."

"I don't think so, either." I turned my attention back to the menu and said, "Their fried ravioli is good."

"Is it ricotta cheese filled?" she asked.

"I think so," I said, looking at her. "Why? Is that bad?"

She nodded. "Ricotta is lumpy and disgusting, like curdled milk mixed with cottage cheese. But you enjoy, buddy."

"Oh, I will," I said, thinking of her Pop-Tart—and empty fridge—and wondering if she was a picky eater.

But as I looked at her—as she looked up at me, wearing a shitty little grin—it held for just a moment too long. Something passed between us, a memory or an awareness, before she cleared her throat and turned her attention to the menu.

Said, "Do they have good spaghetti?"

Spaghetti? What's a spaghetti?

I just stared at her profile, my brain slow to move on and comprehend her words. "No one knows the answer to that question, because who would be stupid enough to order spaghetti from a food truck?"

"I would," she said, still looking at the menu. "I love spaghetti."

"But you can't walk and eat it at the same time, dipshit."

That made her look, and then her grin was back. "Now I have to—challenge accepted—which will be a colossal mistake for which I'll blame you all day. Every time someone looks at the blob of marinara on my shirt, I shall curse your name."

"I thought that was a dress," I said, and the look she gave me—forehead crinkle—made it clear that she was just as shocked by my asinine hyperawareness of her attire as I was. *What the fuck was that?*

"Yeah, um," she said, raising a hand to push her hair behind her ear, "it's a skirt and top."

"Ah," I muttered as I stepped up to the window, needing an escape from that moment of idiocy. I lowered my voice and ordered. "Could I please get the spaghetti?"

I heard her quiet laugh, and then she stepped beside me and said to the second cashier, "I would like the spaghetti, and can I also get a slice of cheese pizza and a piece of garlic bread, please?"

I opened my mouth to comment, when Izzy whipped her head toward me, pointed a finger, and said, "Don't say a word—I'm hungry, okay?"

I didn't know why, but I couldn't *not* smile. I looked at the freckles on her nose and said, "What would I even say, Iz?"

Izzy

"So let me get this straight," Blake said, his face relaxed behind dark sunglasses as he walked beside me. He was looking straight ahead, his hands in the pockets of his perfectly pressed suit pants. "The house that you accidentally 'forked,' which I can't even believe is a thing, was being watched by the FBI."

"Yep." I took a sip of my soda as we walked back to work. "Forked the wrong house, which turned out to be the residence of some questionable members of a satanic cult. So not only did we get picked up by the feds, but we were questioned at the station and also got MIPs because we had a bottle of vodka in the trunk."

"Wow." He looked at me then, and even though his eyes were covered, I knew they were squinting, because his dimples were out. "Your high school experience was *very* different from mine."

"When there's nothing to do, you make things happen, Phillips." I saw the Ellis building at the end of the block, and I was bummed it was time to go back. Even though Blake was my polar opposite and the kind of guy (hot, successful) who usually made me nervous, I felt totally comfortable around him.

I had *fun* with him because I was able to relax and be my uncool self.

"I forgot to ask," he said, glancing over at me as we walked around a woman and her French bulldog who was sitting on the sidewalk with zero intention of moving. "Did you get your car back?"

"I don't want to talk about it," I said, rolling my eyes. "In order to get it out of jail, I have to take the title to the impound lot *and* pay a few hundred bucks."

"Oof," he said.

"Oof, indeed," I replied. "Because after that, I get to have it towed to a mechanic, who will probably tell me it's going to cost a fortune to fix."

"No idea what's wrong with it?" he asked.

"None," I said, looking down at the scarred sidewalk as I tried not to think about how little money I actually had in my bank account at the moment. "But I didn't hate taking the bus today, so perhaps this is a chance to reexamine my vehicular needs."

"Yeah, but how far is the bus stop from your apartment?"

"Only a few blocks."

"Do you really want to have to hoof it a few blocks in the snow?" His voice was full of concern as he added, "In the dark? In the rain?"

That reminded me of the dark and rainy night where I'd kissed Blake, and my stomach did a little flip of its own accord. That kiss was in my head on an hourly basis, swear to God. I cleared my throat and said, "No, but I'm also not going to throw a lot of coin into a car that's fifteen years old."

He looked at me—I could see his eyes through the sunglasses now because the sun was hitting the lenses just right—and it felt like he was having some sort of internal conversation with himself as he just watched me. He didn't say anything, and when we stopped at the corner to wait on the light, he said, "What are the rules about car repairs?"

"What?" I tossed my cup into the trash can next to the crossing light and put my hands in my pockets. "What do you mean?"

The light changed, and we started walking again. Blake said, "If you wanted to have it towed to my place, I could take a look at it."

That made me stumble in the middle of the street, which made Blake grab my arm and say, "Easy, Shay."

Easy, Shay. Good God—what was he trying to do to me? Since the moment I'd met him, his entire existence had been an assault on my ovaries. And now he was going to add car fixing and stumble stopping to the dopamine equation?

I needed holy water or garlic stat, although that fleeting sarcastic thought brought to mind an image of Blake having *un*holy water poured over his massive chest like some kind of hot guy wet T-shirt contest participant.

I was disappointed when he let go of my arm, which was a ludicrous reaction, so I said, "I think that's probably not allowable. But thank you."

He gave me an eyebrow raise. "Why not?"

I shrugged. "I don't know, it just seems too personal."

He grabbed the sleeve of my coat and tugged. It startled me, the jerking motion that moved me a little closer to him, but his mouth slid into a smirk before he started pulling me along behind him as he walked toward the alley to our right.

"What are you doing, Phillips?"

"Getting you to listen to reason before we go back to work, *Shay*."

He let go of my sleeve once we were out of foot traffic. He took off his sunglasses, and I felt the gold flecks of his intense brown eyes as he said, "Hear me out. I'm still all in on rule following for us, but you're my friend, Iz. If I can fix your car and save you a fortune, why wouldn't that be okay?"

Because it would feel like . . . something. Something from a daydream about boyfriends working on their girlfriends' cars.

Side note: Every time he called me Iz, a sex angel got its wings.

"Because of money, maybe?" I couldn't think all of a sudden, but I knew there was a reason. *Reasons . . . reasons . . . what are reasons again?* I cleared my throat and said, "You're my boss, so there's got to be a rule about me paying you for services."

"Like I'd charge you," he said, sounding disgusted.

"Well, *I* would have a rule about that, then, Blake," I said, tucking my hair behind my ears and looking up at his perfectly trimmed stubble. "No way would I let you fix my car *without* paying you."

"Then you can pay me with a favor," he said, and I watched as it hit. He'd said it innocently, casually offering to work for nothing, but his eyes got hot when he realized. His voice sounded deeper, rougher, when he continued with "I'm sure I can come up with something."

The air in the alley suddenly got thick and quiet, like we were underwater. The city sounds disappeared, and I swore I could literally hear my own heart beating. I swallowed, but my voice was a little husky when I said, "I'm sure you can, too."

"If we were alone," he growled, his voice nearly a whisper as his mouth lowered to my ear, "I think we could negotiate a very good deal."

"I know we could," I said, my eyelids heavy as I felt his breath on my neck.

Every nerve ending in my body was crackling and straining toward him, and I was almost lost to it, when I heard a car horn in the distance.

Yes, you're in an alley, dumbass!

I blinked fast and muttered, "Which is why we need to get back on the sidewalk *now*."

He smiled down at me. "We're in the center of the city during lunchtime on a weekday—far from alone. I think we're safe."

"You don't think this alley feels private?" I was still blinking, slightly disoriented as he pointed that gaze at me. "I feel all alone in the dark with you here."

The instant those words left my mouth, I regretted them, because Blake's languid smile dropped. His jaw clenched, and he just looked at me for a few long seconds before he said, "Izzy—"

"Ohmigosh—I have to get back." I pasted a grin on my face and took a step away from him, mortified. Obviously I'd been the only one on the verge of combustion, and I needed to get the hell out of there. My voice was too loud and perky when I said, "You may be able to take long lunches because you're Mr. Fancy VP, but this lowly generalist has to be on time. I'm going to sprint back—I'll see you later."

His eyebrows went down again. "Iz—"

"Bye!" I turned and literally started slow jogging, knowing I looked like a moron but unable to stop myself because I needed to put space between myself and Mr. Chest.

All I wanted in my quiet little life was to keep my friend Blake and to embark upon a promising career at Ellis, but if those things were going to happen, I needed to find a way to be cool when I was close to him.

There had to be a way to speak to him without melting into an endorphin-riddled puddle of goo, right?

It wasn't until I got back to the office, sweaty and still embarrassed, that I saw he'd sent a message.

Blake: I have a Plan B, Iz, so don't freak out. Can I call you at six?

Plan B? What did that mean? I sighed and contemplated not responding, but texted, I'll be dining with the Darkling, but I suppose he won't mind if I take a call.

Blake: Excellent. Also, you looked VERY cool jogging through midtown in high-heeled boots, FYI.

Izzy: Oh, I know.

I logged back in to my computer and was just getting started on a head count report when my phone buzzed again.

Blake: I just found a marinara stain on my tie, so I think I've proven my point about spaghetti.

I smiled and shook my head, even though I was alone in my office.

Izzy: Serves you right—the whole thing was your fault (it didn't have to be like that). I have an orange, Saturn-shaped stain on the center of my shirt, so your tie is child's play. #CountYourBlessings

Blake: Have a good afternoon, Scooter's Amy.

Izzy: Same to you, Mr. Chest.

Chapter Fourteen

Izzy

I took a bite of pizza, set down my plate, and lifted the ringing phone to my ear. "It's five fifty-five—you're early."

"Want me to call back in five?" Blake asked.

I wiped my mouth with a napkin and said, "Nah, but you're going to have to listen to me finish this last piece of pizza."

"Pizza again?" He sounded amused. "It's only been a few hours since your last piece."

"Your point?"

"Forget it."

The Darkling jumped onto my lap, and I ran a hand over his fluffy back. "What did *you* have for dinner, Phillips? A brick of kale? Fifteen chicken breasts?"

"Those are seriously your guesses?"

"I used to work with this super-swole guy, and he literally ate five chicken breasts every day." I couldn't remember his name, but one time he'd shown me a video of himself lifting weights, and then he'd been pissed when I laughed at the noise he made. But to be fair, it was a really weird noise. "He ate one breast during each fifteen-minute break, and three for lunch."

"Do people still say *swole*?"

"I don't know, but they should." I flipped on *Little House* and said, "So I bet you had a veggie burrito and sweet potato tots."

The deep, quiet laugh made me snuggle a little deeper into the sofa cushions. He said, "That's *really* specific."

"Wrong?"

"I had a turkey sandwich."

"So basically the same thing."

"Sure." I could hear dishes clinking as he said, "So listen. I was thinking about us."

My fingertips got tingly, and my heartbeat picked up. *Us.* God, did he want there to be an *us*?

"Yeah?" I said casually, gnawing on my lip and waiting for more. The Darkling meowed his displeasure that I'd stopped petting, and jumped down from my lap.

"Yeah. I appreciate your Scooter's presentation and value its merits, but I think we're making things too complicated."

"You do?" I glanced at the TV and watched Ma Ingalls walk into Oleson's Mercantile with a basketful of eggs on her arm.

"Sure," Blake said, and it sounded like he was pounding on something. "We're both adults, right?"

"Right . . . ?"

"So I think we can handle it." His voice was all cool confidence as he said, "Just because we have a little chemistry doesn't mean we're at the mercy of our basest instincts, right? We're not animals."

"Animals," I repeated, unsure of his point.

"There's no reason we can't be friends who do regular friend things. Saying we can't ever be alone is completely negating the fact that we're grown-ass people capable of ignoring the occasional spark."

So he saw our burning, palpable attraction as an *occasional spark*—good to know.

I didn't know what to say, so I asked, "What is that pounding noise?"

"What?"

"The pounding," I repeated, irritated I felt disappointed that Blake's discussion of *us* wasn't a desire to find an *us*. "What is that pounding?"

"Oh," Blake said, sounding confused. "I'm making cat food."

Fuck me, I thought. Wooden stake, holy water, garlic—all of it would never be enough. The man was making homemade cat food. "Your cats are too good for Meow Mix?"

"Too old and pukey for Meow Mix," he replied.

"Ah."

"Is there a reason you changed the subject, Shay?" he asked, his voice quiet in my ear.

"Not at all," I said, a little too bright and cheery. "I totally agree that we're not animals."

He coughed out a laugh. "Oh-*kay*, but what about the rest?"

I exhaled before saying, "I mean, yes—of course we can handle it."

"You have my word, Iz," he said, tone gravely serious, "that no matter how alone we are, I will always behave as if we're standing in front of the board of directors."

"Oh." *Always.* "That makes me feel so much better. Thank you."

Blake

I thought getting it out in the open would make me feel better, but it didn't.

The way she definitively said, *That makes me feel so much better*, confirmed what I'd suspected, that Izzy would never be comfortable being friends with me if she was afraid of something physical happening. I'd meant to assure her that she could let her guard down, but I felt . . . fuck, *something* about how relieved she seemed.

"Now that we've gotten that out of the way," I said, scooping the cat food out of the mixing bowl and pressing it into the airtight container with a rubber spatula. "Let's talk about your car."

She sighed, and the speakerphone sent her breath across the expanse of my kitchen. "Let's not."

"Iz, listen to me. I don't want to get in your business, but my dad is a mechanic. I grew up around cars. There's a good chance I can fix it."

"Oh, my God, you have a dad?" she said, always the smart-ass.

"Ha ha," I said, picturing the asshole who'd taught me about cars when it was one of his court-appointed "dad" weekends.

"Blake, I just can't."

"I thought of a favor," I said, grabbing a towel to wipe the outside of the Pyrex bowl. "If you need that to make it okay."

She said, "I'm scared, but lay it on me."

I put the cat food in the fridge, then took the bowl to the sink and started filling it with soapy water. "I have to go to Boston on Wednesday, and you could take care of my cats while I'm gone."

She didn't say anything, but I thought I heard her squeak.

"Did you hear me?"

"Yes. Um." She cleared her throat and said, "What exactly would that entail? Because pouring food into a bowl is not the equivalent of labor-intensive automobile repairs."

"Oh, trust me." I washed my hands, then turned off the water and let the bowl soak. "They're very high-maintenance."

"Tell me everything," she said, sounding interested, which made me smile. She was so weird.

I went into the living room, sat down on the couch, and turned on the TV. Both of the cats were immediately on my lap; it was like they were on guard, just waiting for me to sit. They liked to paw around to get comfortable, but I put my hands on their backs and helped them settle into a sit so they didn't drive me crazy. "Goodyear is blind, so everything has to be routine or he just walks in circles, meowing, because he can't figure out what's going on."

"Oh, my God, that's the sweetest thing I've ever heard," she said.

"When you walk in the door, you have to say his name a few times, so he knows you're there. I usually pick him up and pet him when he finally appears, just to ensure he knows everything is okay."

Izzy squeaked again, which for some bizarre reason made me happy as I scratched Goodyear's head and looked for something to watch.

"He likes his food—which I keep in the fridge—warmed up. He also needs his food and water to be in the exact same spot at all times, or again with the circles."

"I'm so in love with your cat, Phillips, you don't even know," she said.

Which made me grin like a dipshit, all alone in my fucking living room. "He has pills that I have to crush and put in homemade applesauce, which he licks off a plastic spoon."

"While you hold it?" she asked.

"Why do I feel like this is a cat-lady version of phone sex?"

She started laughing—hard—and said, "Oh, my God, it *so* is, Blake. *Tell me what you're wearing when you're holding the spoon. Does he lick it fast or slow?*"

She started cackling, and I couldn't help but laugh right along with her as I switched and gave Hole's chin a scratch. "You little fucking deviant, quit using my elderly cat's needs to scratch your weirdo itch."

"My apologies, Mr. Chest." She cleared her throat and said, "Please continue."

I flipped past *Little House* and wondered if she was watching. "My other cat, Hole, is diabetic, so he needs two injections a day."

"Are you kidding me with all of this?" she said, still laughing a little.

"I'm afraid not," I said, wondering if it was too much for her.

"This is very incredible." I could hear the smile lingering in her voice. "Also please explain your cats' names."

I stopped on *SportsCenter* and said, "I found Goodyear under my tire in the parking garage, and I found Hole in a hole behind my parents' house."

"Your lack of naming convention inspiration is truly remarkable."

"Thank you."

"Not a compliment."

"Sure it was."

"I am *dying* to see what your little guys look like," she said, sounding excited. "Sign me up for the cat sitting, bro—I'm a thousand percent in."

"I can barely move at the moment because they're all over me."

"What color are they? Are they fluffy?"

"You really *are* a cat lady, aren't you?" I looked at the boys and said, "Want to flip to FaceTime so you can see them?"

Izzy

Yes.

No.

I don't know!

I was dying to see his cats, but could I just FaceTime without preparation? I stalled with, "Can you do that, mid-call?"

"Sure," he said. "You just hit the button."

I did a quick self-appraisal—sloppy bun, glasses, *YOUR MOM* T-shirt. I was a mess, but since he'd admitted to feeling nothing for me except friendship and a random spark, what did it matter?

"Show me the cats, then," I said, feeling nervous as I waited for the switch. Apple did its magic, Blake accepted the Face-Time, and then—

Oh, dear God.

There was Blake, only he looked *nothing* like VP Blake. His dark hair was messy, like he'd changed shirts and hadn't cared to fix it afterward. He was sitting on a beige couch, wearing a faded red KC T-shirt that read *0:13* in yellow numerals. The cotton tee looked soft and worn, and it showcased that beautiful pec-cleavage-ridge thing that put the Chest in his Mister.

But worse than all of that gorgeousness? There were two cats curled up against his abs, one gray and one black, and his big hand was wrapped underneath them, holding them in place.

Was it hot in here? It felt hot to me all of a sudden.

"Nice shirt," he said, smirking as his dark eyes crinkled at the corners. "Where's the Darkling?"

I raised the phone so he could see the cat sitting on the back of my neck. That made his lips slide into a full-on grin. I said, "So tell me which one is which."

"This little pain in the ass is Hole," he said, gently lifting the gray cat's chin to the phone. "He's a hair ball nightmare and likes to sit on my ear when I'm sleeping, so I really should've dumped him back in the hole a long time ago."

I only half heard his words because I was obsessed with his face. The way big, powerful Blake looked at his feline friend as he talked shit about him made me a little weak in the knees.

"And this is Goodyear." Blake raised the fluffy black face to the phone and said, "I'm fairly certain the universe dropped him under my tire as some sort of punishment for my sins."

"Or as a reward for the one good thing you've done in your life," I said.

"Not possible. And there's more than one," he said.

"Doubtful."

"So," he said, resettling the cats against his midsection. "Are you watching *Little House*?"

"You know it," I said, surprised he remembered.

"Is that your plan for the rest of the night?" he asked. "Charles Ingalls and pizza?"

"Oh, I'm sure I'll switch to binge-watching old seasons of *Top Chef* soon, but Charles is always with me in my heart."

The cats jumped off his lap and ran out of my line of sight. He shook his head and said, "A bird just landed on the railing of my deck. Somehow Goodyear always knows something's happening and blindly follows Hole."

"Show me your deck," I said, then laughed when he gave me an eyebrow raise.

I elaborated, "D-E-C-K, deck."

"Ah," he said, and then he stood and was moving. He was walking as he looked into the camera and said, "I'll show you my big deck, and then we're going to make a plan for your car."

"Bossy," I said, a little hypnotized by his FaceTime eye contact and his deep voice saying *my big deck*.

"Only to the stubborn," he replied.

I heard him open the sliding door, and then he turned the camera around.

"Wow." He obviously lived in the center of the city in some

kind of high-rise, way outside of my price range. "I bet you could kill someone with an apple from that height."

He turned his phone back around and gave me a you-are-ridiculous look as he walked back inside. "Now, about your car."

"Okay, my car. I will take the title to the lot after work tomorrow and get it out of jail."

"I can give you a ride, if you want." He collapsed back onto the couch, and in a second, the cats were on top of him again. I couldn't help but notice he didn't even flinch it was so natural, and that was unfairly adorable. "And then we can have it towed to my garage."

I still felt weird about that. "Um, okay, as long as you promise your cats will be the worst for me."

"Oh, absolutely they will. They are the bane of my existence," he said, sounding like he loathed them while they sleepily purred against his body.

Blake

"What the hell is that thing behind you?" I asked, knowing full well what it was.

She looked over her shoulder at the workout tower and said, "That? It's a workout *thing*."

"A *thing*, huh?" It was almost midnight, and we'd been FaceTiming for hours. It hadn't been intentional, but we'd started watching the same episode of *Top Chef* somewhere around nine and had essentially been binge-watching together ever since.

I said, "I bet you don't even know how to use it."

She scowled at me. "Yes, I do."

"You have scrawny arms—can't believe you. Sorry."

She rolled her eyes at me through the camera, then stood. *Like I knew she would.* "Watch and learn, Mr. Chest."

Things went blurry for a minute, and then I was staring at the machine, so she must've propped her phone against something. She came into view in that stupid T-shirt and black leggings, and I leaned back against the couch and enjoyed the entertainment.

"Now, don't be jealous of my strength, Blakey," she said, dancing around like a boxer getting ready for a fight. "This isn't something everyone can do."

"Right."

It was weird, I thought as she acted like a dork in front of the camera with her messy hair and nerd glasses. Skye had been charming in a perfect sort of way (when she wasn't lying to me). She was gorgeous and elegant. I'd been crazy about her, ready to marry her, but I'd never felt this . . . *charmed* by her.

It was probably just because I actually had fun with Izzy. I was *friends* with her, whereas I hadn't really been with Skye.

Talk about a marriage red flag.

Izzy wrapped her hands around the handles and brought up her legs in front of her. "You lift your legs, Phillips, and it strengthens the core. See?"

She brought her legs up and down.

"*That* is how you're using that thing?" I shook my head as she beamed proudly while dangling from the exercise apparatus. "What about the other side?"

"What?" She dropped her feet to the floor and let go of the handles.

"You're supposed to grab the top of the other side and do pull-ups."

She looked up at the pull-up bar, then back at the camera. "I mean, I suppose you *could* do that if you're a pathetic little workout monkey, but this machine is for your core, dumbass."

"It is not, *dumbass*." I crossed my arms and said, "It's for pull-ups, and the part you're using for your core is for back pull-ups."

"That doesn't even sound real, back pull-ups," she said, walking toward her phone and carrying it with her as she sat back down. "You don't know what you're talking about."

"I have the same machine, Shay," I said.

"Then show me or it's not true, Phillips," she replied, her stubborn chin raised.

I stood and started walking toward the spare bedroom. "Fine, but you're about to feel *really* stupid."

Izzy

Holy crap—his bedroom.

I saw it in a flash as he walked down the hall with the camera facing forward, but it was too quick for me to register anything other than a very big bed.

Of course he had a big bed.

He flipped on the lights in another room that appeared to be an office/workout room. There was a big desk, along with a treadmill, an exercise bike, and a workout tower exactly like mine.

He set the phone down—I assumed on the desk—so it faced the tower.

"Oh, my God, am I going to discover the secrets of Mr. Chest's chest?"

"You wish," Blake said, and then he reached up with his long arms and grabbed the pull-up bar. Without a word, he started doing pull-ups as if they were the easiest thing in the world.

"Booooo," I said, unable to stifle the giggle that escaped as my eyes were treated to Blake's Feats of Strength. "That's lame. Total weak sauce."

"I haven't heard that expression since middle school," he said while not slowing or ruining his perfect form.

"I don't think I've said it since then." I couldn't help but notice the hard strip of stomach that was exposed by his raised arms. Not only that, but his shorts hung low on his hips, so low that I could see that jutting hip bone thing that was pretty much an anatomical aphrodisiac.

Sweet holy hip bones, I need smelling salts.

"Stop it, before I puke," I said. "Your form is atrocious."

He dropped himself to the floor and beamed at the camera, smiling in a way that made me feel like he knew how hot I was for him. "Sure it is."

"What about the other part?" I asked, but I felt like a perv as I said it because I was basically just requesting that he perform another Feat of Strength. "I think you made up something called a *back* pull-up . . . ?"

He went around to the other side and started doing dip-down things that made me want to bite his apple-bottom biceps, so I said, "Oh, those. I did like a hundo this morning."

He dismounted, winked, and said, "Okay, Iz."

I rolled my eyes and said, "Don't you have some chickens to eat or something?"

"Trying to get rid of me?" he asked, turning off the light and heading back in the direction of the living room (or so I thought from this initial FaceTime visit to his apartment).

"I probably should—it's pretty late," I said, not wanting to get off the phone but knowing it was the responsible thing to do.

"Yeah, I suppose you're right," he replied, a serious expression crossing his face for the briefest of seconds. His eyes seemed to search mine as he said, "I'm sure you have more pizza to eat, anyway."

"There *are* a few leftover pieces," I agreed, and there was something so warm and comfortable about our mutual teasing that I was already homesick for it, even though we weren't even off the phone yet.

We made plans for him to pick me up the following day, after work, to get things rolling with my car. But after the call was disconnected, I couldn't settle down enough to even consider sleep. I was wired, all keyed up from hours of Blake, and I kind of didn't know what to do with myself.

I turned off the lights, lay down, and was trying to force sleep when my phone buzzed on my nightstand.

I rolled over and picked it up.

Blake: You awake?

I grabbed my glasses and slid them back on my nose before responding. Sadly, yes. Wide awake.

Blake: Good.

Izzy: Mean.

Blake: I was thinking—you should probably come over to my place tomorrow.

I gasped and sat straight up in bed. *Whaaaat?* He wanted me to come over? How was I even supposed to respond to that?

Blake: I leave for Boston really early Wed. morning, so I should probably show you everything you need to know about the cats.

That's right—the cats. I rubbed my fingertips over my eyebrows and sighed. Texted, That works. After we go to the impound lot?

Blake: Yeah. I was thinking I can order a pizza for you to inhale while you meet the boys.

I was trying to keep my brain from overload, but I was going to be eating dinner with Blake tomorrow. Just Blake and me, alone in his apartment. With his very big bed. And his pull-up abdominals. *Gahhhh.*

I was trying to get a grip on that when he sent another text.

Blake: Would you consider staying at my apartment while I'm gone? I feel bad asking, but I hate leaving Goodyear alone even more. And this way you won't have to keep coming and going; way easier.

Stay at Blake's apartment?!

I responded: Um.

Blake: It's close to work, too, so you won't have to mess with the bus. Three-minute walk.

I wanted to say yes, but it felt like a bad idea. A terrible idea. A colossally bad, terrible idea. My phone buzzed yet again, and I felt my cheeks go warm when I read his message.

Blake: I AM BEGGING. I'll even let you sleep on my brand-new (being delivered Wed.) California king (with adjustable firmness) that is touted as the equivalent of sleeping on a cloud—that's how desperate I am.

Staying at Blake's apartment. Sleeping in Blake's bed. *What in God's name is happening?* Was I having a dream? I slapped my cheek and no—not a dream.

Izzy: Can I use your building's amenities?

Blake: Of course.

Izzy: Can I eat pizza in your new bed?

Blake: Of course NOT.

I pulled back the covers and got out of bed. I might as well go grab a book, because there was no way I was going to go back to sleep now. Life just got really interesting, and my brain was preparing to explode.

I texted as I walked into the living room: I'll do it, but I'm very afraid of falling in love with your cats.

It took a few minutes for Blake to respond, and his words did something to my already riotous belly.

Blake: Don't be scared, Iz. Just take a deep breath and let yourself fall.

Chapter Fifteen

Izzy

"Do you want a receipt?"

God, no, I thought, depressed by the amount of money I'd just paid to get my nonworking car out of jail. I put my credit card back in my wallet and said to the guy behind the counter, "No, thanks."

"Young's will be picking up the vehicle within the hour," Blake said, all-business, and I looked at him. When had he called the towing company? He was still in a suit and tie, all VP vibes, and there was something ridiculously attractive about the authority he exuded.

"Sounds good," the lot attendant said, nodding. "They know where it's going?"

Blake answered in the affirmative, but also gave the guy the address of his garage, just in case.

I looked down at my dirty Chucks, which were right next to his perfect butter-soft leather dress shoes. I knew I looked like a total wreck next to him. But I'd decided, when I got home from work, that a wise thing to do would be to change into scrubby clothes, wash my face, and pull my hair back into a ponytail.

Blake told me he'd never make a move on me—and I totally believed him—but I also figured I'd be less inclined to overthink our spark if I knew I looked awful.

"Ready?" he asked, one eyebrow raised, and I nodded and turned toward the door.

Once we were in his car, I said, "You live downtown, but the address you gave for your garage is out in Springfield. Why so far?"

"I don't work on cars that often," he said as he maneuvered through traffic, "so I opted for the less expensive option a little further away."

"So, it's not the garage you regularly keep your vehicle in."

"No." His big hands turned the steering wheel as he went around a corner. "My building has a garage for parking. The Springfield bay is just a little project stall for repairs."

"Oh," I murmured, trying not to imagine him leaning over the hood of a car with his hands wrapped around wrenches. "Do you have coveralls?"

He glanced over at me. "No."

"Gloves? Safety glasses?"

"What are you doing here, Shay?"

I shrugged and said, "Just trying to picture you working on cars but it's impossible because you're so . . ."

I waved a hand, gesturing toward his *GQ* looks and the interior of his luxury SUV.

"Well, you won't have to picture it for long," he said, switching lanes, "because I'm going to make you keep me company when I work on your hot rod."

I crossed my arms and said around a laugh, "What if I don't feel like it?"

"Too bad," he said with a small smirk as he kept his eyes on the road. "I expect you to feed me, entertain me, and assist me while I bring your car back to life like some sort of mechanically inclined god."

"Oh, I'll be doing *something* to you while you work," I said, then instantly realized how it sounded. That was *not* what I meant. I meant physical harm, not sex acts!

He didn't say a word, but his jaw clenched, and I felt like acknowledging what I *didn't* mean would make my suggestive suggestion even more suggestive.

Or something.

Shit.

"But be careful what you wish for," I charged forth with, refusing to let it get weird. "Perhaps I shall read aloud from my favorite novel or sing the entire *Hamilton* score."

"Why do these ideas not surprise me?"

"Because you can tell I'm artistic?"

"Because I can tell you like to irritate me." Blake pulled into a parking garage in the center of the city, leaving me to assume he lived in the high-rise above it. When he parked, I got out of the car without a word, trying to act like I wasn't crazy impressed by his address.

He gestured toward an elevator enclosure, and we walked in that direction. When he pressed the up button, I asked, "Can your cats have tuna?"

He looked over at me. "Why?"

"Just curious," I said, pulling the pouch of StarKist out of my hoodie pocket. "Can they?"

"Yes," he said. "But they already have food."

"This will buy their insta-love for me, though," I said.

"I wouldn't hold my breath."

The elevator dinged, and the doors slid open.

"Why?" I asked, watching as he stepped in after me and pushed the button for the ninth floor. "They don't like tuna?"

"They don't like people," he said.

"Oh, well, I'm not people," I replied, watching the doors close. Floor numbers started popping up on the display as the car went up. "All cats love me."

"We'll see," he said, pulling his phone out of his pant pocket and unlocking the screen.

"Yes, we *will*," I muttered.

That made Blake look up from his phone. His eyes were a little squinty, like he was thinking as his eyes moved over my face. He asked, "Pepperoni or combo?"

"Pepperoni," I said, looking down because sometimes his eye contact was a little *too* direct.

When the elevator reached the ninth floor, I followed Blake down a long hallway with ivy-patterned gray carpet. Modern sconces on midnight walls illuminated our way like fairy lights on a dusky garden path. He stopped in front of 964 and pulled his keys from his pocket.

"I like your door," I said, then wanted to smack my hand over my mouth for sounding so dumb. But it was ridged with heavy wood panels and a huge brass knocker, like it was the entrance to a grand estate instead of an apartment.

"Thanks," he said, unlocking the door and holding it open for me. "Is it weird to say that the minute I saw it, I knew I was going to lease this unit?"

"Super weird, actually," I said, breezing past him and into his apartment. "It could've been a door made gorgeous on purpose, just to disguise that it's actually a portal to hell."

"Wood door—didn't have to worry about that," he said, and I felt the tiniest of shivers crawl up my back as he hovered somewhere behind me. I heard the door close, and tried to tell myself that it was no big deal, being alone with him in his apartment. "Hell's portal would require fireproof metal."

"I suppose," I said, stepping over so he could lead. "Unless that's what they want you to think."

He stopped beside me. Gave me a questioning eyebrow and asked, "Who are *they* in this situation?"

I shrugged. "You know—them."

He looked like he was going to smile, but instead he put his keys on the table just inside the door and said, "Hey. Goodyear."

I turned and stared, looking for the cat. Blake walked farther into the apartment, and I followed on his heels, reaching into my hoodie pocket to open the tuna pouch.

"I'm home, buddy," Blake said, and I shook my head from my spot behind him. The man was seriously a fearsome thing to behold as his deep voice called to the cat in sweet softness.

Silver bullets, maybe? Perhaps silver bullets were my only chance for survival.

The cat meowed and came around the corner, a sweet little fluffer who headed straight for Blake as he lowered his big body to a deep squat and said, "Hey, bro."

Blake scooped up the cat and stood, turning to look at me. He rubbed the cat's head, and I stepped a little closer.

"Hey, Goodyear," I said, reaching out a hand to pet him.

He hissed and made a little cat-growl noise, instantly backing me up.

"Told you," Blake said, sounding pleased as he kept rubbing Goodyear's head.

"It's only because we just met," I countered, rolling my eyes and pulling the tuna out of my hoodie. "He'll love me soon enough."

"Don't bank on it."

"Are you going to show me around your apartment or what?" I asked, waving the pouch of seafood around in hopes of a feline response.

"Oh, don't be snarky," he said, treating me to a full smile. "If he could see your face, I'm sure he'd love you."

"He'll love me anyway." The cat seemed entirely unmoved by my fishy offering. "Where's the kitchen?"

"Follow me." Blake led me through a living room that had huge windows, a gorgeous buff-colored midcentury sofa, a wall of bookshelves, and a thick off-white area rug that looked like nap perfection.

"That view does not suck," I muttered to myself, looking out at the city as I followed him.

When we walked into the kitchen, I had two thoughts.

The first: Blake was an entirely different kind of adult than I was. His kitchen was large and modern and didn't have any random items sitting out. No empty Amazon boxes; no cans lined up on the counter, waiting to be recycled; and not a single dish was resting in the sink.

I needed a time machine so I could go back a few days and be mortified as he visited my small and not-pristine apartment.

The second: He had to have a cleaning service. There was just no way a young, busy guy had time to make his place shine quite that brightly.

I was a big believer in the five-second rule, but in Blake's kitchen I'd go a full thirty.

"So this is where you'll find their food." He opened his chef-quality refrigerator and pointed to the bottom shelf. "The orange containers."

"Is the color indicative of something? Is orange cat-specific?"

"No," he said, pulling out a container and opening it.

"I thought maybe the O stood for something like *oh, no, it's not for people.* Or *oops, this is horsemeat.*"

That made his mouth kick up just a little. "*Only for felines?*"

"Exactly."

He looked at me for a long second, his dark eyes all over my face, and I was about to ramble incoherently to ward off awkwardness, when he said, "The boys like their food warmed up—which I know is ridiculous, so spare me the mockery. I put it in this microwave for forty seconds."

He gestured to the sink, and when I followed his finger, I saw that just to the left of it, under the counter, was a built-in microwave that looked old and crappy—it had a turn dial, for God's sake. He opened the door, put in the food, and started the noisy old machine.

I raised my eyes to his in disbelief. "Do you . . . have a separate microwave for them?"

He gave a casual shrug and looked a little uncomfortable. "It felt wrong to cook cat food where you cook human food, so I bought an old microwave at Goodwill to use for their dinner."

I couldn't *not* smile at him, because he was beyond adorable. "Did you know that you're a cat lady underneath your fancy suit?"

"I am not," he said, flipping me off before taking out the food. I was impressed by his ability to hold an entire cat in his left hand while doing other things with his right.

"Oh, I think you are. This level of pet care is seriously—"

"No." He raised his eyebrows and gave me a Stern Daddy look. "I hate these little pains in the asses, but it's easier to just do what they want so they shut up and leave me alone."

I tried not to smile, but it was impossible. "If you say so."

"I do," he said firmly, and I coughed to cover my laugh.

He walked the food over to a mat in the corner, where he dropped the bowl and the cat. Another cat—Hole, I presumed—appeared out of nowhere to join Goodyear for the feast.

"I think I can handle this. Doesn't look too tough," I said, watching them go to town on their food. I glanced over at Blake, and he was loosening his tie. I felt frozen for a second, immobilized by the movement that seemed intimate, like something I shouldn't be seeing.

I said, "If you want to go change out of your work clothes, I promise not to rifle through your things."

"But can I believe you?" he teased, pulling off his tie and unbuttoning that restrictive top button. I heard his words, but my eyes were stuck on his throat. They didn't want to move, for some reason, but I blinked fast and forced them up.

"Sure," I managed, slightly dizzy. "Why wouldn't you?"

He raised an eyebrow, reminding both of us of my Scooter's theft, and I rolled my eyes.

"Okay," he said. "But if I catch you digging, there will be consequences."

"So intimidating," I quipped.

His phone rang as I said it, and when he took it out of his pocket and looked at the display, he let out a little groan. "I have to take this—it's work."

"Perfect. Go take it in your room but shut the door so I can rifle in peace."

He gave me a look that was *almost* a smile before raising the phone to his ear. "This is Blake."

Blake

When I walked into the kitchen twenty minutes later, I didn't expect to see *that*.

Izzy was sitting on the island, dangling her legs back and forth while eating a slice of pizza and watching another old episode of *Top Chef* on my TV.

It wasn't that she was doing anything unusual or wrong, it

was that she looked so unbelievably at home. Like she belonged there.

I got that fucking buzz in my gut that I'd been interpreting as an annoying don't-be-an-idiot alarm bell as I approached her.

"I like your shirt," she said, giving me a smart-ass smile as her eyes stayed on my Frank Reynolds *So anyway I started blasting* T-shirt.

"I've got basketball tonight, and this is our uniform," I explained.

"So it's obviously quite serious," she said, grabbing a half-empty bottle of Stella from the counter and lifting it to her mouth. "Want one of your beers?"

"Yes. Thank you so much." I walked over to the fridge and grabbed one, then returned to the island. The bottle opener was beside her on the counter—*right* beside her—and her smell engulfed me as I grabbed it and uncapped the beer.

What the fuck was that—shampoo? Lotion? Perfume? It was like vanilla and baby powder but hot.

"Your cats love me now, by the way," she said, and I had no idea if she was kidding or not.

But it was always that way with her.

"Do they," I said, opening the pizza box and grabbing a slice.

"Well, no—but they will. I have a plan," she said, picking up a crust from her plate.

"And that would be . . . ?" I asked, raising the piece to my mouth while watching her nose crinkle as she grinned at me. I was still fucking obsessed with her nose crinkles.

She tilted her head. "Between me and the boys."

"Is that right?" Someone on the TV was crying because

their pork belly was too dry, and Hole was weaving in between my feet, but all I could do was stare down at her smiling face.

Dear God, she was so fucking pretty.

It wasn't about her looks, though, as asinine as that sounded. She was pretty because she was alive and chaotic and funny and smart. Her eyes fucking sparkled and her nose crinkled and her mouth slid into smiles as if that were its default.

I looked at her lips and remembered what it felt like to kiss her. How it felt to have her sigh into my mouth and hold on to me as if she, too, was fighting the battle of endless imaginings.

"When do you medicate the fluffy guy?" she asked, her voice breathy as her eyes traveled all over my face.

"Whenever I want," I replied, telling myself to move back while leaning a bit closer and resting one palm on each side of her on the butcher-block counter.

"Do you think he'll take it from me?" she asked, her voice even quieter.

"Fuck, yes," I said, hypnotized by her mouth and her words and the way her eyes kept fluttering down.

"Good," she said in a near whisper, and I could almost feel the softness of her breath against my lips.

"So, um," she said, blinking fast before breaking eye contact to look up at the TV. "*Shit.* Um. Where do you keep the apple-sauce?"

Applesauce. Applesauce. What is applesauce again? I straightened, took a full step back, and felt like I was waking up from a dream.

"Applesauce," I repeated, my brain scrambling to catch up. "Is in the fridge."

What the hell had just happened? When had I dropped my slice of pizza on the fucking countertop?

I went over to the fridge, opened the door, and got out the jar of applesauce and Goodyear's meds. Without looking back at her, I grabbed a plastic spoon and yogurt container from the drawer and went to find the cat.

"He's in here," I said, finding Goodyear on my chair. I took a deep breath. *Nothing happened. Izzy probably didn't even notice that you were a millisecond from kissing her.*

I heard her feet as she jumped down from the island, and she looked totally normal and not freaked out as she came out of the kitchen and walked toward me. Yes, her cheeks were pink, but it was warm in there.

Really fucking hot, actually.

"Okay, show me how you slip the cat a mickey." She shifted her weight to one leg and crossed her arms.

"Okay." I showed her how to smash a pill in the bottom of the yogurt container and stir in applesauce.

When I picked up Goodyear and sat down on the chair, Izzy said, "Wait—you do this on an off-white chair?" She looked horrified. "What if you spill?"

"I don't," I said, wanting to laugh as she continued to look aghast.

"Note to Iz—sit on floor when you do this," she muttered. "Continue, please."

"Thank you." I scooped up the medicated applesauce and held out the spoon, to which Goodyear immediately lifted his fuzzy little face and started taking it down. The guy had a thing for applesauce.

"He *really* likes applesauce," she said, dropping to a squat beside me and watching Goodyear go HAM on the spoon. She reached out a hand and petted his head, which made the cat give her a closed-mouth growl while he eyeballed her but kept licking.

I *did* laugh at that, and she looked up at me, grinning and crinkling her nose.

Shit. Suddenly I felt like I couldn't breathe.

And when she took the spoon from me to try feeding him, I realized I'd made a terrible mistake.

A gross miscalculation.

Because having her in my house, surrounded by my things and sleeping in my bed and leaving her what-the-hell-is-that-amazing-fucking-smell smell all over the place—well, that had the potential to change everything, regardless of whether or not anything physical happened between us.

And there was a tiny part of me that didn't hate the idea of that change.

Damn it, I thought as that traitorous cat started purring.

It was just so fucking hot in that apartment.

Wasn't it?

I was so focused on her at that moment that I didn't hear a key jangling in the door, leading me to nearly have a heart attack when Jason and AJ burst into my living room a second later.

"Why aren't you ready?" Jason said, looking at Izzy with his eyes narrowed, like he couldn't believe what he was seeing.

"I texted like five times to warn you," AJ said to me, shaking his head apologetically. "The Bricks are playing in the game before ours, so Jace wants to go early and heckle."

"Come on, are you kidding," I said. Jason was so obnoxious.

I glanced at Izzy, and she was looking up at my brothers with a curious grin.

"Izzy, these are my brothers. The loud one is Jason, and the slightly less loud one is AJ. Guys, this is Izzy."

"Nice to meet you," AJ said.

"Nice to meet you, too," she replied with a smile.

"You're giving Goodyear his meds, and the psycho isn't even hissing?" Jason said in disbelief, watching my cat eat the laced applesauce from her spoon. "Who the fuck *are* you, Izzy?"

I was ready to jump in and explain away his behavior, but before I had a chance, she said around a smirk, "You're a grown-ass man wearing matching shirts with your brothers. Who the fuck are *you*, Jason?"

Chapter Sixteen

Blake

"Haven't I told you enough?"

"Nope," Kylie said, raising her hand to signal to the server she needed another beer. "Because it doesn't make sense to me yet."

I sighed and looked at Jason. "Can't you do something about your wife?"

"You know that I cannot," he said. "And I don't want to. Your idiocy is giving me life."

"My *idiocy*?" I repeated. "Care to explain how my friendship with this person is *idiocy*?"

Because my brothers showed up early, my plan for giving Iz a quiet ride home had been tossed aside, and the four of us ended up piling into Jason's old truck. They'd talked Izzy into going to our game first, which she seemed to have fun at, and then they convinced her to join us for wings.

They'd been fairly chill all night, but in the five minutes that

Izzy had been standing by the door, taking a phone call, I'd been subjected to a speed round of interrogation.

Kylie had forced me to divulge every tiny detail of my strange new friendship.

The way we met, the way we'd come to be friends, the way we were very intentionally carving a path that would never lead to romance because it was against the rules.

"It's obvious you have chemistry and you're her boss," Jason said matter-of-factly, grabbing a chip from the towering nachos in the center of the table. "So your stupid rules and plans are idiocy. All it's going to take is a single moment, and everything will change."

"No, it won't," I said, irritated. "We aren't animals, for God's sake. We can control our behavior and our environment."

"Oh, really?" he countered with his eyebrows up, looking at me skeptically.

"Really," I said defensively. *Of course we can control them— we have to.* "And you've got crumbs in your beard."

"Really?" he said, lifting his chin and *not* wiping away the disgusting specks in his beard.

"Oh, *really*?" AJ teased from the other end of the table, grinning while lifting a taco to his mouth.

"You're *really* fucking annoying," I said, laughing in spite of myself. "Really."

"Okay, but hear me out," Jason said, holding up a hand. "Things with Skye were great until secrets and scheming came into play, right? I know in this particular scenario you and Izzy are scheming *together* instead of her behind your back, but fucking around with the truth is always a mess."

He gave me a look, *that* look, the one that said everything.

"Always," AJ added in agreement, nodding.

And they weren't wrong.

We'd grown up with a father who played fast and loose with the truth, all the time. My parents divorced right after I was born, and I couldn't remember a time in my life when he wasn't hustling reality. He lied about why he couldn't pick us up on his scheduled day, he lied about why he couldn't come up with his child support payments, he lied about promised vacations that never happened, and he lied about the slew of girlfriends who came in and out of our lives.

He fibbed about little things, and he lied about enormously important things; the man was an equal-opportunity liar.

But our mom was always rock solid.

She'd never bad-mouthed him, but as soon as we were old enough to see his dishonesty for ourselves, she quietly used his behavior as a life lesson for all of us.

She taught us that nothing was as important as trust.

Which was part of what made it so incredibly ironic when he showed up out of the blue last year and tried making a play for the insurance money left behind when she died, but that was another thing entirely.

"Well, the part I don't understand is why you aren't just doing what you want." Kylie shrugged and said, "You're consenting adults, and your employer isn't your mommy, right? Just date on the down-low; no one has to know."

"Nope," AJ said, shaking his head. "Terrible way to start a relationship."

"Not the move," Jason agreed. "At all."

"That's just too unethical, Ky," I added, knowing I could never do something that I wouldn't tolerate from another Ellis employee. "I can't."

"Well, those ethics aren't going to snuggle up with you at night, Blakey," she said, rolling her eyes.

I reached for my beer, not enjoying the way that comment made me feel. It sounded an awful lot like what Skye said the night I called off the engagement.

You see it as this strong moral fiber, Blake, but it's just control—do it my way or it's over. Honestly, you're just as controlling as you said your dad was. He controlled the narrative with lies, but you control the narrative with your inability to forgive. Have fun sleeping with that rigid unforgiveness for the rest of your life. Alone.

"Shhh," AJ said as Izzy started walking toward the table. "Here she comes."

Her eyes met mine as she came around the table and took the seat beside me, and something about the way she smiled at me made me want to pull her chair a bit closer.

Instead, I looked at my brothers and said, "Hurry up and finish because I've got an early flight in the morning."

Chapter Seventeen

Izzy

Blake: Fun fact—I hate flying.

I looked at my phone and smiled as I waited in line at Scooter's. I texted, That's because you're a control freak.

Blake: A. No, I'm not. B. I don't need a diagnosis, I need a distraction.

Izzy: You think I'm free to just drop whatever I'm doing to entertain you?

Blake: Be honest—you're in line for coffee, aren't you?

Izzy: That's terrifying. Did you put an AirTag in my purse?

Blake: No, I stuck it to your back like a modern-day "kick me" sign. Also, you told me the first time we met that you waste money at Scooter's every morning.

I ordered my coffee, swiped my card, and moved over to the waiting area. Josh had dropped me off because I hadn't wanted to ride the bus with my overnight bag, the bag I was hauling to work with me because I was going to Blake's swanky apartment when I got off work.

I was excited about the view, the challenge of making his cats love me, and walking to work in the morning like I was the fashionable protagonist in an NYC sitcom, but I was also nervous for some inexplicable reason.

I looked down at the phone and texted, Do you have a window seat?

Blake: Nope. Wedged in between a talker and a hummer.

I snorted and texted, A talker, a chest, and a hummer walk into a bar . . .

Blake: Funny girl.

Izzy: Thank you. What time is your bed being delivered, btw?

Blake: Sometime before two; the doorman will let them in. NO PIZZA on the bed.

Izzy: If a pizza falls on a bed in a forest and the owner of the forest bed isn't there to see it, does it make a sound?

Blake: It doesn't matter because you're not eating on the bed, Shay.

Izzy: Chill, bro—it's hypothetical.

Blake: I WILL KNOW.

Izzy: You're adorable when you use all caps. VERY POWERFUL.

Blake: I'm FaceTiming you tonight at 6:01 and I expect a detailed visual tour of the bed.

Izzy: I'm FaceTiming YOU tonight at 6:01 and I expect a detailed visual tour of your ass.

I quickly fired off a follow-up text.

> **Izzy:** NOT LITERALLY. "Your ass" as in a "your mom" joke. You get it, right? If you moon me via FaceTime I shall report you to the FCC.
> **Blake:** I don't think you need that coffee.
> **Izzy:** You're not the boss of me.
> **Blake:** I am literally the boss of you.
> **Izzy:** I don't think I need this coffee. I have to get to work.
> **Blake:** Have a good day, Iz.

Nicknamification, in my opinion, was the absolute sexiest. Call Isabella Shay by her last name, or Iz, for the love of God, and she melted like a pat of butter on a pile of hot potatoes. I let out a dreamy sigh in response to his *Iz* before responding with You, too, Boss.

"I still don't understand why it's ten o'clock there, and the plastic is still on," Blake said. "What are you waiting for—are you a night owl?"

I was definitely *not* a night owl, and I was getting very sleepy on his big, comfy couch with his cats snuggled in a pile against me, but I just hadn't been able to bring myself to unwrap his new bed yet. It just seemed . . . obtrusive. *He* should be the one to pull off that protective plastic, not me. "No, but I'm far too comfy on this sofa to get up. And these guys might revolt if I do."

"Traitorous little shits." He made a face at me—we'd been FaceTiming for exactly one hour and forty-two minutes—and leaned his head back on the headboard. "It has to be hot as hell in there if you're still running the fireplace *and* the boys are on you."

"Nah—I've got the patio slider open," I said, wishing our call wouldn't have to end soon. Because in addition to the fact that he was pretty much my favorite person in the world to talk to right now, I was kind of enjoying the view.

Yes, he was handsome; the man had a face that inspired erotic letters to the editor. *It was late, and the only other person in the office was the ultrahot billionaire CEO.* But I found myself marginally obsessed with the fact that when put-together VP Blake wasn't working, he was kind of a mess. His hair was always tousled, like he'd forgotten it existed once he removed his tie, and the man seemed to live in faded T-shirts and hoodies.

It was such a contradiction, like beefy Superman being a nerdy reporter, that I felt kind of lucky that I got to see the laid-back side of him.

I suspected not many people did.

Or maybe I just *hoped* that not many people did.

He narrowed his eyes and said, "You're seriously opening the windows and running the heat at the same time?"

"I just love the sound of the city, but hate being cold," I said, shrugging and looking over at the windows. There was something about the lights and the downtown sounds that made me never want to go home.

Well, that and the fact that his apartment was straight-up ridiculous.

For starters, he had an obscenely huge bathtub, as well as a shower that was the size of my entire bathroom. As if that weren't enough, there were built-in Bluetooth stereo speakers wired throughout the place, so I could turn on my favorite playlist and have it stream across every single square foot of that dreamboat apartment.

Monstrously large TV, world's cutest cats, a massive kitchen; why would I ever want to leave? Instead of vacating when Blake returned, I might just barricade myself inside of sexy number 964. Surely I could get in an extra twelve to fourteen hours of luxuriating before the SWAT team finally kicked down that beautiful door and pulled my ass out.

"It's genius, if you think about it," I said, snuggling under the blanket as the autumn breeze blew through the apartment. "By the way, I forgot to tell you—your brother and his wife were here when I got home from work."

I'd been fumbling for the keys in the hallway when the door swung open. I'd nearly jumped out of my skin, but Jason and Kylie were so warm and friendly that we'd ended up chatting in the hall for like thirty minutes.

Which was weird, because I usually didn't know how to talk to strangers.

But they were just so real.

I was a little envious of how close they all seemed. I pretty much only talked to Alex a few times a year, and even then, it didn't feel like we really knew each other as anything more than acquaintances.

Blake and his brothers, though, seemed to know every single thing about each other.

"They were?" He looked surprised. "I'm so sorry, Iz. Sometimes they swing by to use the building's indoor pool, but usually they let me know first."

"No, no," I said, regretting saying anything because he looked so apologetic. "It was no big deal at all. Apparently you've been holding one of Jason's trophies hostage, and he wanted to grab it while you were gone."

"Fucking loser," he said, shaking his head and smiling. "It's not *his*. It's the traveling fantasy football trophy that *I* won last year, but he still can't accept it."

"According to him, there was a little controversy with the finish."

"He's a sore loser—that's the only controversy."

He started telling me about the trade dispute, but I could see he was tired. Whatever he was working on in Boston was confidential—he wasn't able to share anything with me—and important, so I knew I should probably let him go so he could sleep.

"Listen, I'm going to go flood your bathroom by overfilling that decadent tub, so I have to go. Are you planning on text bombing me all day tomorrow, too, or was today just a onetime annoying event?"

Please say yes. We'd spent the entire day in a meaningless text thread of sarcasm and meme besting, and it had been amazing.

He sat up in the bed and leaned closer to the phone so his face filled the entire screen, and said, "If I stop now, you might get the wrong idea and think I'm being nice to you. And we can't have that, can we?"

I tried to play it cool but failed miserably. I was beaming into the phone when I said, "God, no, that would be the *worst*."

Chapter Eighteen

Blake

I'd never been so happy to see my building in my entire life. I held my key card up to the pad, rolled my suitcase through the lobby, and impatiently waited for the notoriously slow elevator.

The trip had gone well, and the merger was now official; everything had gone according to plan, work-wise.

What hadn't gone according to plan, however, was Izzy.

I'd sent her that first text to tease her and to get my mind off the flight, but I hadn't intended on opening a new corridor of our relationship. Though we'd had random textual conversations before my trip, the conversations had usually begun with a purpose. A legit reason for us to be texting.

Now, however, we were rando texting buddies.

I fucking hated that idiotic moniker, but Iz had said it fifteen times over the past few days, just to irritate me, and it had taken root. She was such a little shit, and now I said things like *rando texting buddies*. Obviously our friendship was causing me to shed brain cells.

She texted me about what she was wearing, the noise her coworker made when she chewed potato chips, the macaroni and cheese she'd made in my kitchen, and her thoughts on the mayor's plan to launch a streetcar project.

I texted her about Patriots fans, airport bathroom hand dryers, the book I was reading, my grandmother's phone calls, and my opposing views on the mayor's streetcar proposal.

We'd texted the entire three days I'd been in Boston and FaceTimed every night. I'd even FaceTimed her when I called my grandma on the hotel room phone, just so she could hear how unorthodox my favorite relative was.

Basically, she'd become like one of my buddies. Hell, I was just as comfortable talking to her as I was with my brothers, only with her I got little gut punches when she did certain things. Smiled, laughed, talked about my bathtub, snuggled with my cats; shit like that gave me a pinching pain just above my kidney.

Which I ignored because it was irrelevant.

I pulled out my phone and tried texting her again as I got into the elevator. I am in the building now.

I'd been texting her since 5:00 a.m., when I decided to change my flight and come home a couple hours early. But she hadn't responded. I didn't want to scare her by showing up unexpectedly, but I was also dying to get home and get started on the weekend.

Of course, the only real plans I had were to go for a run, watch football, and fix Izzy's car, but after the past few days of nonstop work, that sounded fucking amazing.

I unlocked the door, opened it slowly, and said, "Izzy?"

I stepped inside and closed the door behind me. I could hear the TV, but no movement. I said more loudly, "Izzy? It's me. I took an earlier flight."

Was she asleep? Perhaps the new bed was *that* good, so comfortable that it rendered the sleeper comatose. *Please, God of Insomnia, let that be the case.*

I took two steps into the living room and said, "Iz, I'm ho—"

My mouth snapped shut when I saw her.

For some reason, the sight of her sleeping on my couch made that pinching feeling so sharp that it almost hurt. *Fuck.* I quietly approached as my gut burned.

Her hands were tucked under her cheek, her hair wild across my pillow—*my* pillow—and a disconcerting emotion I couldn't identify settled on my chest like a brick as I looked down at her. Protectiveness? Longing? Fondness?

Something about seeing her there, cocooned in my blanket, asleep on my couch, made me homesick for . . . *something*.

Fuck, I was a mess, and I was also a fucking creep, watching her sleep like I was goddamn Joe Goldberg.

"Izzy." I dropped to a squat, moved my mouth a little closer to her ear, and said, "I'm home, Iz."

"Chest." Her mouth turned up into a smile, even though her eyes stayed closed, and she turned her head and pressed her lips against mine.

Shit, shit, shit.

"Iz," I said, moving my face away from hers, "wake up."

"I *am* awake," she purred, reaching out and bringing my face back to hers with both hands on my cheeks.

Before I could think, she kissed me, her mouth soft and warm as she opened her lips under mine. I held myself still, unsure of what to do when my head was exploding.

Was she even awake?

"Kiss me, Chest," she said against my mouth, a smile in her voice. "Unless you don't want to."

She moved her hands down to my neck, and the movement threw my squat off balance. I caught myself by bridging one arm over the back of the couch and one on the front, and Izzy apparently took that as a move. She wrapped her arms around my shoulders and pulled me closer, and all of a sudden I was on my knees beside the couch, my upper body leaning in as she bit down on my lower lip.

I'm done, I thought—maybe even said out loud—as I opened my mouth wide over hers, wanting to fucking consume her. She made a noise in the back of her throat that shot heat through me as her hands moved to my chest and her mouth went wild.

She kissed like sex and battle, like domination and competition, like going all fucking out and leaving nothing on the motherfucking floor, holy *shit*. I wanted more—wanted it all—as I felt her fingers flexing, gripping the front of my shirt.

My hands clenched the sofa as her smell—vanilla and something sexy—burrowed into my senses and made me drunk on fumes. I opened my eyes, needing visual confirmation that this was really Izzy, destroying me like I'd imagined her doing a hundred fucking times.

Hell, yes.

I nibbled on her bottom lip and said her name—no, I *rasped* her name, because apparently I'd lost the ability to speak clearly, and her eyes fluttered open.

They seemed absurdly blue as she blinked up at me, a sleepy smile on her mouth.

But then her forehead got a tiny crinkle, just between her eyebrows, and the smile disappeared.

"Oh, my God. Blake," she said, blinking fast and removing her hands from my body like it'd been burning them. She sat up on the couch, gave her head a tiny shake, and said, "Shit, shit, *shiiiit*. I am *so* sorry."

Chapter Nineteen

Izzy

I pushed my hair out of my face and had no idea what to say.

Shiiiiiiiit.

Had I seriously just attacked Blake without his consent? *Seriously?!* He calmly sat down beside me on the sofa, like I hadn't just behaved like a maniac, and I wondered what time it was.

And what the *hell* had just happened.

One minute, I'd been having a sexy dream about him. He'd been kissing me—the world's hottest kiss, for the record—and in my dream, he'd said my name in a total sex voice.

But then I'd opened my eyes and he was there, leaning over the couch, looking down at me with those unreadable dark eyes as I freaking clawed at his chest like . . . *shit* . . . like some aggressive animal with claws that I couldn't name because my brain was no longer functioning.

I wanted to die of embarrassment.

"I was having a dream, and it was super realistic," I blurted out, not expecting him to believe me but desperate to convince him. I didn't want to lose him, so I had to make him understand that nothing had changed between us.

His jaw was hard, his eyes intensely on me as I said, "I don't know how you got here, but somehow my brain thought your presence was part of the dream. I kissed you, but I was kissing someone else in my dream, I swear. Please believe me that I would never, ever make a move on you."

He didn't say anything, just swallowed, and I knew I'd ruined everything.

"Come on, Blake—say something. Tell me that you aren't mad, or grossed out, or, God—that I didn't make you feel violated. This was just a very real, very bizarre mistake, a misunderstanding of epic proportions, and things with us are technically no different than they were last night when we watched *Top Chef* together on FaceTime."

"Izzy."

"I meant it when I agreed with you that we're both adults and can control ourselves, and this random moment of macking was entirely the fault of my unconsciousness."

He looked at me for a long moment, his jaw clenching and unclenching, and I hated that I'd caused that serious expression on his face. I cleared my throat and said, "If I could take it back, I would. I swear it—"

"Who was it?" he interrupted.

"What?"

"Who were you kissing in the dream?" He almost looked pissed. There was an ego blow somewhere in there, tied up in his very unhappy response to my pawing, but I was choosing to ignore it.

He was watching me, waiting for the answer, and I knew everything would be rectified if I could just spew out a name. *Think, think, think.* But just like that, every name on the planet was erased from my mind. Well, every name except Ronald McDonald, but that wouldn't work. I cleared my throat and said, "You don't, um, you don't know him."

I rolled my eyes at myself.

"But you do?" he asked.

I sat up straighter on the couch and turned so I was facing him. "He's just a celebrity. No big—"

He tilted his head. "Which celebrity?"

"You're going to make me say it?" I asked, wanting off the hook but also wanting to kiss his ass into forgetting what just happened.

"Say it."

"You want a name?" I stalled. "You want me to say his name?"

"Name him, Shay."

I groaned. "Come on, Phillips."

"If you don't tell me his name—"

"Fine. Tom Colicchio!" I nearly shouted it, and then I crossed my arms over my chest. Nodded my head and said, "Yes, I was kissing *the* Top Chef."

"Tom Colicchio." He gave me a look that told me he knew I was lying.

So I nodded again, doubling down. Rubbed my lips together and added, "I guess you could say we were having our own little quick fire."

"Are you ready?"

"What?"

He stood, and I noticed he didn't look mad anymore. He pulled his phone out of his pocket and glanced at the display. "I'm starving, so I thought we could drive through Bruegger's when I take you home. Bagels sound good?"

He was sure in a hurry to get me out of his apartment. I nodded, but couldn't stop myself from saying, "So we're okay?"

"Of course." He put the phone back and held out a hand to help me up.

"Thank God." I grabbed his hand and let him pull me to my feet, but every cell in my body ceased to exist except for those in my fingers. His big, warm hand swallowed mine, and the slide of his hot skin on mine was electric and sexual and—*shit*.

It made me literally look down at our hands before quickly letting go.

Dear *God*.

"But, Iz?"

"Yeah?" I shook out my fingers at my side.

"The way you kissed Tom Colicchio," he said, his dark eyes hot, "was fucking sinful."

"Dude, come *on*." Josh held his arms out at his sides before letting loose with a high kick. "That seems like bullshit. Like a flimsy-ass reason for you both to be alone with each other."

I ducked my head as my cousin swung his leg around. I was sitting in the grass of our front yard while Josh and six of his friends practiced some sort of martial arts–yoga–stretching thing. They were all silent as they meticulously followed the leader's movements, so I took the opportunity to sit beside him and tell him my entire situation.

Captive audience and all that.

"I know it sounds that way, but it actually isn't," I explained. "He's this, like, bigwig who totally believes in the values and ethics that go along with his role. He would never get involved with someone who reports to him, because it's *wrong*."

"Is he religious?"

"No—I mean, I don't think so. I think he's just a good human."

"Well, if it's that perfect between you two," the guy to my right said, hissing out his words as he slowly lowered to a squat-like lunge, "why don't you just find another job somewhere else?"

"Butt out, Stan," Josh said, raising his left leg and rotating it. "She shouldn't have to quit."

"But if she's still new to the company, it makes sense," Stan muttered, giving me a know-it-all look.

"But if she's still new to the company," Josh replied, also lowering his body toward the ground, "she needs this huge opportunity more than he does, right?"

I wrapped my arms around my legs, resting my chin on my knees. "You guys just did a great job of getting to the heart of it. But you missed the finer point."

"We did?" Stan asked, his limbs shaking as he held his pose.

"What did we miss?" Josh said, letting out a long, quiet groan as the sun reflected off his forehead.

"If I were to quit my job, which I totally don't want to do

because I love it and it seems like it holds so much potential, what would that say to Blake?" I pictured his face as he'd leaned over me on the couch, and I sighed. "Wouldn't it seem desperate, that I'm willing to quit my job for him even though we've never even gone on a date?"

"No," Josh said, at the exact minute Stan said, "Yeah, totally."

I gave Josh a look, which made him point at his friend and say, "No one ever listens to him. Stan's always wrong."

Stan raised his eyebrows, giving me a long, meaningful look. *Stan is right.*

"Can I steal your I-swear-it-was-a-dream move, by the way?" the group leader asked, smiling as he effortlessly held his leg up against his ear like he was a Rockette. "Sounds like a patented Roy move."

"Who's Roy?" I asked.

"He is," Josh said, pointing at the leader.

"Shut the fuck up and breathe, Roy," Stan said before doing what appeared to be the splits.

Chapter Twenty

Blake

I slid my feet into my Nikes and was reaching for my keys when my phone buzzed. At a glance I could see who the email was from, and I didn't want to open it for multiple reasons.

For starters, it was Saturday morning. *Ever heard of work-life balance, Brad?* I had a lot of respect for my boss, but the man worked 24-7, and I was *not* about that. I worked my ass off, too, but I also valued my free time and refused to let it get polluted by constant emails and phone calls.

But more importantly, I needed to pick up Iz and go work on her car. I was a little out of sorts about the way things ended yesterday morning, and I wanted to right the ship. I'd been pissed as hell when Izzy wouldn't tell me the truth about who she'd been dreaming about—which was irrational, I knew—but then it hit me.

She'd called me Chest. She called me by my name. Sort of.

She might've been having a dream when we kissed, but she'd been having a dream about *me*, not Tom Colicchio.

And that'd made me happy as a goddamn elf, all day long. I'd gone right back to text bombing her, acting like nothing had happened, and she'd even FaceTimed me that night as if I were still in Boston.

But the kiss—holy shit, THE kiss.

The kiss had been playing on a constant loop in my head, and I'd be lying if I said I didn't want to just forget the world and find a way to make it happen again. And again.

But that wasn't possible, and that was fine.

We were destined to be friends, or some other bullshit platitude that was destined to fucking kill me.

I grabbed my keys and headed out, thinking of Iz's I-like-your-door comment as I locked the dead bolt.

I opened Outlook and started reading the email as I walked down the hall, and kept reading as I got in the elevator. I hit the "G" button, the doors slid closed, and I clicked on the attached document.

Now that the merger had gone through, there was a new org chart. Leadership had reorganized the business units since the company had doubled in size, which made sense.

But when the color-coded chart opened and I looked at my division, my ears started buzzing.

Human Resources had shifted, and that department no longer reported to me.

When the elevator doors opened, I sprinted to my car.

Chapter Twenty-One

Izzy

"He just pulled up." I watched through the window as Blake got out of his car and slammed the door. He was wearing jeans and a gray sweatshirt that made his chest look ridiculously wide, and of course, his hair looked like he'd driven all the way over with his windows down. I let go of the blinds I'd been peering through and turned around. "He's here."

"Are you surprised?" Josh asked, not looking away from the monitor in front of him. The Darkling was on his lap as he sat in my desk chair, playing some stupid game on my computer because his was glitching. "That he showed up when he said he was going to show up?"

"No, but I don't—"

Blake knocked on the front door.

"Gah!" I froze and gasped. I whispered, "What do I do?"

"Open the door, numb nuts," Josh said. "This isn't hard."

"Shhh—and yes, it is." I tugged on the bottom of my fuzzy

red sweater—which I'd paired with boyfriend jeans—and tucked my hair behind my ears. "What if he wants to talk about it?"

"You just told me that you guys texted all day yesterday."

"Yeah, but texting is different," I explained, leaning down to pick up the remote control that had been cat-batted onto the floor. "Face-to-face, after I attacked him on his couch, is—"

"Quit being a pussy," Josh said, his eyes still on the computer. "And open the damn door."

"Fine." I walked over, grabbed the cat off his lap, and turned toward the door. "But I'm taking the Darkling for protection."

"Why would you take the cat to the door?"

"Because I don't know if I can deal with him looking at me like I made a move on him," I said, squeezing the cat against my shoulder as he tried jumping down. "Darkster will be a good distraction."

"You are such a dumbass," he muttered as I walked over to the door and grabbed the handle. I shifted the cat in my arms and pulled open the door.

"Hey." It was a small word, a casual one-syllable utterance, but the way Blake said it made my breath catch. His dark gaze moved all over my face, like he was searching for something specific. He looked tense, and I couldn't stop myself from glancing at his mouth and remembering how it'd felt on mine.

"Hey," I replied, turning my attention to the cat in my arms before Blake had a chance to mistake my eye contact for a desire to talk.

"Listen, Iz, I need to talk to you—"

"Sup, Physical Challenge?" Josh yelled from behind me.

Thank you, Josh.

"Josh." Blake sounded surprised by Josh's presence, but I wasn't about to look at him. "How's it going?"

Josh said, "You know."

I had no idea what to do next, so I looked at Josh.

"I'm just about . . ." he said, rapidly hitting keys on the keyboard. He muttered, "Yes, fucker," before looking up, smiling at us, and saying, ". . . to take off."

"No," I blurted out, desperate to not be alone with Blake. "You don't have to go."

Josh pushed back the wireless keyboard and stood. "There's a bacon sandwich upstairs that's calling my name."

"I have bacon," I said, glancing back at Blake, who was watching me with his eyes narrowed.

"Yeah, but what kind of bread do you have?" Josh asked, rubbing a hand over his stomach. "I only like bacon on Wonder Giant."

"I have Wonder Giant," I blurted, relieved that I actually had the stupid bread that my cousin wanted.

"Do you have any mayo?" he asked.

"I think I have—"

"She's out of mayo," Blake interrupted, his voice firm. "And bread."

Josh's face split into a huge grin as his eyes went from Blake to me. "Message received."

"But—but I have both," I said, but it was too late. Josh, that jackass, totally betrayed me. He walked around me and out the door without even looking back.

Shit.

I didn't look at Blake as I closed the door behind Josh, but when I turned around, he was there, crowding me against the door.

"Why are you trying to avoid me?" His voice was thick and deep as he looked down at me.

I rubbed my lips together and said, "I'm not—"

"Isabella Shay." He moved, and before I knew what he was doing, he took the cat from my arms and dropped the Darkling onto the floor.

"Blake Phillips." I meant to say more, maybe, but my heart started thumping as he stepped a little closer.

I looked up at his hot eyes and felt a little lightheaded when he said, "I'm going to fucking lose my mind if you don't let me talk to you."

"So talk," I said, intending to sound unaffected but failing to pull it off when my voice came out breathy in almost a whisper.

"You'll find out on Monday that Ellis bought out a company called Everett Holdings in Boston—which is why I was there."

"Okay," I said, trying to pay attention, but the close proximity of his body was all I could focus on.

"Ellis reconfigured its org chart afterward, to absorb new employees under the existing leadership umbrella."

I wasn't sure why he was talking about work, but I was glad. Maybe focusing on work would help me stop focusing on *him* and the way it felt to be so close to him.

"I saw the chart this morning, and HR is no longer in my division."

"What? Who do we report to now?" I asked. I liked my job, but a new boss could ruin everything. "Someone from Everett or—"

"Not me."

"Oh, well, that's specific," I quipped, wondering how this would affect my job. "You don't have any idea at all?"

"Izzy." He set his palms on the door, one on each side of me. "I'm trying to tell you that we can be more than friends. If we want to."

I gasped. "What?"

His Adam's apple dipped when he swallowed, and then he said, "I'm fine with staying the way we are, though, so no pressure if that's what you want."

He watched me, and God, the look. His jaw flexed and our breaths mingled and the world held still for a second when our eyes locked. We moved together the tiniest bit, a nearly imperceptible sway, as if he were a magnet and I was steel.

My throat felt dry as my eyes traveled over his face. I managed to breathe out, "I, um, I would very much like to explore more than—"

His mouth cut me off, landing hard on mine as he inhaled sharply, like he'd been woken from a dream. He angled his head and went deep, and I forgot what every kiss before this felt like. I couldn't hear or see or breathe anything but him; he was my center.

His mouth ate at mine, kissing me like he'd been denying himself and was finally indulging, and I raised my hands and set them on his chest. Grasped at his sweatshirt, needing to get closer. To get more.

His palms stayed planted on the door as his body pressed against mine, as he stepped even closer. I could feel the heat of him, of that solid, warm body, and I felt hungry. Starved. I fisted his hoodie and bit down on his lower lip, which made him grunt and press closer still.

"That kiss yesterday gutted me," he said against my lips. "And it's all I've thought about since."

"I have to confess," I said, looking up into those dark eyes, "that the dream was actually about you, not Chef Tom."

"Oh, I know," he said, his lips turning up into a dirty, delicious smile.

It made me brave.

"And about that kiss," I said, thrilled at the thought of him being even half as obsessed as I'd been. "I dreamt about it last night."

"Tell me," he said, moving his mouth down to lick at my neck.

"Can't," I said, melting as he nipped my skin and made me burn all over. "Too embarrassing."

"Hot?" he asked, his tongue sliding over the spot he'd bitten.

"Oh, yeah," I sighed, letting my head fall back to give him better access.

"Tell me anyway," he growled, his voice raspy in my ear as he nipped my earlobe. "Where were we?"

"In your room," I said, struggling to form words as he kissed my throat. "New bed."

He raised his head and looked a little wild-eyed. "Naked?"

"So naked," I said, and the look on his face when I said that told me that we were about to have sex against my front door.

And I'd never wanted anything more.

My hands found the bottom of his hoodie and slid underneath, touching the taut, hot skin of his shredded stomach—holy *shit*. He sucked in a breath as his palms gave way to his forearms on the door, putting his body flush against mine without the tiniest bit of space between us.

"Iz." I felt the heat of his gaze before his mouth went back to mine, feeding me unbridled kisses that made me push myself against him. He picked me up, and I wrapped my legs around his waist, taking every hot kiss he delivered as he carried me toward the hall. My fingers drove into his hair, and I wondered how it was possible to feel so much.

I was weakened by it, the power of my want, while at the same time feeling strength in every meeting of our mouths. I wanted nothing in the world but Blake, nothing in the world but the two of us in that moment. It didn't seem possible, but he was everything to me in that white-hot minute.

He made a sound in his throat, but instead of walking into my bedroom, he turned.

He walked through what seemed like the kitchen, but I was too lost in his lips and the way his teeth toyed with my lower lip to confirm, and then—

Then he set me down on the kitchen table.

I opened my eyes—which was far more difficult than it sounded—and he was looking down at me with so much sex in his eyes that I felt dizzy. His face was flushed as he said, "I have an idea."

Holy *shit*, Mr. Chest wanted kitchen table action? I tried to sound chill when I removed my fingers from his thick hair, and I tried to sound casual as my blood pressure hit what must've been a catastrophic range, because my hands started shaking and my lips felt tingly. "Change of plans, Phillips?"

"Yeah." He ran a thumb over my cheek and said, "I want to take you out."

Blake

I watched that little wrinkle form between her eyebrows, like she was confused.

Yeah, I got that. I was alone with Izzy and we were finally free to do whatever the hell we wanted, yet I was pumping the brakes. *Idiot much?*

But the thing of it was, I really liked Iz. I liked being friends with her, regardless of the shape of her body (perfect) and her beautiful face. I liked the smell of her hair and the way her nose scrunched when she grinned, but I loved her smart-ass fuckery even more.

So much so that now, on the eve of our relationship being suddenly green-lighted and wide open, I was nervous that rushing into sex might somehow screw everything up.

I said, "I can't believe I'm saying this, but going from zero to one hundred seems unwise. Should we maybe pause for dinner?"

Izzy blinked up at me before she said, "Wait. You're hungry?"

"No, *numb nuts*," I said, reveling in the smile that curved her lips when she realized I'd heard her cousin through the door earlier. "I'm asking if you'll go to dinner with me tonight."

"Well, I don't know," she said, tilting her head and giving me that playful look that made me want to mess up her hair or tickle her until she fell down. "Where are you going to take me?"

"Wherever you want," I said, realizing I meant it. I looked at that upturned face and felt a little unnerved by how willing I was to give her whatever she wanted, do whatever she requested.

"So, Paris for dinner sounds good," she said, reaching out a hand to tug on the strings of my hoodie. "But only if we wear berets."

"Negative. No one looks good in a beret."

"Audrey Hepburn did," she said, and I was so fucking into the way I never knew what was going to come out of her mouth that it had become problematic. I texted and called her way too often, but honestly, talking to her was all I ever wanted to do. I said, "Debatable, and no berets."

"Fine." She grinned, giving me her full-scale smile as she leaned back on her arms. "How about dinner in Tuscany?"

"You're picky," I said, leaning down to rub my nose against her collarbone because something about it was driving me wild. "And real Italian spaghetti is nothing like what you're used to. I'm afraid you'll starve."

I lifted my head and wondered how a smart-ass smirk could make me feel so unbalanced.

"So Italy is out, then, because obviously spaghetti is the only possible dinner item." She pursed her lips, like she was seriously considering our options, and said, "Then all that's left is Johnny's down on L Street, I guess."

"Perfect," I said, needing to kiss her again.

I lowered my mouth, hypnotized by the way she looked at me, and just when my lips touched hers, she said, "But I can't go with you to your garage now."

I pulled back from the kiss. "Why not?"

"You know." She shrugged and rubbed her nose against mine, soft and slow as her breath touched my lips, and it caused a strange physical reaction. The movement made something in my chest pinch, and now I was convinced I was losing my goddamn mind. Surely it was my libido talking, because chest pinches in response to physical contact were not a real thing for grown-ass adults.

"I do *not* know," I managed, pulling back a little farther. "You're bailing on me?"

"Here's the thing, Mr. Chest," she said, scooting over on the table just enough to drop her feet to the floor and stand. I watched as she tucked her hair behind her ears, took a deep breath, then hit me with, "If I see you in coveralls with a wrench in your hand, there's no telling where the afternoon will go. And as lovely as that idea sounds, I really want to go on a date with you tonight."

I didn't get it at first, and then she tilted her head and raised an eyebrow.

"Damn it, Shay," I bit out through gritted teeth as sexual images of Izzy and me on the trunk of her car came at me, "I told you I don't have coveralls."

That made her snort and tap her forehead with her index finger. "But you do up here."

I couldn't hold back the smile, just like I couldn't stop myself from reaching out and giving her ponytail a tug. "So I have to go to Springfield by myself because you're a little pervert?"

She shrugged again and said around a giggle, "So it would seem."

"That's not fair."

"Life isn't fair."

"You're an asshole," I said, pulling my keys out of my front pocket. "Did you know that?"

"An asshole who will FaceTime you throughout the entire repair." She slid her fingers through mine and pulled me behind her, through the kitchen and toward the door. Her small hand in mine, tugging me along, caused that fucking idiotic chest-pinch thing again, which would've pissed me off if she hadn't made me laugh by saying, "The only difference will be that I cannot digitally goose you while you lean over my engine."

"You would've goosed me?" I asked, releasing her hand to mess with the tendrils around her face that had fallen out of her ponytail. "Digitally?"

"You know what I mean," she said, laughing and batting at my hands. "I was referring to the method of communication, not the method of goosing."

She went up on her tiptoes and kissed me then, and I was still grinning like an idiot when I climbed into my car and put the keys in the ignition. I was about to pull away when the phone buzzed in my pocket.

I expected it to be my little smart-ass, texting her usual bull-shit from the window, but it was an email from my boss instead. I was miles away from caring enough to read it—it was after hours, for fuck's sake—when I saw the subject line.

Re: Reconfigured Org Chart—V.2 (revised)

"Son of a bitch." I got that feeling in my gut, the one that told me I was going to fucking hate that attachment, and I rubbed my temple with my fingers. *Shit, shit, shit.*

But just as I was about to click the attachment, I closed the email app instead.

"Nope," I muttered to myself, putting the phone back in my pocket and buckling my seat belt. I pulled away from the curb, stood on the gas pedal, and made the decision to ignore my messages until Monday morning.

Chapter Twenty-Two

Izzy

"Yeah, baby, right there," I moaned.

"Shut up," he grunted through gritted teeth.

"But, honey, the way your shirt is riding up so I can see your lower back is just working for me," I said, really doing my best to sound disgusting. "I know I told you I'd stop, but it's impossible for me to keep from losing my shit when you're tossing all of this car repair porn in my face."

"Has anyone ever told you," Blake panted, obviously struggling to do something to the new alternator he was installing in my vehicle, "that you're an obnoxious pain in the ass?"

"Oh, tons of people. All the time. But don't change the subject."

He laughed but kept working. "What exactly is the subject? Your idiocy?"

"How aesthetically pleasing this whole video chat is." I looked at the FaceTime display and saw we'd been talking for almost two hours—basically the entire time he'd been working on my car.

It'd felt like five minutes.

I'd never in my entire life had as much fun as I had with him. It was like our brains were in sync. He always got my weird sense of humor and played with me in the most delightful way, which was probably what made our whole maybe-taking-this-to-the-next-level thing so petrifying. What if it ruined everything?

"I can't tell you how glad I am that my work is getting you off," he said, and my stomach dipped.

Somehow hearing him say *getting you off* was a turn-on.

But everything about him was a turn-on.

"Listen, I've got to go," I said, clueless as to what I was going to wear to dinner. I wanted to look good, but not trying-too-hard good. "I've got a date tonight with a guy I met at Scooter's, and I want plenty of time to get ready."

"Is that right?" He looked away from my engine and directly into his phone, which he'd propped on top of his rolling toolbox. "Good-lookin' fella?"

"You could say that," I said, smiling like a lovesick teenager.

"Smart?" He set down his tool and wiped his hands on his thighs.

"Oh, not at all," I teased, laughing when he gave me a shocked look. "He requested a physical challenge during Billboard Assholes, if you can believe that, and he also puts chia seeds in everything. I mean, who does that, right?"

"How the hell do you know about the chia seeds?" he asked, looking amused.

I shrugged. "When I took care of your cats, I couldn't help but notice you had the industrial-size bag in your pantry."

"You snooping little shit," he said, picking up the phone so he could move it closer to his face. His eyes twinkled. "What else did you notice?"

"Okay, confession," I said, but not feeling embarrassed at all. I never really did with him. "I did snoop, but like, quick glancing looks into drawers—I didn't touch or rifle through anything."

He didn't look like he believed me. "What's the coolest thing you found?"

I thought about that for a second before saying, "Your drawerful of glasses. I took a picture of myself in every single pair."

"You're the shittiest liar; you *just* said you didn't touch anything." His mouth slid into the teasing grin that I'd decided was my favorite of all his smiles. (The current top five were teasing grin, sexy smirk, sarcastic near smile, full-on sunshine, and you're-an-idiot-but-it-amuses-me lip twitch.) He said, "And you wore my glasses, weirdo?"

"I didn't wear them, I tried them on," I clarified. "And who has eight pairs of glasses? I think you might be a sociopath."

"I wear glasses every day, even if I wear contacts for a few hours, so eight pairs for three hundred and sixty-five days seems minimal to me." He tilted his head and said, "If you ask me, the person with only one pair is the nutjob."

"No need for name-calling, and no one asked you."

"So what's the least cool thing you found, then?"

"Aside from the buttload of chia?"

"How much chia constitutes a buttload, Shay?"

"Count the ones in your pantry and that's the answer, Phillips."

"Least cool thing. Go."

"Okay, the thing I found troubling in your apartment was the geriatric sex book."

He coughed out, "Excuse me?"

I grinned at his horror. "There's a book in your hall closet that looks like it came out in the 1950s, and it's called *Delicious Sex*. I mean, I'm all for honing your craft and reading all the resources, but I don't think—"

"Holy shit—was it on the bottom of the closet, in that stack of books on the floor?" he asked, pressing his fingers to his temples.

"Yeah."

"Oh, God. Those books belong to my grandparents." He squinted at me, looking queasy. "There's seriously a sex book in that stack?"

I started laughing. I'd been about to accuse him of lying, but he looked far too disgusted for me not to believe him. I said, "Not just a book about sex, but a book about delicious se—"

"Stop it." He shook his head and pointed at me. "Your snooping has ruined Nana and Papa for me, you little shit."

"Yeah, I'm gonna go now," I said around a laugh. "See you at six?"

His mock rage slid into a soft smile. "See you at six."

Blake: I can see you peeking through the blinds.

I smiled as I watched him walk up to the stoop, looking

down at his phone. Stepping away from the window, I texted back: I was watching two squirrels get married, egomaniac.

Blake: Sure you were. Open the goddamn door.

I took a deep breath, ridiculously nervous. Just hours earlier, I'd been nervous to see him because I'd been embarrassed about kissing him. Now I was nervous because we were going on an actual date and would likely be doing even more kissing by the end of the night. I was tied up in anticipation and excitement and terror, because something about the night felt big.

I slid the phone into the pocket of my tweed skirt (a cute new skirt that perfectly matched my white ruffly pirate shirt with an open cardigan), crossed the living room, and pulled open the front door.

Blake stood there, looking beautiful, which was nothing new. Perfectly combed hair, knee-weakening cologne, and a V-neck sweater / button-down shirt combo that showcased the hell out of that mile-wide chest and spectacular pecs; the man could serve a look.

But those things were nothing—*nothing*—compared to the way he was looking at me. He looked the way I felt, like he was filled with anticipation and intensity, and that was enough to make me want to faint.

Especially when he was holding a bouquet of bright yellow daffodils.

And smelling like something I wanted to bite.

"Hi," I said, feeling breathless and incapable of words.

He smiled and held out the flowers. "Hi."

"I love daffodils. Did you know that?" I tried remembering if I'd ever told him that as I took them from him. "Thank you."

"I didn't know," he said, his voice a little quieter than usual. "But you're welcome. My mother always said that daffodils are like two flowers in one, so, uh, that's why I chose them, I guess."

I nodded. "Let me just put them in water," I said, walking away from him and trying to find calm as I headed for the kitchen. "And then we can go."

"Sure," he said. He cleared his throat, and then he added, "I also have some other flowers that the florist talked me into. I, ah, I don't think they're really a thing for a dinner date, but she was kind of bossy and insisted you'd want them so I . . ."

And he just trailed off.

That made me stop in the kitchen doorway. I turned around, and Blake was still standing just inside the door, holding a . . . wrist corsage?

"Is that for me?" I asked.

He looked embarrassed and gave a little half shrug. "Yeah, but it's totally fine if you don't want it. The lady—"

"Oh, I want it." I rushed back to him and looked down at the pretty yellow and white roses. I hadn't gone to any formal dances in high school but had always wanted a corsage. "It's gorgeous."

"Really?" He looked down at me with wrinkled eyebrows. "Are you messing with me?"

"No," I said, getting a little sidetracked by the curl of his black eyelashes. "I love it."

"Well, let me put it on, then," he said, his eyes on mine as he lifted my wrist with his free hand and attempted to slide on the corsage. But the elastic band got hung up on my ring, and then again on my pinkie finger.

I looked down and saw the tiniest shake in his hand.

"Are you . . . *nervous*?" I asked, unable to believe it as I looked up at his face.

"No," he said dismissively, and immediately followed it up with, "Actually yes. Fuck."

That made me smile through my nerves. "Me, too."

"It just feels important," he said, looking down and straightening the flowers on my wrist. "Tonight, that is."

I nodded. "Weird, right?"

He returned his gaze to my face. "Very."

"But that's dumb," I said, my anxiety taking over. "Because it's not."

"It's not?"

"No," I said, rubbing my lips together. "You're just feeding me so I don't bite your arm off, and I just happened to wear makeup and a proper bra for the occasion. No bigs."

He raised an eyebrow. "Proper bra?"

"An undergarment," I explained, shifting my weight to one foot as my big mouth took over. "With wires inside of it to push the ladies up and make them more appealing to the male gaze."

He looked like he wanted to smile. "And you don't usually, um—"

"Yeah, no." I waved a hand and said, "I don't have a lot to work with upstairs, so I'm all about comfort. Sports bras and bralettes are my jam."

Shut up, you idiot! I always rambled when I was nervous, but this was perhaps my first overshare of which foundation garments were my fucking jam.

Blake cleared his throat. "I see."

"Oh, God, did I just ruin the illusion?" Why was my mouth so vomitous all the time? I said, "Was my admission akin to a man opening a date by sharing the details of his micro-penis? Should we just call it a night now, before you have to spend money on dinner when you know you don't want micro-peen?"

"For fuck's sake, Iz," he said, half smiling with a confused crease in his eyebrows.

"Oh, my God, I did!"

"I don't give a shit about your micro-penis, okay?" He grabbed the front of my cardigan with both hands and pulled me closer, frustration and amusement shining in his brown eyes. "I spend hours every day obsessing about all of you, every little bit."

"You do?" I said, my voice barely there.

"Yes, I fucking do," he said around an exhale. "So you can't talk about your underthings without making me crazy. Without making me think about your skin and your body and the way you'd look in goddamn lace."

Dear *Lord*. I felt winded, instantly rendered oxygen deficient by the forceful heat behind his words.

My hands rested on his chest. "How did you manage to call my bits little, tell me I have a micro-penis, yet still make me want to give you a standing ovation?"

"I'm a hell of a good presenter."

"I'd say so," I said. "No wonder they sent VP Blake to Boston to finish the merger."

"Yeah." He got a wrinkle between his eyebrows, like he was distracted by his thoughts, and he swallowed.

"I'm ready to be fed now," I said, and that seemed to make him forget about work.

We left the apartment, and when Blake opened the door for me, I rolled my eyes. "I appreciate the chivalrous gesture, Phillips, but I promise you that I know how to open a car door."

That made his mouth split into the full-on sunshine. "Praise Jesus. A woman who knows to pull the handle."

His face was right there, right above mine, and I desperately wanted him to kiss me.

"By the way," he said, lifting a finger and tracing my eyebrow with the softest touch. "It is killing me not to kiss you, but I don't want to mess up your pretty red lipstick."

"Please destroy it," I blurted out. "Unless you're chick—"

All ten of his fingers slid into my hair, and he kissed me like it actually *had* been killing him. I raised my hands to his hard jaw and kissed him back with everything I had, hoping to make him feel even half of what he delivered whenever his lips met mine.

Going up on my tiptoes, I pulled his head closer, taking the lead as I attempted to consume every addictive bite of Blake that I could get. He growled into my mouth, his fingers flexing, and the heat of it all made me burn.

Kissing Blake was so much more than just kissing, and I suspected nothing would ever compare. It was teeth and tongue and lips and breath, teasing and sliding and utter oral chaos— an onslaught, and hands down the most erotic activity I'd ever participated in.

Aside from sex itself.

"Get your ass in the car," he said, his lips barely above mine, so close that I could still feel their impression, "before we get arrested."

"Kissing isn't illegal," I whispered, rubbing my lips against his.

"But what your kisses make me want to do against the side of my car is."

Blake

"So I was thinking," Izzy said, and I could see in my periphery that she was turning toward me in the passenger seat.

"God help me."

"On a normal first date, the two people get to know each other slowly. But since we already know each other, maybe we should do an information speed round."

Her mind was always whirring. It was dizzying and fascinating, all at once. I said, "Please explain."

"Okay, so usually there are things that people want to know but cannot ask. About exes, family stuff, how many babies the other wants—off-limits topics that make you sound crazy or desperate if you ask them, right?"

"Right . . . ?"

"So how about, at dinner, we allow all questions. Because obviously if you ask me about an ex, I know you aren't a potentially jealous psycho. And if I ask you if you want to get married someday, you know I'm not trying to tie you to the altar and baby you up."

"I don't think that expression is correct."

"But you get me, right?"

"Sure." I pulled up to the red light and looked over at Izzy.

She looked so incredible that I'd had to force myself to stop looking at her after every sentence we exchanged. If I didn't make a conscious effort, I might never stop staring, and I'd never want her to think Date Izzy was any better than every other version.

Because Iz was the sexiest person I'd ever met—all the time. In her messy ponytails and smudged glasses, in her skirts and heels at work; I was painfully attracted to her, no matter what.

But it had way more to do with her brain and her heart than her appearance.

She was smart and funny, warm and sweet.

Every day—hell, every *conversation*—exposed me to more of the inner workings of her brain, and I was constantly blown away. She had her own brand of generosity that was all about kindness and acceptance, and I was starting to wonder how I was lucky enough to even *know* her, much less take her out to dinner.

But tonight—holy shit. Her long hair, that lipstick, those legs in that skirt; all of it together would tempt anyone with eyeballs. But combine it with the punch of her quiet perfume and the fact that she'd gotten dressed to go out with *me*, and I was fucking on edge.

"Okay," she said, leaning forward to turn up the volume on the radio. "As soon as we order, it is on."

Chapter Twenty-Three

Izzy

"Obviously you're close with your brothers. Is it like that with the rest of your family?" I asked, breaking my roll in half. "I'm picturing an entire clan full of bearded Jasons."

"That is a terrifying thought," he said, picking up his low-ball glass. "And Jason and AJ are the exceptions in my family, actually. I don't talk to my dad, and my mother passed last year. I'm pretty close with my grandparents on my mom's side but only talk to my dad's parents on holidays."

"So you are an American family," I said, picturing Tom Hanks and Meg Ryan in a bookstore.

He raised an eyebrow. "Did you seriously just throw a *You've Got Mail* quote at me?"

"Did you seriously just recognize it?" I said around a laugh. "That is crazy impressive, Phillips."

"Not in the slightest," he said, and he took a drink of his Scotch.

"I'm sorry about your mom, by the way," I added, hating the thought of him ever being sad.

He shrugged. "Cancer sucks. Next question."

I was glad his face was soft, because if it wasn't, that answer would've made me feel like a prying ass.

"Okay, next question," I repeated, trying to come up with a good one. "Um, have you ever been in love?"

He set down his glass. "No."

That surprised me. "Really?"

He gave his head a little shake. "I was engaged not that long ago, but after the fact, I was able to see that it wasn't the real thing."

"Really?" I grabbed my wineglass, fascinated by the thought of Blake with a ring. "What happened after the fact?"

He stared at me for a long minute, like he was weighing his thoughts, and then he said, "I realized that I had stronger feelings for one of my friends than I ever had for her."

"Oh." I stared back at him, my heart beating in my throat as I tried to sound calm. "Is that right?"

"Yes, it is."

"Interesting," I managed, feeling so flustered I didn't even know how to string words together. It felt like he was saying something huge, but what if that was just my brain shorting out from being in such close proximity to him? What if I was absolutely inserting myself into his conversation because I was drunk on his face? I cleared my throat and said, "Well, you must've thought you were at the time."

"I did." He looked directly at me, not evading my gaze whatsoever, and laid it all out there. "Skye and I got along great and it felt right, but then things changed. I don't want to get into the details of a past relationship, but I guess you could just say we had different values in the end."

"Values," I said, nodding. "Like, she was super into NAS-CAR and you're an F1 guy?"

He smiled and leaned a little closer. "Like, she was super into lying a lot and I was not."

"Ah." I was dying to know what she looked like. "Please tell me it wasn't in an I'm-in-a-hurry-so-I'm-stealing-a-latte kind of way."

He did a little eye roll that was adorable. "No, it was in an I-text-and-hang-out-with-my-ex-but-lie-about-it kind of way."

"Oh." I swallowed and felt bad for prying. "Did she cheat?"

He shrugged and said, "No idea. The lying was enough to kill the relationship."

"I see," I said, mostly because I didn't know what else to say.

"My turn." Blake leaned forward a little, the light from the table's candle reflecting in his dark eyes. "Have *you* ever been in love, Iz?"

That was an easy one. "Nope. Never. Not even close."

He raised his eyebrows, waiting for a story, and I wished I had one. Somehow, a tragic tale of heartbreak would feel like more of a success than the truth. "I've never even gone out with someone more than twice since high school, so I'm—as Halsey would say—bad at love."

"Who?" he asked.

"Halsey," I replied, taking a bite out of my roll.

"Is that a friend of yours?"

"Oh, my God, she's a singer," I said, trying to politely talk with roll in my mouth. "You've seriously never heard of Halsey?"

"Does she sing anything I'd know?"

"Um, 'Bad at Love,' for starters."

That made him smirk as he watched me chew. "Which is your theme song. Full circle right here, ladies and gentlemen."

"Cute," I said.

Then he asked, "Why don't you date?"

If this little speed-round game wasn't my idea to begin with, that question might've felt intrusive. I shrugged and said, "I'm not big on talking to people I don't know."

"But you never shut up."

"Because I know you."

"Online dating?"

"I've got the apps but I've never done more than scroll." I felt like a loser, like it was obvious I was a total loner, so it was time for the next question. "My turn. Kids and marriage—in or out?"

"Are you trying to tie me to the altar and baby me up, Shay?"

"I don't think that expression is right," I said around a laugh.

Which made Blake laugh, too, and I loved that it was like that with us. So strangely comfortable, when I was rarely comfortable with anyone.

"I mean, I guess I'd like to have kids and a partner someday," he said as casually as if I'd asked him how spaghetti sounded for dinner. "I'm not in any rush, but I fucking love Jason and Kylie's kids."

"So you're saying as long as your kids are as cool as theirs," I said, trying to picture Jason as a dad.

"Then I'll totally be all in," he finished with a grin. "But if they suck, I'm for sure out."

"Of course."

That was the end of the question portion of the date. We fell into ourselves after that, leaning on the sarcastic banter that was our language of choice as we talked about nothing and everything.

I discovered he loved animal documentaries (though the man was straight-up terrified of monkeys), hated snow, and was a volunteer "watchdog" at his niece's school, which basically just meant that he had to volunteer one day a year doing whatever the principal told him to do. The smile on his mouth when he talked about little Ellie made me slightly dizzy.

It wasn't until our plates were cleared and we were enjoying a post-dinner glass of wine that things changed. Blake was talking about one of the new machines at the gym, and I said, "Y'know, I haven't gone back there since the day I saw you in the elevator."

"Why not?"

I knew I should shut up, but the wine had loosened my tongue. I ran a finger over the rim of my glass and said, "Because if I go all the time, my routine visits will gradually dim the memory of that first time. And I don't want to ever forget that elevator ride."

His smile disappeared, his expression turning serious.

"I mean, I know it's no big deal now—you're Blake and I'm Izzy. We're friends. But at the time, it felt like this great cosmic coincidence, that I would run into Mr. Chest from Scooter's, and I always want to remember the magic of all that crackling potential."

He didn't say anything. At all. He just watched me.

"Obviously I'm drunk," I teased, rolling my eyes and lifting the glass to my lips. "I shall shut up now."

"Don't," he said. "I think about it every single time I step into that elevator."

"You *do*?" I asked, unable to be cool. "Seriously?"

"Hell, yes," he said. "I rotate between the memory of what it was, and the fantasy of what it could've been."

"You fantasize about the elevator?" I leaned forward on my elbows. "I do, too. All the time."

His eyes dipped down to my mouth as he said, "About you hitting the stop button?"

I ran my tongue over my bottom lip. "That's where it starts."

"Tell me where it finishes, Shay," he said, quietly and calmly. No one around us would ever guess that he was asking me to share a sexual fantasy. No one who'd ever known me would guess that I would.

"With my hands on the wall," I said, stuck somewhere between shyness and exhilaration as I dared to say it all. "And with you behind me, most of the time."

He raised his eyebrows like he was amused, but his jaw was rigid. "Most of the time."

"It varies, y'know?"

"Yeah, I fucking *do* know," he said, and my stomach dipped.

"So tell me," I said, intimidated and totally turned on by his blazing eyes. "Where it finishes for you."

I didn't know what I'd been expecting—Blake wasn't the kind of guy to back down from a challenge, so *of course* he'd answer—but it wasn't "your back against the elevator wall, your legs wrapped around my waist, and my name on your tongue."

"Ah," I managed, unsure of how to behave as my body spontaneously combusted over after-dinner drinks. "I, um, I think I like yours better."

"Do you want more wine?" he asked.

"No, thank you."

"Do you want to go?"

"Yes, please."

Blake

I pulled into the parking garage as Iz rambled about the song on the radio. The drive to my place had been off, the two of us unusually quiet as thoughts of sexual fantasies pinged through the air.

Izzy tried to jump-start a conversation, but it wasn't meant to be. I was fucking incapable of thinking about anything other than the image she'd put into my depraved mind. After pulling into my spot and turning off the car, I finally dared to look at her.

"This'll only take a sec," I said, referring to our stop-off to inject the cat.

"Like I don't know that," she teased. "I did it last week, remember?"

I swallowed, my throat dry as hell. Yeah, I remembered. We got out of the car and walked to the elevator bank, and I couldn't help myself. I grabbed her hand and laced my fingers through hers, needing to touch her.

She grinned at me and said, "You couldn't stay away, could you? You just had to touch me."

I didn't even bother denying it.

Izzy hit the up button, and her thumb rubbed back and forth over mine as we waited. "I think the boys will be happy to see me."

"Nah, they'll hate you again. Short-term cat memory." The doors opened and we stepped inside.

"There is no such thing, and those two are hopelessly devoted to me."

The doors slid closed. "Please don't sing *Grease*."

Izzy pressed the button for my floor with her free hand. "I wish I had tuna in my purse."

"Said no one ever," I replied.

The elevator started moving, and it hit me like a freight train. I watched the numbers lighting up, hyperaware of Izzy's scent and how close she was and the size of her hand in mine. In the fucking elevator. She looked at me then, and something in her eyes was different.

"Blake," she whispered, like she was going to say something, but she didn't.

I turned toward her, just the slightest bit, and I knew she was thinking the same thing. I could feel it in the way she looked at me. The air crackled, we stared each other down for a long second, and then everything exploded.

Izzy

Blake's huge hands came up to my face as his mouth came down on mine. I kissed him back with ferocity while I pushed my body into his, moving him—both of us—closer to the stop button.

"Fucking yes, Iz," he said against my lips as I reached around him and depressed the button. The elevator jerked to a stop, causing us to stumble. Blake took advantage of the impetus to move, turning us and pushing me up against the wall.

Was this really happening? Was I really pinned against him in the elevator while he kissed me like he wanted to eat me whole? I kissed him back with the same unhinged intensity that he was giving me, snaking my arms around his shoulders, crazed with lust.

His hands slid up the backs of my thighs, stopping at the bottom of my skirt as he whispered, "Is this okay?"

"Don't you dare stop," I said, needing him like I needed oxygen at that moment. Every nerve in my body was buzzing and connected to the points on my skin where his hands were resting.

"Shay," he panted, his fingers tightening before sliding higher. I bit down on his lip and moaned into his mouth when he touched me—holy *hell* the man knew what to do with his hands—and I lost the ability to formulate logical thoughts as he made me climb.

It got frantic as the alarm started going off, reminding us of our limited time before maintenance showed up. A cacophony of zippers and wild hands and ripping wrappers joined the jangling elevator bell as he lifted me in his hands and then—finally—he was there.

Blake

"Oh, God," Izzy moaned, her heels bringing me in closer as her head fell back against the elevator wall.

"Holy *shit*." I gritted my teeth and froze, my knees nearly buckling from the feel of Izzy surrounding me. Nothing had ever felt that good, and when she opened her eyes, I felt her gaze in my every molecule.

"Blake," she bit out as I started moving, her eyes closing as she met me move for move. I could feel her fingers grasping me through my shirt and sweater, and it made me fucking burn. She'd been in every one of my fantasies since the day we'd met, but the reality of sex with Izzy was a thousand times better.

She breathed, "You do not suck at this, Phillips."

"Nor do you," I quipped, my entire body overcome with that annoying emotional pinch as I looked down at her face. I was in the middle of the hottest sexual encounter of my life, a mind-blowing escapade against the wall of an elevator, yet I desperately wanted to kiss the tip of her freckled nose.

"I don't?" she asked, her mouth sliding into a slow grin. She said it like a joke, but there was something wary in her eyes that reminded me what she'd admitted, that she didn't really date.

"Iz," I said, recognizing that I sounded like an asshole as I tried talking through a clenched jaw. But every fucking muscle in my body was tense and taut as our pace got faster, hotter. "Swear to God this is the best I've ever had, and we aren't even done yet."

She pulled my face down to hers and started kissing me, desperate and hungry and wild, and that's when things caught fire. I stopped hearing the deafening alarm as every one of my five senses—my entire consciousness—narrowed in on that one spot where we were joined.

"We should probably stop," she said, panting, sounding like

someone absolutely not interested in stopping. "Before we get arrested."

"I just. Want," I started, *needing* her to finish, and then— like a sex goddess—she gave me exactly what I'd been waiting for. All ten of her fingernails pressed into my shoulders as her entire body tightened and flexed, making me growl out, "*Fucking thank you holy shit*," before following her lead.

"He totally knew," Izzy said, laughing beside me in the hallway as I pulled out my keys.

"*Of course* he knew," I replied, relieved she was able to laugh at the fact that security had opened the elevator doors a mere three seconds after we got our clothes readjusted. I slid my key into the dead bolt and said, "I know *I* couldn't stop grinning like a dumbass, which made the elevator-stuck scenario pretty tough to believe."

"Yeah, you suck at lying," she said, giggling.

"Totally do," I agreed, turning the lock.

She grinned up at me with maximum nose crinkle, and I knew I loved her. It didn't make a damn bit of sense, but I loved her enough that it terrified me.

It was total lunacy.

It was way too soon to feel that much—impossible to love her already—but I knew it with absolute certainty.

"By the way, Mr. Chest," she said, giving me a total smartass smile that made me want to pick her up and throw her over my shoulder. "Have I told you how happy I am that you're no longer the boss of me?"

Chapter Twenty-Four

Izzy

I scratched Goodyear's head and watched Blake freak out.

Technically he was just standing beside me in the living room, holding his cat after injecting it with insulin. But he kept clenching his jaw and pulling at his shirt collar, and he hadn't given me shit since we'd walked in.

In fact, he'd been incredibly polite to me.

"Do you want something to drink?" he'd asked. And then he followed it with "Let me know if you change your mind."

What the hell did that even mean? It was totally freaking me out. Obviously, he was regretting our impetuous elevator liaison and trying to think of a gentle way to tell me that he was not at all interested in a sleepover.

"Y'know what?" he said, barely looking at me as he moved the cat out of my arm's reach and onto the floor. "This shirt is driving me crazy. Bad detergent or something. I'm going to go change."

"Okay," I said, narrowing my eyes and watching as he nearly ran to his bedroom.

I literally felt queasy as I wondered what exactly was up with him. Did he not enjoy the elevator sex? Was I a bad elevator lay? Did he not respect me now? (If that was the case, screw him, but still—ouch.)

Was he nervous I was looking for a relationship?

I started pacing, and as I walked toward the big windows with the gorgeous view, I realized that it mattered too much to me. The why of his strange behavior felt like everything at once, like the world would end if he remained aloof and distant.

Dear God, I cared way too much about what he thought. *No, no, no.* Cared way too much and also felt mildly panicked at the thought of screwing things up with him.

Wait—was I in love with him?

Impossible.

I shook my head and muttered, "Nope," into the empty living room. "More than friends" was light-years away from "in love," and I was just getting confused because I hadn't been "more than friends" with anybody in, like, an eternity.

I hadn't known him long enough to know if he was worthy of sharing my favorite banana bread, much less my heart.

Nope. I was freaking out because he was the hottest person I'd ever been "more than friends" with, and that was it.

Just be cool, moron, and be casual.

Blake

I yanked my shirt off like it actually *was* the culprit, even though my irritation had nothing to do with the oxford. No, my irritation had to do with my conscience and the fact that I had to open that fucking email before I could move forward with Izzy.

As blissful as ignorance had been—seriously, it'd been a top-five fucking day—it couldn't be my excuse.

Especially when Izzy had no idea that everything was likely about to change.

I grabbed a Henley from the closet, pulled it over my head, and as soon as my arms were through the sleeves, I grabbed the phone.

Time to take a look.

I opened the email, dread settling into my stomach. Somehow, I just knew it wasn't going to be good. I clicked on the attachment, and—

"Can't," I muttered through gritted teeth, swiping out of the attachment before I had a chance to see it. I set the phone on my dresser face down and stepped away from it with my hands up like it was a loaded gun.

I knew looking at it was the right thing to do, but the part of me that wanted to fall asleep wrapped around Izzy wouldn't let me. I was too drunk on her, too lost in every crinkle of her freckled nose, to give up the chance to finish the perfect day with a long, perfect night. It was lazy and selfish—I knew that—yet I wasn't strong enough to stop myself.

I dragged a hand through my hair before opening the bedroom door and going back out into the living room.

"About time, bro," Izzy said, and I was surprised to see her standing next to the door, looking down at her phone with her purse over her shoulder like she was waiting around to leave.

She didn't even look up when she said, "I think my grandma with arthritis changes faster than you."

"Are you . . . leaving?" I asked, disappointment slamming into me.

"Yeah," she said, finally looking at me. Her mouth turned up into a smart-ass grin that didn't reach her eyes, and her nose didn't crinkle. Still, she teased, "Our elevator workout made me sleepy, so now I must go crash. And the Darkling needs to be fed."

I let my gaze move all over her, taking in every square inch that I'd hoped to explore. "Didn't you feed him just before we left?"

"Well, yeah," she said, absentmindedly rubbing a finger over her lower lip. "But, um, he eats a lot."

"Ah." I scrubbed a hand over the top of my hair. Apparently Izzy and I were feeling entirely different about the night. *Noted.* "Let me go grab my phone, and I'll take you home."

I went back in my room and slipped the phone into my pocket, but when I returned to the living room, Izzy was crouched down, petting both of my cats while talking to them in the sweetest voice.

That pinching feeling returned with so much force it nearly brought me to my knees, and I couldn't stop myself from biting out the words "Holy shit, you are so fucking beautiful."

Chapter Twenty-Five

Izzy

Blake scared the crap out of me, which made me lose my squat and fall onto my backside.

But Lord, the way he'd said it.

The *way* he'd said it.

He'd said the words through gritted teeth like he meant them so hard. And his intense expression didn't soften as I smiled at my own klutziness. His mouth was firm, his eyes so fierce that I felt the look from head to toe.

"You mean graceful," I teased, because I was not equipped to receive incendiary compliments from someone like Blake.

"Wrong," he said, crossing the room to stand above me. He held out a hand to help me up, and when I let him pull me to my feet, he held on to my hand and didn't let go. "You are so fucking pretty that I have a hard time not staring. Obsessively. Every second that I'm with you."

"Phillips," I said, blinking and hoping I didn't sound as flustered as I felt, "you just can't say things like that to me."

"Why not?" He dropped my hand and ran a knuckle over my cheek, killing me with eye contact as his body seemed to hover in front of me, surrounding me, as his scent snaked around my head and made me hyperaware of his closeness.

My eyes closed of their own volition, and I swayed just the tiniest bit before forcing them open and being too honest. I didn't know why my voice came out as a whisper when I said, "Because it makes me want to believe it."

"Believe it, Shay," he said, his voice quiet as he stepped closer. "Your face is all I've thought about since you scalded my chest with your latte."

"*Amy's* latte," I corrected, my heart beating a little faster as his hands wrapped around my waist and pulled me closer. I swallowed and said, "Does this mean you *don't* regret the elevator sex?"

"Regret the hottest thing that's ever happened to me?" His eyebrows slammed together, and he looked at me like I'd insulted him. "Of course not. Do you?"

I couldn't stop myself from beaming up at him as relief settled over me like a soft blanket. "Not even a little bit."

"Good. Now, Izzy, I am more than happy to take you home," he said, lowering his head to give my neck the softest kiss. "But if you're interested in a sleepover, nothing in this world would make me happier."

"What about a lotto win?" I asked, moving my head so he had better access. "I bet that'd make you happier."

"Wrong," he growled, scraping his teeth against my skin. "I want you more than millions, though it's quite likely I'd regret that decision in the morning."

That made me smile and put my hands on the back of his head. "World peace would surely make you happier."

"You can't pin world peace on me," he said with false indignation, his fingers unbuttoning the top button on my pirate blouse as his tongue licked over my throat. "World peace would of course be sublime, and I would choose it over you because I'm not a selfish monster. But all I want tonight, Isabella Clarence, is this."

"I cannot believe you remember my middle name," I said around a laugh.

"It's so bizarre that it's unforgettable." He unbuttoned another button. "Just like you."

I stepped back—well, as much as he'd let me—and said, "Well, before I can decide on the sleepover, I'm going to need to see Mr. Chest's chest."

His hands stopped moving on my buttons, and his head came up. "The chest is a deal-breaker?"

"No, but I just really want to see it," I said, feeling on more solid footing when we weren't being serious. "I feel like once we start getting busy, I'll be too distracted to look."

"Did you just say *getting busy*?" he asked, reaching over his shoulder to grab the back of his shirt.

"It's better than the alternative."

"Which is?" He pulled the shirt over his head and dropped it onto the floor.

"Doing the nasty—holy *shit*," I said through clenched teeth before my mouth literally dropped wide open. Mr. Chest's chest was absolute perfection.

"*The nasty* is not an alternative at all," he said, reaching out to return to his previous unbuttoning task.

"How about *banging*?" I asked, setting my hands on his sternum and slowly sliding them up toward his shoulders. It was sinful and wrong that he should look so beautiful. It's like they supersized his hot genes when the universe was stringing him together or something.

He was a freak, honestly.

"Too pedestrian," he said. "We're better than *banging*."

"Please don't say *making love*," I objected, watching my fingers move over his sculpted pectorals. "That's so disgusting."

"I would never," he said, flicking open my remaining buttons. "Do I look like a douche?"

"You look like a sex dream," I said, then sucked in a breath when he leaned down enough to drop a hot kiss on my cleavage.

"As do you." He raised his head, his mouth in a mischievous grin. "This proper bra is incredibly hot, by the way."

"An optical illusion that really makes my . . . *you-know-what* pop."

"That's it," he said, grabbing my waist and tossing me over his shoulder as if I were . . . well, something one would carry on their shoulder. I squealed, staring at his muscular back as he said, "If you call your breasts a micro-penis one more time . . ."

"I didn't say it that time," I said, overcome with giggles as my silky shirt slid off my upside-down torso entirely and dropped onto the wood floor. "And whatcha gonna do, Phillips?"

"Not sure," he said, his arm tightening across the backs of my legs as he started walking. "Tape your mouth shut, maybe?"

I couldn't stop laughing as he walked through his bedroom doorway, and I said around a cackle, "But then you'll be denying yourself the magic of my mouth, Mr. Chest, and you don't want to do that."

I meant it as a lighthearted tease about kissing, but realized it sounded filthy.

Blake stopped his forward motion and set me back on my feet a little roughly. His hot eyes were burning every little bit of me when he said, "Your mouth is the very best part of you, Iz."

How did he do that? How did he manage to say things that made my heart swell up in my chest? I tried defusing the moment with "I'd say same, Blake, but those abdominals—"

"Izzy."

I stopped rambling. "Yeah?"

"No jokes." His eyes were just above mine, the planes of his face the center of my existence as he said, "I'm trying to tell you that I—"

A huge crash cut him off, the sound of ceramics shattering from the other side of the doorway, making both our heads turn in that direction.

"What was that?" I asked, suddenly hyperaware of my shirtlessness.

"Fucking cats," he growled, putting his hands on my upper arms and repositioning me just a little. His eyes were all sex as he moved his face closer so his nose touched mine, and he said, "Stay right here and don't move, Shay."

"I'll do what I want, Phillips," I said, ruining my attempt at sass with my inability to not beam up at the man.

His mouth twitched and he said, "If your shirt is back on when I return, there's going to be hell to pay."

"Not scared," I said as he walked out of the room, and then I lost it yet again when he held up a hand and flipped me off without looking back.

No, I wasn't scared, I thought as I watched him go into the kitchen.

I was terrified.

Blake

"Watch the claws," I muttered under my breath as I swept up the broken remains of a glass bowl. I was holding both of the little shits in one hand so they didn't step on any of the shards, and the broom in the other hand as I attempted to sweep up their mess. My reflection in the refrigerator mocked me.

Dress pants, no shirt, two cats—*fucking cool, bro.*

And talk about your shitty timing; I'd finally had Izzy smiling again. I was tempted to just ignore the crash and hope for the best, but then I remembered Goodyear's circle walking and didn't want to be responsible for bloody paws.

Fucking cats.

My phone buzzed in my pocket, and I knew beyond a reasonable doubt that I was not going to check it. An email from the office would destroy my resolve to ignore work until Monday and hope for the best.

But the damn thing buzzed again.

And again. And yet again.

"Fuck," I growled, propping the broom against the pantry and pulling out the phone.

But it wasn't an email. It was a text. Multiple texts.

From Izzy.

Izzy: I'm taking a poll. Are you between the ages of 20 and 40?

What the fuck was she doing?

I responded: Yep.

Izzy: Is your name Blake Phillips?

Yep.

Izzy: Okay so random poll question—are you still nervous?

I glanced toward the bedroom but couldn't see more than the doorway.

She was so weird—I never knew what the hell she was talking about—but for some reason, it made me fucking out of my mind over her. I was obsessed with the unpredictability of her brain.

I answered honestly: No.

Izzy: Oh.

A second passed.

Izzy: Yeah, me, either.

I wasn't letting her off the hook. I texted, Why are you nervous?

Izzy: So I'm not nervous exactly, maybe just shy . . . ?

I reached down and scratched between Goodyear's ears and texted, It's ME. Last week you FaceTimed to prove to me you can do the Napoleon Dynamite dance. If you can do that on camera, you cannot be shy.

Izzy: I think that's the problem—us, in your apartment after a "date," is new. Not at all like us in our normal habitat.

I stood. Replied, I get it. So . . . ?

Izzy: So if we're going to knock boots when you come back, perhaps we should text a little, to remind us of our Iz/ Blake friendship roots.

I was smiling again, like a damn fool. You want me to text you before I sex you?

Izzy: Maybe.

I texted, Okay. So HEY, DIPSHIT, you didn't put your shirt back on, did you?

Izzy: Is that your pre-sex text?

I responded with It is.

Izzy: I actually just buried myself under your covers as is.

I felt the blood rush from my head. Texted, To clarify—you are half-naked in my bed?

Izzy: Correct. I felt all awkward, waiting for you with no shirt on, so the intelligent next step was to dive and bury.

Blake: That sounds positively canine.

Izzy: I will not make a joke about doggy style.

I tried to focus on my phone and not the images she was putting in my head. I texted, Wise decision, considering your unclothed state and your geographical location.

Izzy: Just because I'm half-nekked in your bed doesn't mean I'm at your mercy.

It was getting hot in the apartment again. Believe me, I know. May I ask you a question?

Izzy: I'll allow it.

Blake: How would you like me to proceed? Shall I join you under the sea of blankets, or is there another plan hatching in that cacophonic brain of yours?

Izzy: Confession—the thought of you and I together in this bed makes it hard to breathe.

Something about her confession made my heart twist in my chest, maybe the fact that I felt the same way. I texted, Confession— the thought of you and I together in my bed makes it hard for me to breathe too.

Izzy: Really?

Blake: So hard.

I walked to the bedroom, stopping in the doorway. Izzy was lying on her stomach in my bed, covered by my comforter. Her shoulders and upper back were visible, bare except for the thin black strap across her back, and she was looking down at her phone.

Holy hell, I wanted that so much. Not just the obvious, but the mundane. I wanted Izzy in my bed, scrolling on her phone like it was an ordinary occurrence, all the time.

I texted, I dare you to take off that bra.

I heard her inhale sharply before she responded. Are you in the doorway?

Blake: Yes.

She cleared her throat and texted, I cannot pass up a dare, can I?

Blake: I sure as fuck hope not.

My skin felt hot as I watched her slim fingers reach around her back, unhook her bra, then fling it off the edge of the bed. She raised herself up, onto her elbows, and texted: Better?

My eyes were stuck to her bare back, to her pale, naked skin that set fire to every one of my fantasies.

The reality of Izzy was a thousand times better.

I texted, So much better. Is it weird that I want to lick every bump of your spine?

Izzy: Not as weird as how badly I want to bury my face in your pillow and let you.

Blake: Are you still wearing that skirt?

Izzy: Shhh—my turn, Phillips. I dare you to lose the pants.

I'd never unbuckled and unbuttoned faster in my life. The room was so quiet that the click of my belt buckle hitting the floor confirmed I'd done as she'd asked. She responded with Good boy.

I wanted to ditch the phone and tackle her on the bed, but if this was what it took to get past her nervousness, I would do it. Also, something about it was fucking hot. The vanilla scent of her perfume slithered around me as I texted, I'm gonna need to see that skirt come off, Iz.

Izzy: Confession—It's already off. When you went into the kitchen, I shed the outer layer.

Blake: So tell me exactly what you're wearing this second.

Izzy: Tighty-whities and old man socks.

"That's it," I said, dropping my phone and charging over to the bed. "I'm coming in."

Izzy

I screamed—a cackling laugh of a scream—when Blake's big hand wrapped around my ankle. He dove under the covers and crawled up my body, but the laughing stopped when I felt his hands on my hips, his mouth on the small of my back.

I shivered and let out a sigh that might've been a moan as his lips and tongue moved up my spine, his body poised above mine with the space of a breath between us. When his mouth hit the back of my neck, he murmured, "Those lacy black panties are not tighty-whities, for the record."

I gasped when he bit down on my nape—*dear God*—and said, "I guess I was thinking of yesterday's undergarments."

"Really."

I could feel the rumble of his voice on my skin, and I wanted to see his face. *Needed* to see his face. I turned over underneath the bridge of his arms, and the sight of him hovering above me, with his hair tousled, his eyes all heavy-lidded and hot, made me realize it was the first time I'd ever been knocked breathless just from looking at someone.

"Hey," I said, my voice almost a whisper.

"Hey." He swallowed.

I rubbed my lips together, trying to think of the right words to say, but he cut me off with a kiss. His lips came down, somehow different—yet again—than every other time we'd kissed.

Blake Phillips apparently had an entire dossier of kisses at his disposal and dispensed them with the utmost care. So far I'd had sweet, sexy, and hot, but this one was dirty. Filthy. I'd thought the Billboard Assholes kiss was a sex kiss, but no.

This was a sex kiss.

His mouth was just as hot and hungry, but it had the patience that went along with having all night. It felt like foreplay and tantric marathon sex, all at once, and I stopped thinking and held on for dear life. I brought my arms up and around him, letting my fingers flex into the muscles of his back, needing to bring him closer.

He made a noise deep in his chest—a growl or a groan—as our bodies came together. I could feel every inch of him—chest, stomach, thighs—and I bit down on his bottom lip, instantly impatient for everything his body had to offer.

That was apparently the green light he needed, because it was *on*. His greedy mouth moved lower, licking down the column of my throat in a way that had me pressing and straining to feel more. My arms fell to the bed when his mouth moved south, because it was worshipful and with the kind of enthusiasm that made me feel like a centerfold, as opposed to the B cup I actually was.

"You," I said, digging my fingers into his hair, "are delightfully obsessed with my mi—"

"No." He delivered a nip of punishment that made me squeal, a squeal that turned into a pornographic moan as his mouth continued the onslaught that was making me wild. How was he so good at that? He only got better as he moved down my body, ridding me of the last scrap of my clothing, kissing every bit of me and making me writhe, tremble, gasp, and scream.

And it wasn't just that he was skilled at the tasks he was performing or the way I was fairly certain I had an extraordinary hickey on my hip bone. No, it was that everything he did, every move he made—it felt like all of it was exclusive to us in this moment.

None of these things had ever been done before, not like this.

It was magic that existed only for us and this wildly perfect connection.

His fingers slid over my skin, and I felt them where he touched, but I also felt his fingers in the depths of my chest, the racing of my heart, and the heat of my cheeks.

When he kissed my belly, I felt the heat of his mouth on my flesh, and also in the pit of my stomach.

And, God help me, when he finally came back to me and our eyes met, his gaze was so full of adoration that I felt it in the backs of my eyes.

Yes, when this man looked at me, I wanted to *cry* because I was so into him.

Blake swallowed, opened his mouth like he wanted to say something, and I realized that I was waiting for a profession of love. His flared nostrils and flushed cheeks made him look like a man ready to spit sonnets, and I felt like I couldn't bear the disappointment of what he wasn't going to say.

So I grabbed his face and brought it to mine—hard—and tried showing him how I felt by kissing the ever-loving shit out of him, swallowing down the stupid tears that for some reason were really close to the surface.

He sucked in a breath and went even harder, kissing me like a storm, surrounding me with passion that was inescapable and wild, where shelter was nowhere to be found.

I wasn't sure I was going to make it.

I let go of his jaw, slid my hands down the front of his body, and touched him. *Finally.* He hissed my name and froze, tension hardening every muscle in that big body. He ground out the words "Holy. Hell. Yes. Iz. *Fuck.*"

His hands left me long enough to open a drawer and rip into a wrapper, and in a matter of seconds, he was inside my body. I squeezed my eyes shut and felt all of him, so incredibly good and right and full and hot that I was overwhelmed.

But then he said my name.

"Iz."

I opened my eyes, and he was watching me, looking like every wicked fantasy I'd ever had about him.

I swallowed and said, "Hi."

That made him smile, the sweetest, most affectionate little grin, and he said, "I fucking love you."

My chest burned, my ears buzzed, and I wanted to freeze that moment forever.

But then Blake started moving, dominating my body with that sexpertise of his, and I lost the ability to think. I wrapped my arms around him and held on tight as he made me burn. I might've blacked out at one point, and I definitely forgot how to form words for a solid ten seconds, but I never wanted it to end.

Nothing in my life had ever felt quite that exquisite.

Well, until fifteen minutes later, when Blake wrapped his body around mine, pulled the heavy comforter over us, kissed the top of my head, and turned out the light.

I felt like I was home.

And just like that, the worries that had plagued me disappeared. It was too late to turn back, so I was just going to listen to Blake.

Don't be scared, Iz. Just take a deep breath and let yourself fall.

Really, what else could I do, now that I was falling in love with him?

Chapter Twenty-Six

Blake

I sat down on a kitchen stool and opened Outlook.

The clock on the microwave said two fifteen, but I was still wide awake because my guilty conscience wouldn't let me sleep. Izzy, on the other hand, was totally out, looking adorable with her face buried in my pillow and my shirt on her back.

The sight of her there, sound asleep under my blanket, made me want so many fucking things.

But I couldn't have them. Not yet.

I took a deep breath and opened the email attachment, ready to accept whatever I found. I'd come up with a plan as I lay there with my face buried in her vanilla hair, and now it was time to formulate the strategy and hope she'd be able to forgive me later.

My eyes quickly moved over the chart—*shit, shit, shit*—and disappointment knotted in my gut. Her name was back underneath mine; she was back on my team. I'd suspected it, but see-ing it felt like a punch.

I paced around the kitchen as I texted, Is there any way we can meet up tomorrow? It's important. Your office, Scooter's, your house—wherever.

I knew Brad wouldn't respond in the middle of the night, but that man had bothered me after hours so many times that I didn't even feel bad for texting him this late.

My phone buzzed. *Holy shit—that was fast.* I opened the message.

Brad: Is everything okay?

I sighed and responded, It's fine, I just need to talk to you ASAP.

Brad: I can meet you at Scooter's at six.

I was usually the second person in the office every day; Brad was always the first. Six thirty was his normal start time, which was probably why the man was on his third wife and had chronic high blood pressure. I replied, Six o'clock it is, but let the record show that I texted you the minute after I opened the updated org chart.

Brad: Noted.

I swiped out of my messages and plugged the phone into the kitchen charger. Hitting the lights, I exited the kitchen as the room plunged into semidarkness. The city lights outside the window provided a little illumination, which usually made me feel less alone when I couldn't sleep.

But tonight the lights didn't matter.

Because Izzy was wrapped in my blanket, my shirt on her

body and my socks on her feet. I felt . . . fuck, *whole*, was it? That seemed way too dramatic, but whenever I was with her, I wanted nothing else. I thought of nothing else. Everything else ceased to exist.

When I was with Izzy, I was with the only person who mattered to me.

I walked through the living room, and even that looked different with her there. Her bag on the couch, her shoes on the floor, her shirt lying on the area rug as if she'd undressed on the way to bed.

I was usually a big fan of tidiness. For some reason, though, seeing her things scattered around my apartment made me feel some kind of fucking way.

When I walked into the bedroom, it was amplified to the nth degree. Because there, on the nightstand where I usually set my glasses when I went to bed, were *her* glasses. It felt polarizing, staring at her crooked frames with the smudged lenses, and I had the overwhelming urge to do something to keep them there indefinitely.

Yeah, I was clearly losing it.

I went around the bed and climbed in beside her, doing my best not to wake her. She was out, sound asleep with her hands tucked under her cheek on my pillow. I wanted to look at her, to watch her sleep, but I was pretty sure that was another level of creepy. So I rolled over, settled onto the other pillow, pulled the blanket up, and closed my eyes.

"Everything okay?" she asked, her voice slurred and a little gravelly with sleep.

"Fine," I replied, my eyes still closed.

"You took away my warmth when you left," she said, scooting closer until she was curled into my back. I felt her breath on the back of my neck and her knee snaking between mine as she murmured, "Mm, better."

I swear to God every muscle in my body relaxed like I'd been given the sweetest sleeping pill, and I took a deep breath of Izzy air.

She was right—that *was* way better.

Chapter Twenty-Seven

Izzy

I couldn't believe that VP Blake was still asleep.

It was seven o'clock, I was dressed (in his big T-shirt and a pair of his baggy shorts that I'd had to waist-roll two times) and ready for a run, while Blake lay face down on the bed as if comatose. I would've imagined him as one of those dudes doing burpees at 5:00 a.m., but apparently he liked sleeping in.

And I found that contradiction to be so adorable, God help me. I wanted to jump on his back and bounce up and down, just to irritate him awake and see his sleepy scowl.

After feeding the cats, I left him a note so he didn't overdose Goodyear and quietly left the apartment. I still had his code from when I cat sat, so I didn't bother with a key. It wasn't until my second mile that I finally heard from him. His text notification silenced the Post Malone that was blaring through my AirPods.

Blake: Where did you go?

I stopped and replied, I'm under the bed.

Blake: You don't seriously think I'm going to look, do you?

Izzy: In my head, you did.

Blake: Was I wearing coveralls, little perv?

I snorted and moved off the sidewalk and onto a bench. Texted, First of all, it's LIL PERV. Second, no coveralls this time. This time you're only wearing that pretty chest and a very precarious sheet.

Blake: What makes it so precarious?

I grinned and pictured naked Blake, sound asleep in his bed. Texted, The way it's SOOO close to sliding off and exposing your junk.

Blake: Have I ever told you that you have a way with words?

Izzy: Don't have to—I know it.

Blake: So—where'd you actually go?

Izzy: I'm running. Well, I WAS running until you texted. Now I'm sitting on a bench outside of a barber shop.

Blake: In your skirt?

I offhandedly wondered where that skirt was. Blake had removed it from my body, and I hadn't seen it since. I texted: In your pants. I swear I didn't rifle, but you had a pair of workout shorts folded on top of the dryer so I borrowed them.

Blake: Are they falling off of you? They must be huge.

Izzy: That's what she said.

Blake: That doesn't make sense.

Izzy: That's what HE said?

Blake: Still not there.

Izzy: How about that's what you said when I said I was wearing your shorts?

Blake: FFS, Shay. How much longer will you be running?

I snorted. There was something so rewarding about irritating VP Blake. I texted, Two more miles. But the time varies GREATLY.

Blake: Greatly??

Izzy: Well, it depends on if I'm feeling lazy, or if I see a dog, or if I got railed last night and am out of shape because of it—that sort of thing.

Blake: Did you get railed?

I grinned and noticed that the man sitting at the bus stop was looking at me like I was out of my mind. *Totally fair, dude.* I texted, Seriously, Chest, you wouldn't BELIEVE the night I had.

Blake: Good?

Izzy: I wouldn't want him to know and get a big head, but this man was unbelievably good.

Blake: He knows.

Izzy: Oh, he does not.

Blake: Trust me. You make this noise that sounds a little bit like a sexy guinea pig and you get super bitey; it definitely lets a man know how he's doing.

Izzy: So you know it was good for me because I became vermin-like.

Blake: YUP.

I texted, Well you make this growly noise that rumbles in your chest and your fingers get all grippy, so I know you liked it because YOU became a cat.

Blake: You also know I liked it because I came so hard I nearly blacked out.

"Oh, my God," I said out loud with a squeal, and the bus

stop dude clutched his grocery bag like he thought I was coming for it. I responded with I have to go run before Bus Stop Man calls the cops.

Blake: Why? What are you doing?

Izzy: It's this perverted little cackle, like I'm turned on and also very amused. I imagine it's mildly unsettling to a stranger.

Blake: Do you want company on your run, weirdo?

Izzy: Well yes, but I feel like you might be slower than me and hold me back.

Blake: I promise to try my hardest.

Izzy: I'm sitting in front of Alliance Barbershop. You've got 20 mins.

Blake: I'm still in bed—how am I going to run two miles and be there in twenty minutes?

Izzy: Sprint, dumbass. Or drive.

Blake: Drive, she says.

Izzy: Yes! Drive here, we run, and then we drive to breakfast after.

Blake: I was going to make you breakfast.

I felt all gooey inside, like I was about to melt into a thick puddle of happy honey. I texted, You were?

Blake: Homemade pizza because I know you hate breakfast food.

Izzy: Oops I just made the guinea pig sound.

Blake: Fuck, yes, I'm on my way.

Izzy: YESSSSS.

Blake: I seem to recall you saying that a lot last night.

Izzy: I pretty much chanted it.

Blake: Fucking amazing night, Shay.

Izzy: Agreed, Phillips.

Blake: I'm pretty sure I saw God that last time.

Izzy: No, that was me, silly.

Blake: My mistake, Goddess.

Izzy: #newnickname

Blake: #youwish

Izzy: #drivecarefully

Blake: #iwill

Blake

"How old were you?" I asked.

"Five," she said, toeing off her shoes in the entryway as I shut the door behind us.

"Seems like you should've been old enough to know better," I said, wondering when I'd become the kind of guy who was obsessed with childhood stories. For some reason, with Iz, I wanted to hear every single anecdote that led to her becoming the person she was.

It reminded me of that Taylor Swift lyric *You told me 'bout your past, thinking your future was me.*

"Maybe Scotty was a little shit—did you ever think of that?" she asked, her nose crinkled as she pretended to be pissed. "Did anyone?"

I watched her pull the ponytail out of her hair and then use her fingers to shake it out. Those little mannerisms were somehow *something* to me all of a sudden. I wanted to learn every single one. I crossed my arms and said, "But didn't you say he cried every time he saw you coming?"

"Are you going to talk about Scotty the Shit all day, who probably deserved my tackling backbites, or are you going to show me how to work your fancy showerhead?"

I grabbed her hand, linked my fingers through hers, and pulled her toward the master bathroom.

The run had been entertaining, with Izzy shit talking the entire time about how fast she was while simultaneously telling me to slow down. After that, we grabbed breakfast while walking around the farmers' market (she was too hungry to wait until we got home). I'd wolfed down a breakfast sandwich sold to me by a certified beekeeper who also taught yoga, and Izzy wolfed down a glazed donut she'd found at the gas station across the street.

There had been a brief moment of mortification when the flower vendor told Izzy the "adorable" story of how I'd needed to find the perfect flowers yesterday and was a bit of a psycho about it, but when Iz's lips turned up into a huge grin and she sarcastically batted her eyelashes at me and put her hands over her heart, I'd stopped caring.

"You know," she said as I flipped on the bathroom light, "it'd probably be best for the planet if we just showered at the same time."

"I do love the planet," I said, opening the glass door and turning on the water.

"I knew it," she said, going straight to the counter to brush her teeth with the extra travel brush I'd given her last night.

"But I think you just want to see me naked." I joined her at the vanity, grabbing my toothbrush.

She shook her head and said through a mouthful of toothpaste, "That's a mighty big ego you have, sir."

"I think you want to see my mighty big—"

"Shhh," she interrupted, her eyes crinkling at the corners as she scrubbed her teeth. "Don't say it."

"Say what?" I asked as I started brushing, feigning innocence even though we were both remembering the night before.

The things she'd said.

The things I'd said.

She delivered a look of warning to me in the mirror, but the smile in her eyes ruined it.

"You can't say it now?" I teased, giving my mouth the fastest brushing, because that shower was calling. "Because I seem to recall that pretty mouth saying some filthy things in my bedroom."

Her eyes sparkled with humor, with challenge, as she finished brushing and turned off her sink. Then she stepped out of her shorts, pulled off her T-shirt, and stripped down to nothing. "I'd rather use my mouth for other things. You coming?"

She walked around me and stepped into the shower. I just stood there, frozen with my toothbrush in my hand, looking at naked Izzy as she turned away from the shower stream so the water was hitting her back, and she leaned her head all the way back to get her hair wet.

"Stop staring and get in," she said, her eyes closed.

I was naked in a second and stepping into the shower, my hands reaching for her waist to pull her close. I muttered something, but she cut me off by grabbing the back of my head, pulling me down to her level, and kissing the living shit out of me. The hunger of it, the want, nearly buckled my knees as I squeezed her waist and tried keeping up with her.

Hot water poured over us as heat pulsed through my veins. This . . . *this* I could do forever. I reached around her to grab the body wash, not breaking contact with her mouth as I squeezed out liquid soap and started lathering her back. My hands traveled all over her slick skin, back to front, head to toe.

And I was a fucking junkie for her reactions. A sigh was great at first, but then I needed a moan. When my hands made her moan, my adrenaline spiked, and I could barely breathe from the burning need to hear her scream. And when my mouth delivered that hot-as-fuck sound, I finally felt like I had my fix.

Until she slid down my body, her fingers scraping down my thighs, and she proceeded to make me lose the capacity to think at all.

Chapter Twenty-Eight

Blake

"I told you this would be a great date."

"You were right," I said, doing my best to drink my IPA, but it was extremely difficult when Izzy was walking so fast. She'd decided after our shower that she wanted to take me on a date, and who was I to stop her, right?

Last night was so perfect that I want the opportunity to top it, Phillips.

In my humble opinion, that sounded like one hell of a good time.

Was I surprised when we ended up at the zoo? Yes. Was it hands down the best date I'd ever been on? Also yes. I mean, what was better than beer, food trucks, and wild animals? She bought me snacks, took me on the train, and forced me to lie down in the shark tunnel so I could have "an entirely different underwater-viewing experience."

Everything in the world seemed better with her. More fun. Fucking *happier*.

"What's the hurry, Shay?" It felt like she was practically running. "The zoo doesn't close for an hour."

"I know, but Skyfari closes in twenty minutes."

"Sky what?"

The words were barely out of my mouth when she stopped and pointed, grinning. I followed her finger, and *oh, hell no*. It was one of those ski lift things, where you rode around and viewed the zoo from above.

No fucking way.

I hated heights. I'd hated heights since Jason and I had gotten stuck on a ski lift when I was nine and we'd had to sit still, dangling over the side of a mountain, for over an hour.

It'd been terrifying.

I'd gotten over it and dealt with heights when necessary, but I was definitely not going to subject myself to this nightmarish little zoo ride that was more than likely maintained by a staff of disengaged sixteen-year-olds.

No, thank you, I would rather eat glass than get on that thing. I rubbed my forehead and said, "I don't think—"

"This is my favorite thing at the zoo," Izzy said excitedly, beaming up at me and kind of bouncing a little. "My grandparents used to get mad at me when we came here because all I wanted to do was ride it, over and over again. They'd be all *only one time* and I'd cry inconsolably and then we'd end up riding it for hours."

"What a little shit," I said, in love with the way her eyes danced when she told that story.

"Right?" She wrapped her arms around my arm, and her eyes were all squinty when she grinned up at me and said, "I think it'll be the perfect way to end a perfect weekend, don't you? Just the two of us, watching the sun set from our quiet spot on top of the world?"

I opened my mouth to politely decline, to explain how you couldn't pay me enough to ride the Skyfari, but then she kissed my arm. Just an offhanded little peck that she probably hadn't even realized she'd done, but something about the subconscious gesture wrecked me. I looked down at her and stupidly said, "I do. Let's go."

This is no big deal, I told myself as she bought tickets and handed them to the kid at the gate. Just a quick little ride around the zoo; easy peasy. Hell, there were little kids up there; what the fuck was *I* feeling nauseated about?

I was a grown-ass man.

Izzy was talking a mile a minute as we waited in line, and even though I was listening and responding, nothing was sticking. My eyes were too focused on the lift cars that just kept coming and coming.

When we reached the front, Izzy grinned. "Here we go."

"Yeah," I said, forcing my lips to smile as we walked over and stood on the white loading line. The car came around and scooped us up, and then a blond kid who looked no older than fourteen—*Ryker*—latched the bar for us.

Yeah, this is a terrible idea, putting our lives in the hands of a Ryker.

I wrapped both hands around the bar and looked straight ahead, needing to see anything but the ground below.

"Hey, Blakey," Izzy said as the kid stepped back and our car started climbing that cable, "scooch closer."

And then she wiggled a little closer to me, dear *God*, making the car rock.

"Stop that," I hissed, glancing over at her out of the corner of my eye.

"What?" She was looking at me in confusion, which tracked. I'd sounded like a total lunatic.

"There was a sign that said you shouldn't rock the cars," I said calmly, forcing myself to sound normal. "So we should probably follow the rules."

"I think they mean don't shake them back and forth on purpose," she teased, sounding (rightfully so) like she was amused by how seriously I was considering the Skyfari regulations. "I'm pretty sure you're allowed to move."

"Yeah, but it's best if you don't, though," I said, injecting boredom into my voice. "Sitting still is probably the way to go."

"Blake." Her voice was less confused and more concerned now. "Are you okay?"

"Sure," I said, forcing myself to move my head just enough to smile at her. "You?"

"I'm good," she said, her eyes narrowed as she watched me. "Having fun?"

"Yes," I said, swallowing as I saw the other cars, the ones heading back toward the starting gate, moving off to her right.

Something about seeing how high *they* were made my stomach drop.

Why the hell am I being such a pussy?

"Ooh, look at the rhino," she said, looking down at the ground beneath us. "That thing is massive."

"Yeah," I said, turning my head back to the forward-facing position, gripping the bar, and closing my eyes behind my sunglasses. "Enormous."

"Is that an ostrich?" she asked, and I felt the weight shift when she leaned a little to look down. "I wouldn't have thought they'd be friends."

"Yeah, same," I managed, freezing every muscle in my body to offset her movement, definitely not looking down at the animals.

"Blake."

"Hmm?"

"There aren't any ostriches. Are your eyes closed?"

I sighed but still didn't open them. "Maybe just a little. I'm tired."

"They're *squeezed* shut, you liar," she said. "What is going on with you?"

I sighed again, keeping my eyes closed because in addition to not wanting to see how high we were, now I didn't want to see her looking at me like I was a nutjob. "I maybe don't love ski lifts."

"What?"

"It's no big deal," I said, working hard to maintain a relaxed voice, "but they just aren't my thing."

"So why are you *on* one?"

Because you kissed my arm. That wasn't a rational answer, so I went with "You wanted to and I thought maybe I liked them now."

"Look at me," she said, and she sounded like she wanted to laugh. "Blake."

"I don't want to," I said, keeping my eyes closed. I honestly wasn't sure if that was making it better or worse, but I knew the zoo geography enough to know we had to be getting close to the monkey island, a place I definitely didn't want to hover over.

"Okay," she said, clearing her throat. "Um, maybe if you . . ."

She didn't trail off, but my ability to listen to her did, because the lift stopped.

It fucking *stopped*.

It wasn't supposed to stop, it was supposed to keep circling around and around. That was its job, right? To keep moving on a constant loop? I wasn't sure what was going on, but why would the ski lift just stop?

Ryker, what the fuck?

"Try opening your eyes?"

"I'm good," I said, swallowing. "Really. Don't worry about me, I'm good, just look around at the zoo and have fun while we wait for this thing to start moving. I'm fine, I promise."

"Well, you don't *look* fine," she said, her voice soft. "Your knuckles are literally white and you're sweating even though it's starting to get cold. How can I help you?"

I loved her more at that moment than it was right to love her this early in our relationship, and I really wanted to open my eyes and look at her face.

But that seemed to be physically impossible for me.

It was like my eyes were glued shut.

"I promise I'm okay, Iz," I said, "I just really need this thing to start moving. Why isn't it moving?"

"Oh, this happens all the time," she said calmly. "Nothing's wrong, I promise. Sometimes they'll have to stop and, like, clean out a car because a kid spilled, things like that. I know because I *destroyed* a lift car with an ice-cream cone when I was seven."

That made me smile in spite of this hell. "So on-brand."

"Right?" she said, and I could hear the smile in her voice. "It was like a hundred degrees, I was with my brother, and I dropped a large cone the instant we took off. By the time we got back, melted ice cream was *all over* our shorts and the seat, and the sticky chocolate was even dripping down onto people walking below."

"Nice."

"Do your brothers know about your aversion to heights?" she asked.

"Oh, yeah," I said. "Jason is exactly the same."

"Okay, what's his phone number?"

Obviously she was going to call him, which wasn't going to help anything at all, but I was so incapable of any thoughts other than *what the fuck, Ryker* that I gave her my brother's number.

A second later, I could hear the FaceTime ringing.

Oh, shit. She's FaceTiming him.

I thought he wouldn't answer because he wasn't going to recognize her number, but then I heard, "Yeah?"

"Hi, Jason, um, I'm sorry to FaceTime out of the blue, but I'm with your brother and we have a little situation."

I forced my eyes open and turned my head just the slightest, only to see Jason's face on Izzy's phone as he said, "What's wrong? Is he okay?"

"He's fine," she said, and then she turned the phone toward

me. "But we're on the Skyfari at the zoo, it stopped for a moment, and he seems a little tense. I thought—"

"Why the fuck are you on that thing, Blake?" Jason was yelling—*when wasn't he*—and he sounded seriously offended by my situation. "Do you have a death wish? Did someone force you to board at gunpoint?"

"It's not *that* high, Jason," Izzy said calmly. "And I called you because I thought it might *help* Blake."

"Yeah, you dick," I said, shocked that it was somehow a little funny to me. "Help Blake."

"Blakey is an idiot and cannot *be* helped," Jason said, but he was shaking his head and grinning. "You got on a ski lift by choice, man, come *on*."

"Aren't you going to tell him that it's no big deal," Izzy said slowly, "and that everything's going to be fine?"

"He'll know that's a lie," Jason said. "Didn't he tell you about the last time we were on one?"

"Jace," I warned, nearly having a heart attack when the lift started moving again. "Don't."

"He did *not*," Izzy said, sounding amused.

Jason launched into the story in the way only Jason could, adding f-bombs as adjectives, adverbs, and even proper nouns.

"Our dad—King Fuck—let us go alone, if you can believe that shit."

I stared at his stupid face as he told the story, and Izzy laughed her ass off.

"Blakey wouldn't stop bawling, and the sound of that little shit screaming and crying was driving me nuts. Like, I was terrified, too, but the kid was *howling* so loudly that I wanted to gouge my eardrums out. So I started making up this story about the girl he had a crush on."

"Rachel Devos," I said, laughing because I'd forgotten all about the story. "Holy shit, you told me she was super into daredevils, and that as long as we didn't die, our story was going to make her totally want me."

Izzy started laughing at that, and Jason was grinning as he kept talking.

"It worked, though, because you stopped sniveling and started scheming, right?" He said to Izzy, "This little scrawnball was making plans on how we were going to be casually talking about it when we walked to school—because Rachel's mom made her walk with us."

"Poor girl," Izzy said.

"No, I think she learned a lot from us," Jason countered, which made Izzy laugh even harder.

"A lot she's probably trying to forget," I said around a laugh.

"All I know is that by the time we got rescued from the lift, I swear to God our ski pants were frozen to our bodies because we'd both peed our pants so many fucking times. I mean, it had been *hours* and we'd gone hard on the create-your-own-drink Coke machine beforehand."

"That thing was so cool, though," I added.

"Mom fucking hated it because Dad let us have as much as we wanted."

"Hey, Jason, we have to go," Izzy said, turning the phone back to herself. "We're almost back to the gate now."

I looked in front of us and I could see Ryker. We were almost finished, praise Jesus.

"Well, tell my brother to quit doing stupid shit," my brother said. "And stop taking him on death-defying dates, Izzy, okay?"

"Okay," she said, grinning. "Goodbye, Jason."

My knees were a little wobbly when we stepped off the ride, and it felt like I was waking up after sleeping, to be honest. The late-day sun, the people, the noise—it'd all disappeared for a bit, it seemed.

But the one thing that hadn't disappeared was *her*. I refused to overthink what she'd done and what had just happened, because that would force me to recognize the patheticness of all she'd had to witness, but the fact of the matter was that she'd rescued me.

Izzy had seen me at my most vulnerable, and she'd rescued me in the very best way.

"Hey." I grabbed her hand and pulled her away from the zoo sidewalk and into the trees. I didn't stop until her back was against a tree and her face was in my hands. I let my eyes drink in every detail of her face—those eyes, those freckles, that mouth—before saying, "Thank you."

She blinked, long lashes like butterfly wings, and her lips turned up. "You're welcome."

"Will you be embarrassed if I kiss the living shit out of you at the zoo?"

Her eyes squinted as she grinned and shook her head. "Bring it on, *Blakey*."

Chapter Twenty-Nine

Izzy

"Seriously? You really think Patrick Mahomes is the guy?"

"He had four hundred twenty-five passing yards last week," Blake said, cracking open a peanut shell. "It's a no-brainer."

"Last week is last week, this week is this week," I countered, tugging on the bottom of the Beastie Boys T-shirt I'd stolen from Blake's closet that morning and had been wearing since we got home from the zoo. It was getting chilly and I was going to need to put on pants soon, but the game had just started and I was too comfy to go all the way into the bedroom.

"Wow." Blake gave me a look and tossed a shell in my direction. "*So* profound."

"Profundity is my forte."

"*Profundity* isn't even a word."

"Googling, dipshit." I laughed and opened Google. We were each sitting on opposite ends of my couch—because I'd forced him to scoot over as punishment for calling my fantasy football team "abysmal"—but then the Darkling had ruined everything by settling on Blake's lap so he couldn't come back to me.

I loved what an unwilling cat lover he was.

"Boom—profundity," I said, reading the definition aloud, but he just shook his head and tossed more peanuts in my direction.

After the zoo, he'd brought me home so I could feed the cat and, well, go home. But instead of saying goodbye, I'd invited him in to watch football, which we'd been doing ever since.

It felt like we were both trying to stretch out the last waning hours of our weekend together.

It'd been so perfect it was terrifying.

"I need a soda," I said, getting up. "Want something?"

His dark eyes were all over me, a smile on his lips, and I muttered, "Pervert," before rolling my eyes and going into the kitchen. Blake walked in when I was closing the refrigerator, and the sight of his socks on my tacky linoleum floor made me happy.

Incandescently happy.

So weird, right? But VP Blake in his stocking feet was a glorious sight to behold.

Because I felt like I'd gotten to know an entirely different person over the weekend, a person I was even more interested in than VP Blake *and* Mr. Chest. For example, as odd as it sounded, seeing him get totally tripped up by his fear of heights made me feel insanely close to him.

Like I really *knew* him.

"You want a Dr Pepper?" I asked.

"Actually, I should probably take off. Tomorrow is going to

be a stressful day at work, so I should be a good boy and get a decent night's sleep. You know, since some little shit kept me up all night."

Disappointment settled over me, even though we'd both said over our living room pizza picnic that we needed to stay at our respective apartments with work hovering in the morning.

"Yeah, get out," I said. "I'm done with you anyway."

"Nope." He wrapped his arms around me and squeezed tightly, lifting me off the ground as he added, "We're only getting started."

I tried to be cool, but it was impossible not to smile at that because I just freaking adored him. I adored him and wanted everything.

So I looked away from his face before he could see my naked adoration, and I changed the subject.

"Did you know that when you set me on the table yesterday, I kind of thought you wanted to sex me up? On the butcher-block dinette?"

His gaze moved over the span of my face, like he was trying to see if I was serious or not, and then he lifted me higher and carried me over to the table. My heart started racing as he gave me a look, plopped me on the table, pushed my knees apart, and stepped closer.

"Were you into it, Iz?" he said in a quiet growl as he dragged his teeth along my jawline and his hands slowly slid the oversize T-shirt up my thighs. He raised his head and asked, "Were you down for some table action?"

"Yes," I sighed, looking straight into his eyes. "I seem to be into everything when it comes to you."

Something in his face changed when I said that. All at once he looked sweet and serious, and he leaned closer and rested his forehead against mine. He swallowed and said, "I know the feeling."

"It's bizarre, right?" I whispered, raising a hand to his stubbled jaw.

He closed his eyes for a half second, leaning into my touch, and when he opened them, they were bright and hot and intense. "Fucking bizarre and so fucking perfect, Iz."

His mouth found mine as his hands made quick work of my clothes, and I took care of his pants while never breaking contact with that power kiss.

In mere seconds he was right where I needed him, consuming my mouth as he crashed into me on the kitchen table, and I felt emotional as I locked eyes with him, somehow homesick for him at that very second even though the moment hadn't yet passed. He rocked into me, making me wrap my legs around him to hold him closer, squeeze him tighter, to try to lock up his body the way he'd locked up my heart.

"Fuck," he hissed, sliding his hands underneath me and changing the angle to where it was no longer physically possible for my eyes to stay open. Or for me to think. He was so good, so in tune with every little thing that I didn't even know I wanted, that I just dug my heels and nails into him and let myself fall into the blissful escape.

Chapter Thirty

Blake

Izzy: You awake?

I smiled as I read her message. Yes, I was lying in bed, in the dark, but I was definitely still awake. I texted, We literally hung up the phone four minutes ago.

Izzy: Well you fell asleep really fast last night, so . . .

Blake: No, that was you, Princess Snore.

Izzy: I don't snore.

Blake: No comment.

Izzy: Quit lying about things, liar.

I pictured her, face down and sound asleep beside me. I texted, Isabella Shay, I'm not saying you snore, but if you did, it would be the most adorable sleepy sound I've ever heard. Like a motherfucking kitten.

Izzy: Flipping you off.

Blake: Grabbing your finger and sucking.

Izzy: ABORT MISSION! THIS IS NO WAY TO GET SLEEPY!

I sat up, grinning like a dumbass, and fluffed the pillow. Texted, Is that why you texted? So you could get sleepy?

Izzy: No. I texted to say that no matter what happens, this weekend was perfect.

What was that? Did she know about the new reorg? I sent "No matter what happens??"

Izzy: I just mean that regardless of any other thing that happens in my life, in the world or in the universe, this weekend will be preserved in my heart as perfection.

Well, shit. I felt that in my stomach, in my heart, and in my mind, because it was exactly how I felt, too.

I love you. I wanted to say it, and not in the idiotic *I fucking love you* way I'd already done when we first slept together. I was sure she'd chalked that one up to me being overjoyed to have her willing body in my bed, the equivalent of me saying, *I love having sex with you.*

No, I wanted to tell her a hundred times that even though it was too soon, I was in love with everything about her.

Maybe I'd tell her tomorrow, after everything went down. Yes, it was too soon, but I was starting to not care that nothing about us made sense.

I love you, Iz. It's what I felt in my core, but instead I texted, I love your profundity, Iz.

Izzy: And I love hearing you acknowledge the word profundity. Goodnight, Mr. Chest.

I lay back on the pillow, looked out at the city lights, and texted, Goodnight to you, Scooter's Amy.

Chapter Thirty-One

Blake

Izzy: Two things. Number 1—I miss gas station donuts and co-ed showers.

Same, I thought as I stepped out of my car and hit the lock button on the key fob. There was a chill in the early morning air, the subtle fall warning that winter was on its way, and for once I was glad I was wearing a suit jacket.

Izzy: Number 2—Hope your stressful day goes better than expected. I'm not prying, but I'm assuming it has to do with the merger and the resultant revised org chart. In which case I'm sorry for your discomfort, but also not sorry.

I put my keys in my pocket and texted, Nor am I.

I didn't want to say much, but I also didn't want *her* worrying about the shit that was going to go down at Ellis; that was *my* problem. I added, It's a mess, but just know that I will NOT let work get in the way of us.

Izzy: US? 😏

I pushed through the doors at Scooter's, more determined than ever to find a way to make it work. I texted, US.

"Are you kidding me right now?" Brad sat back in his chair, looking at me like I'd lost my mind as the sound of steaming milk suddenly seemed deafening. It'd been nice when I'd been discussing Izzy, providing a loud, foamy layer of privacy, but now it just added to the tension in my neck.

I asked, "Which part are you referring to specifically?"

"All of it—*shit*." The older man smiled and gave his head a shake. "You moved in fast as hell after version one, didn't you?"

"I know, I know," I said, recalling the way I'd literally sprinted from the building when I thought I was safe to date Izzy. I reached up and tugged at my collar, which suddenly felt too tight. I hated sharing my personal life with anyone from work, but since I wasn't willing to lie, it was the only way. I'd told Brad everything, and I just hoped Izzy would forgive me for not asking her first.

I considered Brad a friend; I knew I could count on his discretion, regardless of what the man's business decision was on the matter.

Still, I was nervous. This was new territory for me.

Brad said, "You never talk about your personal life, so I'm assuming this must be important to you."

I nodded. "It is."

"Well, then," Brad said, sitting back in his chair and crossing his arms. "I have good news and bad news."

I clenched my teeth—gnashed them together, really—before saying, "What's the bad news?"

Brad's eyes narrowed as he looked at me and said, "The same as the good news. As you know, we're eliminating some duplicate positions, post-merger."

"Yes." I never liked letting anyone go, but the reality was that when Ellis bought out smaller companies, they usually ended up with too many employees in certain roles and had to downsize.

"Well, the Boston branch was heavy on admin, so most of the cuts will be from there. However, there are some senior positions from that location which we'll keep."

I knew this already. "Brad, I was the one who—"

"Isabella Shay is a new employee, with far less experience than the generalists in Boston, but her wage is the same. So it makes sense that hers should be the eliminated position."

I felt like I'd had the wind knocked out of me. "*What?*"

"You signed off on the plan when you were in Boston, Blake." Brad wore a patient smile as he took off his glasses and adjusted one of the sides. "But the spreadsheet only had employee numbers, not names."

Fuck, fuck, fuck. "Holy shit, I didn't know."

"That's right, you didn't." Brad put his glasses back on and glanced at his watch. "Think about that. You knew—and still know—that it's the right business decision if you take emotions out of the equation. There isn't a single solid reason why we would change the plan."

I dragged a hand through my hair, frustrated because *shit*— Brad was right. It *was* the right move. If I weren't involved with her, I would absolutely put Izzy on the top of that list.

Anyone in my position would.

"Don't take this the wrong way, but maybe this is a good thing, if you really like this girl. Now you don't have to worry about your jobs getting in the way."

Not helping. I seriously felt sick to my stomach, because I already knew there was nothing I could do. If I tried to save her job, it would be seen—rightly so—as a conflict of interest and the by-product of my emotional attachment to her. Brad might be my friend, but he wouldn't overlook the obvious.

"Listen, I have to go." Brad picked up his coffee and stood. "I'm sure I don't need to remind you that regardless of your relationship, this is top secret until Human Resources takes care of it tomorrow morning. I trust you'll keep it to yourself?"

I nodded. "Of course."

I watched Brad leave, and then I just sat at the table, feeling numb.

The cuts were happening tomorrow morning. I knew that because *I* was the one who'd stared at the spreadsheet for hours before making the decisions. *I* was the one who'd called Pam and scheduled when and how the separations and severance packages would be handled.

Ellis was generous with severance, and I was proud of the kind, helpful way our HR team provided assistance to departing employees. I hated layoffs, but the way the company took care of people had always made me feel marginally better.

The way it worked—the way it'd always worked—was that everyone in the know kept it entirely confidential until it went down. That way no one could be tipped off in advance and do something crazy; I'd seen it all, so I knew firsthand that the key to separations running smoothly was to keep everything quiet.

But how the fuck was I supposed to do that? How was I supposed to *not* tell Izzy?

I'd always looked at the integrity of my role through a simple lens. It wasn't uncommon for me to have to give depositions and make statements under oath; workers' comp claims, harassment, unlawful terminations—those were things that happened under the umbrella of Administration and HR.

So I'd always conducted myself as if every decision I made could be questioned under oath. *Because it could.* If I was always honest and followed the rules, I'd never have anything to hide.

It'd always seemed remarkably black and white to me. I could testify under oath that I'd never shared confidential information with an Ellis employee because I never had.

But how could I follow the rules and keep this confidential when all I wanted to do was protect Iz?

Izzy

I walked into the conference room, trying my hardest not to look too happy, like I was a deranged elf or something.

But it was tough.

Because it felt like my world had changed over the weekend, like it'd grown bigger, its colors painted brighter. I was ridiculously amped by the promise of it all.

Obviously, I knew that Blake was just a guy and it might not work out.

It *probably* wouldn't work out, honestly, if you played the odds on the dating game.

But why not jump into these moments of wild promise and roll around in them? I was going to make lovesick snow angels in these swoony times and not allow odds and reality to creep in and destroy the magic.

Pam came into the conference room and started talking about the acquisition, which I'd expected. I felt cool, that I had this knowledge ahead of time (although, to be fair, it appeared as if half of the department had been involved in the paperwork side of the merger).

Pam started talking about benefits for the Boston employees who were coming on board, so I had to take a lot of notes; this was going to give me quite the workload, but I was still in love with my new job, so I was excited. But when it was clear the woman was wrapping up the meeting, I couldn't help but notice that she'd yet to mention the org chart.

I was *so* tempted to ask, but I didn't want to accidentally say something that hadn't been announced yet. The last thing I wanted was to sabotage myself. After the meeting, I was spared from having to ask, when Heather, the HR assistant, asked Pam, "Do I need to merge the two org charts?"

Pam shook her head and said, "Blake already did it this morning. It's on the shared drive."

I stood there, waiting for Pam to say he was no longer our boss, but she didn't.

Weird, right?

I went back to my office and opened the Excel spreadsheet of all the new employees that I'd need to reach out to, ready to dig into the work. But I couldn't stop myself from checking the shared drive. I opened the org chart document, and it only took about five seconds for me to see that Blake was still on top, with Pam underneath him, and me underneath Pam.

"*What?*" I muttered out loud, to myself. Maybe it wasn't updated—no, it appeared to have been updated by Blake at seven that morning.

Oh, no.

I dropped my hands to the desk. What did that mean? He was my boss again? If he was, did that mean we were done? Finished after two days?

Why had it changed? Why hadn't he told me?

I pulled out my phone—no messages, which wasn't a surprise, since we didn't really talk during business hours. But . . . what did it mean?

What was going through Blake's mind?

I wished I could just text him and ask, but I didn't want to interrupt his stressful day with self-centered questions about how it affected me.

Surely it was fine.

Surely he was on top of it.

I inhaled through my nose, forcing myself to relax. I trusted Blake, and that everything would work out.

I got lost in the reports after that, forgetting everything but work. Pam was in meetings somewhere else in the building, so it was easy to just fall into the work without interruptions. But when my stomach growled and I looked at the clock, my mind went right back to Blake. Because it was Monday—Caniglia's food truck day.

I stood, grabbed my coat, and reached for my bag. He probably wouldn't be there today, but if I happened upon him and we shared a lunch, perhaps he'd feel like enlightening me.

If not, I'd just stress eat until I puked.

Six o'clock.

I stared at the clock above my TV, still stuffed from the Blake-free stress eating. It was probably late enough to text him, right? He was most likely still at the office, but it was technically after the workday.

I texted, Are you still at work, Chest?

Blake: Yup

I didn't like one-word answers with zero punctuation; that made me very nervous. I replied, Was the day as stressful as you thought it'd be?

Blake: Worse

I really, really, *really* needed an emoji or a superfluous exclamation point to reassure me that everything was fine. I texted, Well I'll stop bugging you so you can leave.

Blake: Tks

I hated being that girl because I *hated* that girl, but staccato brevity wasn't our normal mode of conversation. I couldn't shake the feeling that something was wrong, that he was distancing himself from me.

Especially when he hadn't taken a break to have lunch at Caniglia's or at least text me when he surely knew I was trudging toward an Italian feast.

I scarfed a piece of leftover pizza before going for a run with

Josh, who was always willing to accompany me if it was getting too dark. Normally we both wore headphones and tuned each other out, but that night, I found myself totally unloading on him. I told him everything, mostly because I knew he liked Blake, so it felt safe to share with him.

But then he said, "Shit, Physical Challenge isn't looking too good all of a sudden."

"*What?*" I almost tripped and landed on my face when he very matter-of-factly said those words.

"Think about it," he said, looking down at his Apple Watch. "Either Blake lied to you about the org chart to get in your pants over the weekend," he started, making me roll my eyes at his disgustingness, "or he found out about the changes at work today and is freaking out and hoping you'll let him go back to only being coworkers."

"Those aren't the only options," I said defensively, because I'd been forcing myself not to think that very thing. "He could be so busy that he hasn't had a chance to discuss this with me."

"That doesn't change what I said," Josh replied in that know-it-all tone that made me want to slug him. An hour later, after I'd showered and had checked my phone fifteen times, his words kept replaying in my head.

And as much as I wanted to deny them, I couldn't. Because regardless of what happened with the org chart, Blake was now my boss again, so it was incredibly possible that he would be ending our entanglement.

I finally gave in and texted a trivial, low-key message: The Darkling vomited on Josh's couch and now he's holding my pillows and blankets hostage until I pay to have it professionally cleaned.

It was true—*that dick*—and it was something that would amuse Blake.

But an hour later, still no message.

And that kind of pissed me off. I understood a stressful day, and I also understood that his obsession with ethics might prevent him from continuing our relationship, but he didn't need to ghost me. I would've assumed our weekend had elevated us to a place where ghosting was no longer a possibility. He was obviously home from work by now and capable of using his huge fingers to smash out a polite response.

Asshole.

After putting in a few hours on the benefits paperwork, I plugged in my phone and went to bed. As I laid my head on a throw pillow from the sofa and covered myself with just the sheet (freaking Josh), I decided that if Blake texted me overnight, I didn't even want to know. I put that thing on silent and turned off the lights.

Despite myself, I really wished I could vent about him to my best friend, Blake.

Blake

"What the fuck are you looking at?" I glared at the cats, who were huddled together on the couch and staring at me as if disappointed by my actions. I was sitting at my desk, sipping straight Scotch—as I had been since I'd arrived home—while trying to figure out how the hell I was going to proceed.

I couldn't tell her. I *couldn't*. It went against my business principles, and surely Iz would understand that. She would, right? Izzy would totally understand.

I'd ignored her texts all night, though, because acting normal was impossible on the eve of her termination. I couldn't in good conscience do the whole banter thing, laughing with her while knowing what was waiting for her the following morning.

So radio silence was my only option.

It was almost midnight, and I was still clueless as to what to do. Because if I continued to avoid her until after she was terminated, it's not like she wouldn't know that I'd known. She *would* know, and odds were high that she was going to be pissed that I hadn't warned her or at the very least responded to her messages.

So what was my plan? Wait until I knew she'd left the building with her COBRA paperwork, then text, *You up?*

All I knew for certain was that I missed her. It'd only been twenty-four hours, yet I was dying to see her face and smell her hair and listen to her ridiculously amazing takes on the world.

Fuck it. Izzy was more important than ethics, God help me.

I picked up my phone and sent her a text: I really need to talk to you before work tomorrow. It's important.

Chapter Thirty-Two

Izzy

The buzz of my phone woke me up, even though I'd been in the lightest of sleeps since turning in. I looked over at it in the darkness, and it was him.

I sat up and swiped through the lock screen.

Blake: I really need to talk to you before work tomorrow.

It's important.

"Fuck *me*," I croaked, turning off the phone and setting it back on the nightstand. I rolled over and let the tears of disappointment fall, mourning the relationship we'd barely even begun. I knew it was coming all day, but that didn't soften the blow.

I took a deep, jagged breath. I'd respond because I wasn't a jerk, but not tonight and probably not before work in the morning.

If he could ignore me for hours, I could do the same.

Only, when my alarm went off at six, he'd sent three more texts.

Two a.m.: Please call me first thing in the morning.

Four fifteen a.m.: I'm already up, so you can call whenever.

Five thirty a.m.: It's important, Iz.

Wow. I felt the *Iz* in the very core of my heart. He'd ignored me all day yesterday, and now, when he wanted to make sure the work bases were covered, he used that nickname?

Screw him.

I silenced my phone and dumped it into the bottom of my purse when I went into the living room to grab clean underwear out of the laundry basket. I didn't really need to have the phone handy since Blake was the only person who ever texted me anyway, right? I showered and got ready for work, feeling miserable the entire time.

I was pathetic.

But when I got to Ellis and stepped into the elevator, I realized that I wanted to text him. To hear what he had to say and give him a chance to explain. Blake had always been a good friend—he was a very good person, that was clear—so he deserved my trust and patience.

There was no reason to assume the worst.

I rifled through my bag until I found my phone. I texted, What's up? You get tired of ghosting me and need an Izzy fix?

I kept the phone in my hand, expecting a quick response. What I hadn't expected, though, was for Pam to be standing outside of my office when I got off the elevator, pacing like she was waiting for my arrival.

"Hey, Pam," I said, hoping I hadn't forgotten an early meeting or something. "How's it going?"

She frowned before saying, "Fine, thanks. Can I talk to you in your office?"

Blake

I pulled the phone out of my pocket as I exited the conference room.

Izzy: What's up? You get tired of ghosting me and need an Izzy fix?

Holy shit, she'd responded. I felt my pulse kick up as I hit the button to call her.

It went directly to voicemail. *Shit.*

I glanced at my watch—nine thirty—and realized I was probably too late. Pam liked to get separations out of the way first thing in the morning, so Iz was probably already gone.

I pushed through the door to the stairwell and started down the stairs toward Izzy's floor. It was a stupid move, running to her office, but I felt like I had to know that fucking instant. I sprinted down four flights of stairs before straightening my tie, checking my phone, and then stepping onto the HR floor, trying my best to look casual and professional.

"Blake," Adam Carter, one of the new IT guys, said with a nod, walking down the hall as if it was entirely normal for me to be skulking about in stairwells.

"Adam," I muttered in response before turning the corner.

"Hey, Blake." Pam stopped walking. "I was just coming to see you."

"Yeah?" I said, looking past her, in the direction of Izzy's office.

"Yes. We finished all twelve of the separations."

That made my gut clench, which was stupid as fuck because I'd *known* it was happening. I tried for detached when I said, "Everything go okay?"

She nodded. "The Boston employees didn't seem surprised, for the most part, and I think they were happy with the severance."

"Good," I said.

"I felt really bad for my new generalist, though," she said, pursing her lips. "She seemed shocked."

I rubbed the back of my neck and wondered if I had any more Tums in my desk. I said, "It's never easy, is it?"

"No, but I think she's really young and was putting a lot on this job."

"Ah." I wanted to puke.

"She was one of those applicants who was so . . . *enthusiastic* in her interview that I just had to hire her. She seemed to really love it here."

I swallowed and wished she'd stop talking.

"So what brings you down to our floor?" she asked.

"Uh." I tugged at my tie and seemed unable to come up with a word. Any words at all. *What the fuck is wrong with me?* I said, "I misplaced my phone and thought I'd check down here."

She glanced down at my pants, where I was certain the shape of my phone was obvious.

I said, "I have to go now."

Once I was in the elevator, I pulled out my phone and texted Izzy: Are you okay?

I hadn't realized how certain I was that she wouldn't respond until the vibration of my phone scared the shit out of me.

Izzy: Fine. HBU?

HBU? I responded with I just saw Pam.

Izzy: Ha ha samesies

I hated this. I didn't want work to ruin what we had. I didn't want this hanging between us. I texted, So again—are you okay?

Izzy: I'm fine. Ellis is very generous with their severance packages.

I didn't know what to say to that. I texted, Can I call you?

Instead of her answering, my phone started ringing. Izzy was calling *me*.

I lifted the phone to my ear. "Hey."

"So I have two questions," she said, and the sound of her voice made me miss her like I hadn't seen her in years. "I don't want to be a hard-ass, especially since you've kind of been my favorite lately, but I need answers."

Fuck, fuck, fuck. "Okay . . . ?"

"Okay." She cleared her throat before saying, "When did you find out Ellis was firing me?"

"You didn't get fired, you were part of a workforce reduct—"

"Blake." Her voice was tight. "When?"

Fuck, I didn't want to answer that. I sighed and said, "Yesterday morning."

"Oh—wow." She breathed out a noise between a cough and a laugh that was definitely not good. "More than twenty-four hours."

"Well, I was—"

"Question two," she interrupted, sounding like her teeth were gritted. "Did you have any part in the decision that I should be one of the eliminated?"

I felt even more queasy than I'd felt before. "Yes."

I heard her shocked inhalation through the phone. I said, "But I didn't know that—"

"Nope. Blake." She talked right over me, her voice stiff and distanced. "You have no idea how much I respect your honesty. I'm sure you made the right business decision and didn't let your personal feelings interfere."

I had no idea if she was being sincere or sarcastic, so I said what was in my heart. "Please let me bring you a pizza."

"No." She cleared her throat again and said, "I mean, no, thank you. I have to go."

"Wait."

"What?"

"Are we okay?" I asked, feeling like I needed to brace my arms on my knees and put my head between my legs so I didn't pass out.

"I don't know. I don't really think so."

"Iz." For the third time that day, I had no fucking idea what to say. "Please tell me we can be okay."

"I can't." Her voice was louder now. "Because no matter how I look at this, we're not okay. Josh thinks you fired me so we can date—which I don't actually believe, but that's definitely a shitty scenario to ponder. And *I* think that VP Blake fired his most expendable employee, who he didn't like enough to give a heads-up or at least warn before she stayed up late working on reports that would never be looked at. So no matter what, this feels gross."

"I texted you."

"In the middle of the night," she snapped. "And all you said was to call you. That's not a warning."

"You have to believe me that I didn't know you were on the list until Brad told me yesterday morning."

"But you said—"

"I was looking at employee numbers and data when I made the decision—no names. It wasn't even until I talked to him about us that I realized you were affected."

"Wait, what? You told him about us?"

"Yes," I said, realizing I hadn't meant to share that yet. "I met with him yesterday morning to discuss it."

"Oh, my God, Blake—what if that's why?" She sounded even angrier as she said, "You told him we were involved? What if that made him add me to the list?"

"Come on—it doesn't work that way. It *didn't* work that way. It was already decided before he knew about us."

"*Us?*" I thought I heard her sigh, which made me feel like shit, and then she said, "There is no *us*, Blake."

It felt like I'd been punched, and I wasn't sure I'd heard her right. I knew I had, but she just couldn't mean it.

"Don't say that," I said, knowing I sounded desperate. "Please let me come over so we can talk."

"I have to go."

I stood there for the longest time, just staring at the phone in my hand after she disconnected the call.

Chapter Thirty-Three

Izzy

"To Izzy," Josh shouted, holding up his shot glass.

"To Izzy," his friends repeated, and they all tossed back another shot.

When I'd come home in the middle of the day, crying and carrying my small box of belongings, my cousin had gone into full-on supportive bestie mode. He'd taken me shopping to try to help me forget about my joblessness, and then he'd called all of his nerdy friends to meet us for an epic dinner.

It'd been a good distraction, but not good enough to make me *not* think about Blake.

Because how could he not have told me?

I kept rethinking everything that'd happened between us, and I just couldn't find a way to make it okay that he didn't warn me about the layoffs.

"Drink it, Iz!" Josh yelled over the noise of the bar, and I

did. I tossed back the Vegas Bomb, happily allowing my tipsi-
ness to catch a buzz that I hoped would morph into full-scale
drunkenness.

Because it'd been a *very* shitty day that I'd like to forget.

Josh and his friends forced me to play darts with them, then
cards, and it wasn't until I was sleepy and close to drunk, on the
way home, that the conversation turned 100 percent in my direction.

The whole group was piled into the back of their DD's mini-
van when Josh's friend Chuck turned around in his seat and told
me over the headrest that I was too good for Blake.

"I like ethics as much as the next guy, but you can't keep a
secret like that. Not if you really care about the other person."
He stroked his pencil-thin mustache and said, "You deserve
better."

Josh nodded in agreement from his spot beside me in the
back row, his words just short of slurred when he said, "And he
should've asked you before he told his boss about your relationship. Total dick move, not talkin' to you first."

I nodded. "Honestly, I'm dying to know what he said. Like,
word for word, I want to know."

"Ask him," Chuck said, gesturing to my phone. "Make the
asshole tell you."

That made me giggle. "Should I?"

"Yes!"

I gnawed on my lip before unlocking the phone and texting,
What exactly did you tell Brad about us?

His response was almost immediate.

Blake: I told him that I started dating you the second I saw the updated org chart because I finally could.

That sounded really good to me, even though Chuck and Josh were talking about how douchey of a move that was.

Blake: Can I please call you?

I was about to text *yes* when Josh yelled, "NO."

"Give me that," he said, snatching the phone from my fingers. "No matter what your ultimate decision is, you have to be aloof in the meantime. You can't let that pecker think you're too easy."

I pictured Blake's face and felt melty. *Yeah—I am definitely too easy.* Still, I said, "I don't want to lose him, though."

"You won't," Chuck said. "Just let him spend the night thinking *he* might lose *you.* Trust us on this."

I looked from Chuck to Josh and decided that yes, I would trust them. I sucked at love and relationships, so they had to at *least* know more than me, right?

"Fine. Keep my phone and don't let me have it back, even if I beg."

"Donezo."

I regretted that the minute I woke up the next morning. I reached for my phone, only to discover it'd never been returned.

Awesome.

I sat up and looked out the window, and sure enough, his car was gone. Josh had gone to work and left me phoneless.

"Damn it," I groaned, my head aching as I flopped back onto my pillow.

I lay there for a while, feeling Big Sad about being jobless, but after a half hour, I decided to get up and eat. I was mildly hungover, and the only cure was going to be cold pizza. I climbed out of bed and shuffled toward the kitchen.

Man, did I feel like shit.

I grabbed a slice and a Red Bull from the fridge, then took them over to my desk. After waking the laptop that I always forgot to turn off, I plopped onto the chair and logged in to— *ugh*—LinkedIn.

Because as much as I'd like to spend the day loafing, the tiny balance in my savings account was pushing me to start job hunting immediately.

I clicked on the search window and typed H-R-Gen before noticing the little inbox flag on the side of the screen: **25 New Messages**. I knew they were all spam, but clicked into the messages anyway.

The first one was sent at eight that morning, from someone named Ashley Lea at MOA. I was familiar with the huge insurance company, but no one named Ashley.

Hi, Isabella. We currently have an opening for an HR Generalist, and a little birdie told me that you might be looking. If you're interested, please call me—I'd love to chat.

I took a bite of pizza and read the message again. It looked like a legit message, but that was just a little too good to be true, wasn't it?

I moved down to the next message, which was also sent earlier that morning.

> My name is Emily Fitzgerald, and I'm with Price-Harper
> Corporation. We're looking for a Senior HR Generalist, and
> your name was mentioned with a glowing recommendation.
> Would you be interested in discussing?

I dropped the cold slice onto the table and leaned closer to my laptop screen. What the hell?

I started clicking through the rest of the messages, and they were ALL employers reaching out to *me* about jobs. I couldn't believe it. Pam must've made some calls on my behalf—it was the only explanation. The woman was the *sweetest* and had felt horrible when she'd let me go, so that *had* to be it.

I grabbed the heavy old rotary phone that sat on my desk, a throwback relic that my grandparents kept connected to a landline because *you never knew*. As long as I'd lived there, I'd never used the old phone. Not even once.

Now, however, I was grateful as hell for its existence.

I lifted the phone to my ear and dialed the first number. It was a direct line to Ashley, the VP of HR at MOA, and when the woman answered, she behaved as if she'd been dying for me to call. She said she was *thrilled* to hear from me and would love to chat in person.

Two hours later, I had six very promising interviews scheduled. I couldn't believe my good fortune; like, what were the odds? *How is this even happening?*

But when I was on the phone with the seventh person, a Mary

Cartwright at Citibank who was going to rearrange her entire schedule in order to fit me in, it all started making sense. Mary slipped and mentioned Blake's name—"when Blake called"—and I made the woman slow down and tell me everything.

And that was the moment I knew.

Chapter Thirty-Four

Blake

I pulled up in front of Izzy's building, shut off the car, and texted, I have pizza, McDonald's, flowers, a six-pack, a gallon of chocolate ice cream, a bottle of wine, and a thousand apologies. If you'll let me come in, I'll give you all of it.

She hadn't responded to me since the night before, when I admitted I'd told Brad about us. And honestly—I couldn't blame her for being pissed. I should've asked her permission before going to the top with our relationship, but I'd been so fucking desperate to somehow have both Izzy and my integrity that I'd been impulsive.

And I was never impulsive.

Although, to be fair, I felt wildly desperate and maniacally impulsive at the moment as I sat there in a car full of bribes and a gnawing in my gut that worsened every time my brain said, *It's too late—you've already lost her.*

Lost her. As if I'd ever had her. I'd had a perfect weekend with her, but that was all.

I looked at her apartment window and didn't even know if she was home. Her car was still at my shop, but she was also incredibly adept at finding alternate modes of transportation and weird ways to get herself where she needed to be.

I *loved* that about her. *Shit.* I just liked her so fucking much.

When Skye lied to me, I'd been pissed and disappointed and felt like an idiot.

But somehow today, the possibility that I might've lost the girl I'd only been friends with until a few days ago felt far more devastating than a lost fiancée.

I got out of the car, grabbed the mountain of shit from the passenger seat, and walked up to the stoop. It couldn't hurt to try the buzzer, right? Technically I had the building code, but there was no way I'd be that creep who just let himself into someone else's apartment.

I shifted the stack of stuff and hit the buzzer, but after three times, gave up. I lowered myself to the ground and sat, knowing that if I went back to work I'd just think about Izzy and accomplish nothing. I might as well wait for her.

She couldn't be gone for that long, right? I stretched my legs out in front of me and settled in to wait her out.

"What the hell happened to you, Mr. Phillips?" Bob, the doorman, grinned and looked directly at my loosened tie, rolled-up shirtsleeves, and soaking wet dress shirt.

I just shook my head and kept walking.

Because I'd sat on Izzy's stoop for two hours, like a chump, hoping that if I could just see her, just talk to her face-to-face, I could convince her.

But she never came home.

And I might've deluded myself into thinking maybe she wasn't getting my messages, but right about the time it'd started raining, I'd seen conversation bubbles.

Finally, she was texting me back.

I'd stood there in the rain, my heart pounding out of my chest as I stared at my phone and waited for her words.

Only the words never came. The bubbles disappeared and she doubled down on her radio silence, which made me finally chuck everything into the dumpster and head home.

I was cold and fucking sad as I stepped into the elevator and rode up to my floor. It was barely five o'clock, but all I wanted to do was take a long, hot shower and fall into bed. I untucked my wet shirt and pulled off my tie, jamming it into my pocket as the doors opened and I stepped out.

I was on autopilot as I walked down the hallway, lost in my own head. A million miles away in my own pathetic thoughts.

I was so gone that I very nearly stepped on Izzy.

"Holy *shit*," I muttered, coming close to trudging right over her.

She was sitting in front of my apartment with her back against the door, her legs stretched out in front of her. Her head was leaned all the way back and her eyes were closed.

She was asleep.

I was scared it was a mirage as I lowered to my haunches.

How was she there? Moments before, I'd been filled with disappointment and exhaustion, but now adrenaline was pumping through my veins and I was wide fucking awake.

Hyper-focused.

On her.

Her breathing was soft, and her vanilla scent made me breathe deeply as I looked at her face. I reached out a hand and traced the curve of her cheek with my fingertips. "Izzy."

Her eyes fluttered open, bright and blue with butterfly-wing lashes, and she looked . . . introspective. Her eyes were everywhere on my face—my nose, my chin, my lips, my forehead—before she said, "Where the hell have you been?"

Chapter Thirty-Five

Izzy

Blake's expression was dark and unreadable as his brown eyes seemed to be looking for something in my face. His gaze stayed on mine when he said, "I was at your apartment."

"You were?" I couldn't look away from his intense eye contact, which was exactly at my level because he was crouching beside me. "Why?"

His forehead got a little crinkle, just between his eyebrows. "Didn't you get my messages?"

He'd been sending messages? I said, "Josh has had my phone since last night."

"Ah." He did that flex-unflex thing with his jaw, looking terribly serious. His voice was low and a little gruff when he said, "I thought you were ignoring me."

"Why did you call all those people, Blake?" I hadn't meant to just blurt it out, but the question was eating away at me. "It had to have taken you hours to connect with that many business contacts. Why on earth would you do that for me?"

He looked at my mouth. Swallowed, that Adam's apple moving as if to accentuate the gravity of his thoughts. "Don't you know?"

"Guilt?" I asked, feeling a shiver shimmy up my spine.

"Try again."

I drew in a shaky breath and wished I hadn't opted for the T-shirt dress, because my legs were getting goose bumps. The ability of Blake's face to deliver chills made the comfy-cute garment totally weather-inappropriate. "Charity?"

"Iz." Blake leaned a little closer, where his lips hovered just above mine, and he murmured, "Don't you know that I'd do anything to make you happy?"

I felt the world shift as I looked at Blake's honest face and saw that he meant it. "You should get out of those wet clothes." I climbed to my feet, grabbing his hand and pulling him up with me. "Were you in a wet dress shirt contest or something? Give me your keys."

He watched me, wordlessly pulling his keys out of his pocket and handing them over.

"Thank you," I said, taking them from his fingers, but I felt a little ridiculous when my hands shook as I unlocked the door.

The smell of his apartment when I pushed in the big wooden door—clean and somehow totally his—felt like a welcome.

"I'm going to change," he said, still looking solemn. "Don't go anywhere."

"I won't."

"Better not." His eyes were bright as he said, "I don't want to have to tackle you, but I will."

"You know," I commented, remembering what he'd said about sending me messages. "You could let me use your phone so I can read the texts I missed while I wait."

He kind of froze when I said that, making me instantly regret it. "Forget it. It doesn't matter—"

"No." He pulled the phone out of his pocket and dragged his thumb across the screen. "I just, uh, I guess you could say I was a little in my feelings while I waited for you."

That made me smile. "I cannot believe you just said those words, Phillips."

"Right?" He let out a self-deprecating laugh-cough. "I'm a fucking idiot now."

"Now?"

He finally looked like he might smile—but he didn't. He paused, looking at me, his eyes everywhere on my face, before he held out his phone and said, "Just don't judge me too harshly until I get a chance to defend myself."

I took his phone and felt like I'd won something. "Deal."

He disappeared down the hall, so I walked into the living room and leaned my backside against the couch's armrest. I found my name in his messages—**SBUX AMY**—and started reading from the last text I remembered getting from him last night.

Can I please call you? That was the text I'd received while in the van with Josh and his friends, just before he'd taken my phone.

The next message was from eight this morning. Are you awake?

An hour later: Can I buy you breakfast and we can talk?

An hour after that: I get that you don't want to talk to me and I respect that. But I really wish you'd give me five minutes. Just hear me out, and then you can go back to hating me if you want.

Two hours later: I have pizza, McDonald's, flowers, a six-pack, a gallon of chocolate ice cream, a bottle of wine, and a thousand apologies. If you'll let me come in, I'll give you all of it.

Twenty minutes after that: I'm waiting on your porch. Please don't think I'm a stalker, but I can't focus on anything but you—us—so I might as well just wait until you get here.

Ten minutes later: There is a squirrel approaching and he looks hungry. I'm scared.

Ten minutes after that: Fuck, here's the thing, Iz. I like you more than I've ever liked anyone, okay? I love the language you use and the weird way you think and the smell of your hair and the way you make me laugh and the way you eat pizza more than any human ever should and I miss you.

One minute later: My apologies for the run-on sentence. Also I KNOW that it's stupid to miss you when it's only been a day, but somehow I do.

Two minutes later: I will do whatever it takes to fix this because I think I love you. I know it's too soon and swear to God I'm not some pathetic clinger, but I just—

"Still reading?"

I looked up from the phone, and there was Blake, wearing gray sweatpants and a Cubs T-shirt, and the strength of the feelings I had for him was kind of overwhelming. He watched me, looking . . . nervous, actually, and I felt a little lightheaded.

So I just nodded.

He said, "If you need more time—"

"I think I love you, too," I blurted out.

If it weren't for the way his Adam's apple moved when he swallowed (yes, I was obsessed with that), I might've thought he didn't hear me. His expression didn't change one bit before he said, "What did you just say?"

"Well, I mean, I'm sure—"

"Fucking say it again," he said, closing the distance between us. In a second he was wrapping his arms around my waist and adding, "But slower, Iz. Please."

I set my hands on his chest—*the* chest. Where it all began. I repeated, "I. Think. I. Love. You. Too."

He set his forehead on mine. "It's weird, right?"

I let my eyes close and whispered back, "It's always been weird with us. Since the very beginning."

He pressed a light kiss to the tip of my nose.

"So where's all my stuff?" I asked, very nearly purring as he rubbed his nose against mine.

His mouth finally slid into a big smile, and he said, "The dumpster behind your building."

"What?" I pulled back to give him my best scowl. "You threw it all away?"

"Baby, I was depressed as fuck in the pouring rain," he said, teasing but also sounding serious. "I threw your stuff away with a shit ton of force and a litany of curses, actually."

That made me ridiculously pleased, even as I felt bad for him. I tilted my head and said, "Wait—am I baby now?"

He narrowed his eyes. "Do you want to be?"

"Will you please say the words 'Are you lost, baby girl?'" I said, just to mess with him. "As a sample so I can see if I like it?"

"You little pervert," he said, squeezing my waist and giving me a look of mock anger. "I will not table read from your favorite porn."

That made me laugh, because I hadn't thought he'd remember our tiny discussion about the spicy Netflix movie. "That movie is NOT porn, for the record; I already told you that."

"Just because you say something doesn't mean it's a fact."

"Sure, it doesn't."

"Iz."

"Yeah?"

"Can we stop talking now?"

"I don't know if I can—"

He cut me off with his hands, which pulled me tighter against his body, and his mouth, which landed hot and wild on mine.

Yeah—you don't have to tell me twice, baby. I kissed him back like a madwoman, my body infused with a heady cocktail of relief, gratitude, and primal lust. I panted like I was running as he opened his mouth wide over mine. His big hands came up to the sides of my face, his fingers flexing on my skin, which made me growl.

"Your dress is cute," he said against my lips, "and needs to be gone. I'd take care of it, but I don't think I can do it without ripping it off."

I reached around to the back and undid the zipper, letting the dress fall to the floor as we continued kissing each other like we'd been kept apart for decades. My hands found their way to his thick hair, and then he was picking me up, his mouth still feeding me heat as I wrapped my legs around his waist and he carried me down the hall.

"I love how big your hands are," I breathed, feeling his palms under my ass as he maneuvered me like I weighed mere ounces. "So sexy."

"I love how strong your thighs are," he said, lifting his mouth from mine and giving me a dirty grin. "And the way you always tighten them when I do this."

He lowered his head and bit down on my neck, which made me clench every single muscle in my body, which made him laugh and groan, all at the same time. I somehow managed to pull off his T-shirt as he carried me into the bedroom, and when he climbed onto the bed with me wrapped around his body like a baby koala, my feet managed to plant on the back of his calves and pull down his sweatpants.

"Fucking industrious as hell," he said. He laughed as he rolled onto his back, carrying me with him, and used his own feet to finish the job. "See, this is why I think I love you."

I felt warmth bloom, from the tips of my toes all the way to the top of my head, as he grinned up at me. I settled on top of him, sitting up and letting my knees lower to each side of his hips as I grinned right back. "Because I can take off your pants with my feet."

"No." His smile dropped away, and he raised his hands to the back of my neck, pulling my face closer to his. It felt like his dark eyes were my whole world as his fingers burned my skin. He swallowed and said, "Because you're this fucking gorgeous sweet weirdo that I am obsessed with."

My throat was tight, because for some reason it felt like the most perfect love declaration I could ever imagine.

"It's way too soon to say this, but I know I love you, Iz, just like I know Goodyear needs insulin to live and that I'm allergic to cashews." He was beautiful and earnest as he looked into my eyes and said, "I don't expect you to—"

"But I do." I blinked back tears and nodded. "I know it, too."

His jaw muscle tensed and his nostrils flared before he pulled my mouth back to his.

And then everything changed.

He was still delivering white-hot hunger with his lips and tongue, but it somehow felt deeper, like we were signing our names to an unspoken agreement, committing to something bigger via kisses and sighs. His hands tangled in my hair, and he sat up, like he couldn't get enough and needed to be closer, and I wondered if I could die from an overdose of lust.

I felt like I could and also that I'd be absolutely fine with it.

Blake Phillips was killing me, and I never wanted it to stop. He turned us again so he was above me, and I reveled in the feel of him: the weight of his big body on mine, the slide of his leg hair against my opposing smoothness, the heat of his skin.

The hardness of his body—every ridged, straining muscle—made me wild with need.

I trailed my fingers up his wide, shredded back, my nails pressing into his flesh as I urged him closer. More. I needed more.

Now.

"Blake," I said against his lips, shamelessly digging my heels into his soft sheets, rubbing against him as he continued treating my mouth as if it were a gourmet meal and he'd been deprived of food for a month. I managed to pant out, "*Now*," and "*Please*," without interrupting the delicious onslaught, and then I hissed, "*Yessssss*," when I heard his big hand rifling in the nightstand.

But Blake—Blake didn't stop. No, he continued inhaling me, devouring me, even while suiting himself up. *Hot damn*, I thought, delirious with want. VP Blake was a fucking rock star at multitasking. I closed my eyes and kissed him back with every single ounce of me, and when he pressed inside my body, filling me so perfectly, I already couldn't remember what it felt like to not love Blake Phillips.

Chapter Thirty-Six

Blake

"Come on, Shay—you don't really want to go home, do you?" I called out from the bed as she fetched snacks from the kitchen. It was midnight, and not only was I exhausted, but I really wanted Izzy to sleep in my bed all night.

"Of course I don't," she yelled back, clinking dishes. "But the Darkling needs food."

"Can't you call Josh?"

"He's still pissed about the puke," she said. "He won't help."

I kicked back the covers, got up, and walked into the kitchen. "What's his number?"

"Whose number?" Izzy glanced at me as she sprinkled shredded cheese all over a huge stack of tortilla chips. "Have I ever told you how good you look in a pair of boxer briefs, by the way?"

"You have not, and thank you. Now, your cousin." I watched

as she bent her knees—to be at nacho eye level, I was assuming—and surveyed her chip mountain. "What's his number?"

She spouted it off, still focused on her snacks, and I texted Josh, Can you feed Izzy's cat?

The response was almost immediate. I don't know who this is, but until she pays restitution for the puke, the answer is no.

I really liked Izzy's weird cousin. I texted as I went to find Goodyear, I'll give you fifty bucks.

Josh: No I'm pissed at you. Asshole.

That made me smile in spite of myself. I scooped up Goodyear and texted, Izzy's sleeping over—we're good now.

Josh: If you promise not to dick her around, this one's on the house.

I replied, You're too kind.

Josh: Tell me something I don't know.

I texted, Reheating mashed potatoes can give you botulism.

Josh: Is that true?

I texted, Yes.

Josh: Well thank you for that. Later, Physical Challenge.

I sent, Later, Josh.

I set Goodyear on the leather recliner—stupid cat loved to sleep there but couldn't get up without help—and saw Izzy through the patio door. She was standing on the balcony, gazing at the city, looking like a fantasy in just my long T-shirt and argyle socks.

Okay, looking like *my* idea of a fantasy.

When I pulled open the door, she didn't turn around. She leaned on the railing and said, "I love it out here."

"Same." I stepped closer, wrapping my arms around her waist and trapping her between my body and the railing. I lowered my head, inhaling the sweetness of her neck as I said, "Can I ask you a question?"

"Sure," she said, a smile in her voice as she ground her backside against me.

"Honey," I muttered, nipping at her neck. "Do you think you can keep the noise down if I was to lift that T-shirt, slide down those panties, and bend you over the balcony?"

"Hell, *yes*," she said in a near whisper, sounding half-amused and half-aroused.

"You sure?" I asked, biting down on her earlobe as my hands found her soft thighs. I slowly slid my fingers up the backs of her legs—fuck, she had the softest skin—until I was lifting the hem of the shirt over her perfect ass. "Because you're kind of noisy, and I don't want the COA to kick me out."

"Well," she said, her voice a breathy rasp that made my blood boil. "I guess you have a choice to make, Chest. Risk versus reward."

And then—dear God—she did it herself.

She removed the sexy layer of lace and presented me with a fucking beautiful choice.

"If I say I love you at this moment," I started, feeling dizzy with lust.

"It won't count," she said, widening her stance and making any remaining blood drain from my head.

"Grab the railing," I said, done playing. I was naked in a second, practically begging, "And lean down a little."

"You're not the boss of me anymore, remember?" she said,

looking at me over her shoulder, and then she moaned when I slid inside her.

No, it wasn't a moan. She sighed, but with volume.

I didn't know what it was called, that noise, but I knew it set me on fire every fucking time.

"Do you have any idea," I asked, clenching my jaw as I grabbed her hips and started moving, "how many times I've imagined this exact scenario playing out in my office, on top of my desk, and I was absolutely the boss of you?"

Her breathing was erratic, her fingers tightly wrapped around the railing, but the smart-ass still managed to breathe out, "VP Blake is unethical in his perverted fantasies."

"Only about you," I said, and then I didn't say anything else at all. It got too hot, too good, too overwhelmingly potent for me to remember what the hell words even were after that.

Chapter Thirty-Seven

Izzy

How was Blake's bed so unbelievably comfortable?

I opened my eyes and sighed happily, my head on the soft pillow, my body buried by the heavy down duvet. I was floating in a sea of dream bedding, bobbing in an ocean of warm comfort that smelled like fresh linens, and I didn't want to ever get up.

I rolled over, grabbed my glasses from the nightstand, and put them on. It was dark and I was alone in the bed, but when I sat up, I could see that Blake was in the huge walk-in closet on the other side of the room.

He was standing in front of the full-length mirror in suit pants and a dress shirt, tying his tie. *Dear Lord, the breadth of that perfect chest.* His hair was damp, his feet were bare, and I found myself incredibly smitten as I watched him perform the daily task of getting dressed.

So, this is how Blake transforms into VP Blake.

There was just something so . . . *intimate* about watching him ready himself for work. I froze, careful not to move a muscle and ruin the routine by interrupting. I wanted to memorize every mundane task for future mental playback. He turned to a stack of drawers that were built into the closet, and pulled out a rolled-up pair of socks.

"Good morning, Shay," he said, not looking at me. His voice was scratchy, like he hadn't used it yet, and something about it made me feel warm.

"How'd you know?" I asked, pulling up my knees and wrapping my arms around my legs. "I was so quiet."

He exited the closet, giving me an amused look as he walked toward the bed with only that sliver of light illuminating the room. "That's how I knew. Are you aware of the fact that you are never motionless—like, ever—when you're asleep?"

I shrugged. "I maybe toss and turn a *little*."

"I damn near got seasick," he teased, sitting down on the edge of the bed beside me.

"Did I keep you up?" I asked, wondering how he could look so perfect at six twenty-three in the morning.

"Nah. Your constant motion just served as a reminder that Isabella Shay was in my bed, which made me sleep like a fucking baby."

That made me smile, and then my heart grew three sizes in my chest when he leaned closer and gave me a sweet peck on the mouth, the kind of kiss a man placed on his partner's lips every morning before their days began.

"So, what are your plans for today?" he asked, turning his attention to his socks. Blake unrolled the pair, propped his left foot on his right knee, and pulled on the first sock. "Pizza in bed?"

I switched on the lamp and got up, stretching before walking over to the master bathroom. "I'm going to apply for as many jobs as I can, go for a long run outside, and perhaps take a nap because *someone* didn't let me get any sleep last night."

I flipped on the bathroom light and looked in the mirror. Gah—my hair was everywhere. I grabbed Blake's brush and attempted to get my bedhead under control.

"I'm not sorry, and also, I was thinking I can walk to work today so you can use my car."

I glanced over at him through the doorway. "I'm not going to take your car."

"Why not?" He got up from the bed and walked back over to the closet. "You can use it all day, and then I'll just force you to pick me up after work and stay over at my place again."

I'd be lying if I said that didn't make me blissfully happy. "You shouldn't have to walk to work, and also, um, you drive an Audi."

I heard him doing something in his closet as he said, "So?"

I turned on the water and put soap in my hands. "So it's too nice."

I started washing my face, in love with the smell of his soap, the clean minimalism of his bathroom, and even the fact that his expensive watch was sitting on the vanity beside a bottle of cologne. I felt like I was surrounded by Blake, and it was perfection.

I was just leaning down to splash water over my cheeks and wash away the suds when he appeared behind me in the mirror.

"Is it weird that I'm kind of *into* the idea of you borrowing my car?" His eyes were crinkly around the edges, his mouth soft as he met my eyes in the mirror. "Yeah, it's weird."

I turned around, my face covered in soapy lather, and I said, "Do you know how busy I want to get with you when you're weird?"

That made him full on smile and give his head a shake. "Didn't we talk about the phrase *getting busy*?"

I ran a hand over his tie and the hard chest underneath it. "Sorry. What I meant to say was—do you know how bangable you are when you're digging me?"

"Digging you." Blake put his hand over mine, trapping it against his sternum. "What if you drive me to work, then take the car to your place?"

I could've died of happiness when Blake stood there like that, *not* trying to be cool about wanting to see me again. I said, "I guess that works, but only if you promise not to get mad if I drive too fast."

He laughed, a rumbly chuckle that came from deep within his chest. "I cannot make that promise."

"Well, then I cannot—"

"For the love of God, Iz, rinse off the soap," he interrupted, laughing a little harder as he put his hands on my shoulders and turned me around. "Before you get foam everywhere."

I laughed, too, when I saw the big blobs of soap that were dangling precariously, about to drip off my face. My giggles got stuck in my throat, though, when I raised my eyes to his. Heat, warmth, and something more—wonderfully, perfectly more— hovered between us.

"I'm going to go take care of the boys before you distract me and make me late," he said, kissing the top of my head. "Think you'll be ready to go in twenty?"

I nodded and turned the water back on. "Yep."

"Want to stop for a latte on the way, Amy?"

"You know that I do, Chest."

Blake and Izzy

7:45 a.m.

    Blake: You home?

    Izzy: Yep. Just got here.

    Blake: And my car . . . ?

    Izzy: Totaled.

    Blake: Thank you for taking such good care of it.

    Izzy: I'm seriously obsessed with it. All I want to do is drive.

    Blake: You can, y'know.

    Izzy: I fear I might accidentally commit GTA and disappear from the area if I spend any more time with him.

    Blake: HIM?

    Izzy: That car is a sleek, fast, sexy bastard. TOTALLY a dude.

    Blake: Agree to disagree.

Izzy: How's work btw?

Blake: Fine. I think I might miss you (either that or I need some Tums).

Izzy: Can't you miss me AND need Tums?

Blake: I miss you and need a Tum.

Izzy: I can bring you one.

Blake: Without GTA temptation?

Izzy: Hmmm . . .

Blake: It's only been 30 minutes since you dropped me off. I say we hold off on the Tum delivery.

Izzy: LMK if you change your mind.

Blake: Will do. I have a meeting in a few minutes so I should probably go.

Izzy: I think I'm going to miss you. Or need a Tum.

Blake: Not "think," Iz—you KNOW. Try it again—all together this time.

Izzy: I know I'm going to miss you, Phillips.

Blake: Ditto, Shay.

11:15 a.m.

Izzy: You should come over for lunch. I'll make you something with the ketchup, soy sauce, and American cheese in my fridge if you're nice to me.

Blake: Damn, girl, you really know how to tempt a guy.

Izzy: Right? And I'm wearing my grandma's housecoat at the moment, so I'll even look sexy AF while I cook.

Blake: SO tempting, but I have no car, remember?

Izzy: I could come get you . . .

Blake: I have a meeting at 1:15, so there isn't really enough time.

Izzy: What if I make you ACTUAL food and I wear ACTUAL clothes? Then would you be interested?

Blake: Baby, you could wear any-fucking-thing, serving any-ass-food, and I would be frothing-at-the-mouth interested.

Izzy: Ooh—I'm "baby" again. Will you say it NOW?

Blake: NO.

Izzy: Pleeeeeeeeease?

Blake: What do I get if I say it?

Izzy: My mouth on your . . . 😏

Blake: . . . my what?? My WHAT, SHAY????

Izzy: Say it and I'll tell you.

Blake: SIGH. Ahem. "Are you lost, baby girl?"

Izzy: Gawwwwwwwwd. 😆 Get your ass over here, Chest.

Blake: No car and meeting at one, remember?

Izzy: Yes, that's right. Listen, don't take this the wrong way, Phillips, but I can't wait to see you at 5. I'm literally counting the hours until I can pick you up. Weird, right?

Blake: Absolutely bizarre, yet I feel the exact same way. I think we might've eaten spoiled meat or something.

Izzy: For sure. This whole thing is either love or spoiled meat.

Blake: Well, then—I spoiled meat you.

Izzy: I spoiled meat you, too.

Blake

11:45 a.m.

I pressed the buzzer and waited.

And waited.

I knew she was home because my car was parked out front, but she wasn't answering the door.

I texted, What are you doing?

Izzy: Job applications.

Blake: Aren't you going to answer the door?

Izzy: That's you??

Blake: Yup.

The door opened and there she was, looking at me with a crinkle between her eyebrows. "What are you doing here?"

I straightened from my doorway lean and held out the bouquet of daisies. "My one fifteen meeting was canceled, so I decided to take the afternoon off. Pizza's on the way."

She kept squinting at me. "Who was the meeting with?"

"Brad," I said.

"Why did he cancel?"

"He didn't," I said, wondering what she was thinking as her blue eyes moved all over my face. "I did."

"You canceled your meeting." Her face changed then, morphing from confusion to straight-up fucking sunshine. Her nose crinkled and her eyes squinted and her lips slid into a huge grin. "Get your ass in here, Chest."

She grabbed the flowers and went inside. I followed.

"I'm going to get a vase for these," she said, walking toward the kitchen. "Be right back."

I started to follow, but she stopped, put out a hand, and said, "You can turn on the TV or something. I'll be right back."

"Oh-*kay*," I said, watching as she disappeared into the other room.

I paced around the living room for a minute, but I couldn't ignore the noises from the kitchen. It sounded like she was chasing a mouse or something, like she was running and bumping into walls and knocking things over.

I quietly approached the doorway, and then I got that feeling in my chest again, the pinch, only it was the hardest it'd ever pinched. That fucking pinching feeling nearly brought tears to my eyes as I watched her try to hide . . . everything.

"Iz," I said, and she froze.

"This, um, is just . . ." She looked around at the kitchen, obviously trying to formulate some logical explanation. "Like a cleanup effort—"

"Did you go get all of this?" I asked, not meaning to sound so gruff.

She looked at me like she didn't want to admit it, but also like she knew I already knew. "I don't really think that's any of your business."

"Why?" I walked toward her, *at* her, crowding and stalking and just needing to be *closer*. She took a step backward, but I didn't stop until her back was against the counter, her front pressed to mine. "Did you actually get *in* the dumpster?"

She gnawed on her lower lip and shrugged.

I took her chin in my thumb and forefinger, raising her gaze, loving every expression that crossed the expanse of her face. "Is that the bottle of wine? And the pizza box?"

Some of the things I'd brought her yesterday—the wine, the gallon of ice cream, the flowers—had apparently been rescued from the dumpster.

The flowers were wilted and shredded and limply bending over the sides of a vase she'd put them in. The bottle of wine was in the sink, the label soaked because she'd clearly washed it; there was still a soap bubble on the dark glass. The ice-cream container, the pizza box—they were each sitting on the counter, scrubbed and drying.

Izzy sighed and looked embarrassed. "I just wanted to be able to save them, okay?"

That pinching feeling—*fuck*, it was going to kill me. Because it threatened to drop me as I looked at my dream girl, surrounded by my gifts that she'd dug out of a dumpster because she wanted to save them. *Because I had gotten them for her.*

God help me.

"Isabella Clarence, I love you so much that I can barely breathe. Please never change, okay?"

Her mouth curled into the sweetest smile and she said, "I won't if you won't, Blakey, um . . . shit, I don't even know your middle name. What's your middle name?"

"Clarence." I looked down at her face and tried counting the constellation of freckles on her nose. *One. Two. Three. Four*—

"Shut up—you are lying!"

That made me laugh, because I was *still* shocked by our shared middle name. I watched her excited eyes and knew I'd never get sick of the wild animation of her face. She gaped at me, her pretty mouth wide open, and I said, "Swear to God."

She blinked fast, then gave her head a shake, then wrapped her hand around my tie and gave it a tug. "This is, by far, the most shocking thing I've ever heard. Do you believe in fate, Mr. Chest?"

I swiped my thumbs over the soft skin of her cheeks—*five, six, seven*—and said the absolute truth that I felt in the very center of my soul. "I didn't until I met you, Scooter's Amy."

Epilogue

Six months later

Izzy

"I refuse. I will not do it, no matter what you say."

"Come on, Iz," Blake said, kneeling in front of me. "Just say yes."

"I would rather die," I said, turning my head away from him. I couldn't look at him when he was like that, gorgeous and half-dressed and giving me his hopeful look that was nearly impossible to deny. "And I probably *will* die if I do it."

"I won't let you die." Blake glanced at his watch before saying, "Pleeeeeease?"

I shook my head. "Why did I ever give you Josh's number?"

"Because you wanted to have sex all night and needed him to feed the Darkling, if I recall." Blake stood from where he'd been crouched beside the couch and extended his hand. "Get up and come with me."

"Have I ever told you that you look good in boxer briefs?" I asked, letting him pull me to my feet.

"A hundred times, but flattery won't get you out of this. Come shower with me, and then let's go kick some ass."

"How can someone so smart be so incapable of learning?" I muttered to myself as Blake led me toward the bedroom.

I'd moved in with him a few months ago, probably too soon for normal people but perfect for us. Everything had been amazing since the day I'd hung my Target outfits in the closet beside his Brooks Brothers suits, and I'd never looked back.

I had a great job at Google, working in HR, and Blake had been promoted to an EVP at Ellis. Our office buildings weren't that far apart, so on most Mondays, we still met at Caniglia's food truck for pizza and calzone.

Honestly, the biggest difficulty for us so far had been the cats. The Darkling didn't like either of Blake's cats, and poor Goodyear hid under a chair for the first week that I lived there, terrified. The felines were finally coexisting as of last month— basically because the Darkling never left the bedroom—so peace had kind of been restored.

Josh moved into my old place, thrilled to have an upstairs apartment *and* a downstairs apartment like a total boss. I didn't talk to him as often since I'd left, but he and Blake texted all the time.

Hence the Billboard Assholes challenge that my boyfriend was apparently too weak to refuse.

"Your cousin's idiot friends keep talking smack, Iz, saying

that our win was rigged because I'm good at push-ups or some bullshit like that. Josh needs to clear his name with his nerd squad, and we need to prove that we can beat them at *any* challenge."

"But we can't," I said, and when Blake stopped beside the bathroom door, I raised my arms so he could remove my shirt. "The game is impossible."

"Shay." He gave me a smile, one of those sweetly patient grins, and took off my top like he was my caretaker. "We won before, and we can win again."

"Doubtful," I said, but then it was my turn for shirt removal. I slid his Chiefs T-shirt up, letting my eyes and fingertips enjoy the pectoral exposure. Once it was off, I grinned and said, "Although . . . I kind of feel like I'm winning at the moment."

"Same. And the night we won at Billboard Assholes, Iz?" He pulled me close, his big hands covering my backside and pressing me flush against him. "The game wasn't the win—the kiss was."

I smiled, remembering. "That was going to be our one and only, just to see what it was like."

He made a noise that mocked our foolishness. "It was the gateway drug."

"Are you saying my kiss got you hooked?"

He raised a hand and pushed the hair off my face. "Honey, I was hooked the minute you felt me up at Scooter's, checking for a third nipple in those dirty-ass glasses like some kind of nutjob."

I laughed, felt exactly the same. I'd belonged to Blake since the very second I'd stolen a latte and accidentally become Scooter's Amy.

KEEP READING FOR AN EXCERPT FROM

Maid for Each Other

THE NEXT ROMANTIC COMEDY BY LYNN PAINTER!

Chapter One

WAKING UP IN THE BED OF A MILLIONAIRE

Abi

Was it wrong that a tiny part of me was happy to have a bedbug infestation?

Of course it is, I thought as I sat up and stretched in the decadently soft king-size bed. But who could blame me? The luxuriousness of the million-thread-count sheets alone made it way less of a hardship, not to mention the frothy memory foam pillows. Honestly, I wasn't sure how the wealthy *ever* dragged themselves out of bed in the morning when it felt so good to just lie there, cocooned in expensive linens.

But I didn't have time to languish in the opulence. I needed to get the hell out of there and get to work before Benny fired me.

I carefully made the bed, ensuring it was impossible to tell I'd ever been there. I was going to wash the sheets after I came back later, because I wasn't some kind of psychotic Goldilocks-coded monster who'd secretly sleep in someone else's bed without laundering away my DNA, but just in case someone happened to show up in the meantime, I wanted to remove all traces of the uninvited Abi Mariano.

I'd showered the night before, just to ensure I had time to clean every square inch of the bathroom (a *lot* of square inches, for the record), so I quickly changed and pulled my hair into a ponytail. Five minutes later, everything I brought with me was jammed and zipped into my backpack as I reached for the door- knob and opened the bedroom door.

"Well, good morning!"

I gasped and my hands flew to my heart as I looked to my right.

Oh God, oh God, oh God.

Standing there, in the enormous kitchen of the fancy pent- house, was a silver-haired man and a woman with a sleek black bob. They were smiling—*what the hell?*—but that didn't make me feel any better.

I was completely, totally, absolutely screwed.

The guy was wearing a flawless navy suit that was definitely *not* off-the-rack (hello, rich dude with the pocket square), and she was in one of those it's-just-an-oxford-and-white-jeans-but- they-cost-a-thousand-bucks ensembles. They looked like beau- tiful royals in retirement, perfectly put together, and they looked like they *belonged* in the upscale residence where I'd been squat- ting.

But they didn't look surprised to see me.

"Sorry, didn't mean to startle you," the man said, stepping forward to extend his hand while he smiled warmly. "I'm Charles, and this is Elaine."

"Abi," I mumbled, in shock as King Charles wrapped his big hand around mine and shook it confidently, as if this were okay and I was supposed to be there.

Way to give them your real name, dipshit!

"Abi!" The woman—Elaine, apparently—beamed at me like she'd been breathlessly anticipating my arrival. "It's so nice to finally meet you."

"Yeah, um, same," I said, unsure of what she could possibly mean by *finally.*

Am I in an episode of some pranking show?

Are the cops on their way and the Chuck/Lainey duo before me simply a distraction to keep me from getting away?

"I, um—"

"We helped ourselves to your muffins, by the way." Charles pointed toward the cooling rack on the center island, where the six face-size blueberry muffins I'd painstakingly made from scratch in that glorious gourmet kitchen the night before had now been reduced to two.

THEY. ATE. MY. MUFFINS.

I had bigger problems at the moment, but a tiny batshit-crazy part of me wanted to rage because those muffins had been the most delicious things I'd ever tasted. They were supposed to be my amazing breakfast for the next week. I'd planned to devour one perfect little pastry every morning before embarking upon my far-from-perfect life.

Only now, all but two resided in the digestive tracts of these two beaming socialites.

RIP decadent pastries, and a plague on the house of Charles and Elaine.

"They were so delicious," Elaine gushed, then added, "Declan never told us you were a pastry chef."

"Well," I said, my heart pounding out of my chest as I tried playing along, "you know Declan."

They laughed like that made sense—*what in the ever-loving hell*—and I needed to go. I pulled my car keys out of my backpack and pasted on a huge smile. "Listen, I'd love to chat, but I have to get to work."

"Typical Abi," Charles said in a she's-so-adorable tone, giving me just the nicest grin. "Will you be at the Hathaway dinner tonight?"

Typical Abi?

"I'm, uh, I'm not sure," I stammered, doing a sideways walk in the direction of the front door, desperate to escape. Because the quicker I got out of there, the better my odds were of *not* being arrested for trespassing. "Um, probably . . . ?"

"We won't take probably for an answer, Abi," Elaine said, running a manicured hand—*holy shit, that's a huge diamond*—over her perfectly coiffed hair. "No going to work until you say yes. We're dying to get to know you."

"Um, yes, then." Relief shot through me when I reached the front door and felt the cool metal knob in my palm. *Almost there.* "I will definitely be at the dinner."

I would say anything to escape at that moment.

"Oh, that's wonderful," Elaine said emphatically.

"Fantastic," Charles agreed.

"I have to go now," I managed, pulling open the door and giving them what I hoped was a charming smile. "It was lovely meeting you."

The second I was in the hall and the door clicked shut behind me, I made a beeline for the stairs, ignoring the elevator completely. I wasn't usually a fan of exercise, but I full on sprinted down all twenty flights of stairs, wanting to put as much distance as possible between me and whatever the hell that whole scene just was.

I had no idea why those strangers thought they knew me, but I definitely wasn't going to stick around to find out.

Chapter Two

DISCOVERING THE REAL-LIFE EXISTENCE OF AN IMAGINARY FRIEND

Declan

"Good morning, darling."

"Mom." I leaned down and kissed her cheek before taking a seat between her and my dad at the round banquet table. They'd flown in late last night, so I hadn't had a chance to talk to them before giving my little welcome presentation. "How was the flight?"

"Delayed," my dad said, lifting a piece of bacon to his mouth. "But uneventful. Great speech, by the way."

"Thanks." He was right—I'd fucking nailed it—but I still had the entire shareholder week in front of me, so I wasn't about to get cocky.

The Hathaway Annual Shareholder Meeting, where thousands of investors trekked to Omaha for a week of feeling like stock-owning rock stars, always kicked off with a breakfast meeting at the convention center. This year I'd been tapped to do the welcome address.

"He didn't even bore me while I ate my eggs," Warren said from the other side of the table, picking up his coffee cup. "The kid's okay."

The kid's okay.

It was ridiculous how much those three words meant to me. Because Warren Hathaway, the richest man in America and long-term CEO of Hathaway Holdings, had just spoken those words about *me*. The guy looked a little like the old geezer in that Pixar movie about a house with balloons, but he had a genius brain for business and had been my hero for as long as I could remember.

Right after I graduated from college, Hathaway offered my family (who'd taken my great-grandfather's tiny sofa business and turned it into CrashPad, the nation's largest furniture store) a multimillion-dollar buyout. It'd been a dream come true because not only could my parents retire early and travel the world, but I was absorbed into the Hathaway enterprise and given the opportunity to work my way up in a much larger corporation.

Suddenly the MBA that my uncles had called a waste (*you don't need college to work in the family business*) was guiding me toward the career I'd always wanted.

I'd been an EVP at Hathaway for two years now, but moving higher had been proving difficult because I was under thirty. No matter how hard I worked, it seemed, the guys at the top still saw me as a "young kid," even though I was twenty-eight.

But a disagreement at the QBR last month—where I was right

and CFO Marty Mueller was nearly catastrophically wrong—put me on the map with Warren, and suddenly my career was in new territory.

The old guy and his inner circle seemed to be forgetting about my age and inexperience and actually trusting my knowledge.

Fucking huge.

"We finally met his girlfriend this morning," my mom said to Warren, and it took me a minute to catch up.

What?

"You met his Abi?" Warren set down his cup and gave my mom a grin of commiseration. "I was starting to wonder if she was real, because no one's ever seen her."

"Right?" My mom laughed in agreement.

What. The. Fuck.

She *wasn't* real.

Abi was the name I'd given to my nonexistent girlfriend.

So how had my mother *met* her?

For what it's worth, I never meant to make up a girlfriend. I wasn't some adolescent who was too scared of women to date, for God's sake; I was actually a big fan. But I didn't have any time to commit to all the bullshit that went along with relationships. Work was my focus for now, and I'd worry about things like settling down after I turned thirty.

But when everyone in leadership had a significant other, well . . . desperate times called for desperate measures. I needed the powers that be to think I was settled and grounded and ready to lead the company, so when my personal life became a topic of conversation at the quarterly retreat, I might've casually men-

tioned my down-to-earth-and-wanting-a-family-right-away an-
gelic girlfriend.

Abi.

I'd literally looked at the label on the dessert wine and
named my imaginary girlfriend after a town in France; not a lot
of forethought went into it.

I hadn't intended on keeping the Abi thing going, but it was
convenient. It made my parents happy, my coworkers, my nana;
everyone seemed to take comfort in the fact that I had an Abi in
my life.

Only I didn't.

She didn't exist.

So what was my mother talking about?

"She's coming to the dinner tonight," my dad said to Warren, who'd become his pal over the past few years. "So you can
meet her then."

"She," I said, squeezing the bridge of my nose as my brain
ran wild trying to figure out what the hell could be happening.
"She, uh, told you she's coming tonight?"

"Yes," my mom said, turning in her seat to scrutinize me.
"But she looked surprised to see us in the kitchen when she woke
up, Dex; did you forget to tell her we'd be staying at your place?"

"Oh," I managed, trying my best to not look shocked that a
stranger had actually been in my apartment. "Ah, I didn't think
she'd be there last night. I thought she—"

"I'm so glad she was," she continued, as if I hadn't even spoken. "She's the most adorable little redhead, and she baked a
kitchen full of muffins that were to *die* for."

So this was real. Someone named Abi had slept in my apartment and made fucking muffins.

"Abi can cook, that's for sure," I muttered as my mind whirled. What the hell was going on? I lived in a secure building with a doorman. I had locks on my doors and a security system.

How could this have happened?

Who the fuck was *Abi*?

"I haven't had a good muffin since Ethel passed," Warren murmured, setting down his coffee. "Have your little Abi bring one tonight, okay, Dex?"

"Of course," I said, hearing a roaring in my ears as I gave him what I hoped was a casual smile. "Will you excuse me for a moment? I have to step out and make a call."

"Calling Abi?" my mother asked in a singsong voice.

"I'm definitely going to try and track her down," I said before turning away from the table full of watchful eyes and charging for the door. "Excuse me."

Chapter Three

THE MILLIONAIRE MEETS HIS MAID

Abi

"Would you like your receipt?"

"No," the woman said, grabbing her Lululemon tote bag and heading for the exit of Benny's Natural Grocers without giving me a second glance.

"Have a good day," I yelled before turning to ring up the next customer in line.

I hated this job, this perfectly easy and mind-numbing job. I'd worked at Benny's since high school, so it was comfortable, but every shift just reminded me that my life was stuck in quicksand that I might never get out of.

Hence my second go-round of college.

Hence my need for this job *and* my three-times-a-week overnight job. *Loans, loans, and more loans.*

Hence my propensity for thinking stupid words like *hence*.

"Hi," I said robotically to the next customer, my mouth on

autopilot before I noticed the person in line didn't have anything on the belt. I raised my eyes to the customer's face but then—*wow*.

I might've actually gasped aloud.

Because there were a lot of attractive men out there, but this man had to be the one they were inspired by.

He was tall—like six and a half feet tall—but no one would call him lanky. They would never. Broad shoulders filled out the impeccably tailored suit, and he reminded me of a professional football player when they did the long walk from the bus to the locker room.

Expensive.

Built.

Perfect.

And not to be messed with.

His face made that point even more than his impressive physique, actually.

He had brown eyes—no, green—that were trained on me and absolutely butterfly-inducing with their directness. It was like the man was staring into my soul, I swear to God, and his lips were turned up like he wanted to smile.

I usually didn't notice mouths on men, to be honest, but the bow on his top lip—or maybe it was the fullness of the bottom— drew my eyes downward as if it were a magnet and my irises were flecked with steel.

I could picture that mouth speaking French. Or Italian. I forced my eyes back up and offhandedly thought that this well-dressed man could actually be the cover model for any romance novel about Mob bosses, race car drivers, or grumpy billionaires.

I opened my smitten mouth to say, *How can I help you?* without drooling, when he said in a midnight-rich voice, "Hello, Abi."

"Hi . . . ?" I narrowed my eyes, biting my lip so I didn't smile like a lovesick schoolgirl as I tried figuring out how he knew my name when I wasn't wearing my name tag.

"You don't recognize me?" he asked, tilting his head, a motion that made his thick, dark hair move just a little.

Did I know him? There was no way I could've forgotten that face, right? I tried not to seem too flirty, but Joey Tribbiani's *how you doin'* was totally in my tone when I said, "Should I?"

"I would think so, since just this morning you woke up in my bed and told my parents you're my girlfriend."

"Oh, shit." *Oh shit, oh shit, oh shit.*

"Oh, shit, indeed," he repeated, his eyes judgmental under slashing dark brows as he watched me as if I were a bug he was about to squash.

My heart started pounding, and I was hot everywhere as this man stared me down with pure disdain.

"Benny," I yelled, not taking my eyes off the guy's face. "I need to go on break."

"You just had a break, Mariano," I heard from behind me, where Benny was ordering produce at his desk. He'd been hunched over the antiquated computer for hours, rotating between grunting, sighing, and scratching his bald spot, and I knew he wasn't in the mood for this.

"Mariano," the man quietly repeated, as if memorizing that morsel of information.

"I'm taking a break, Benny," I said through gritted teeth as I turned off my aisle's light. "Whether you okay it or not."

I pulled off my Benny's apron and gestured for the guy in the suit to follow me as my pulse skyrocketed. I'd been panic watching the door all morning, expecting the police to show up and arrest me for breaking and entering. It wasn't until an hour ago, when I ate my lunch at the table beside the big green dumpster, that I foolishly convinced myself no one would ever know it'd been me.

I'd been stupid enough to allow myself a deep breath.

"Swear to God I'm gonna fire you one of these days, Abi," Benny yelled as I walked away from my register.

"No, you're not," I yelled back as I tried not to hyperventilate. "No one else would put up with you."

"At least hurry, will ya?"

"I'll see what I can do."

I could sense Mr. Suit following me as I led him through the back of the store and out the door that opened to the back alley. Bright sunlight, warm air, and the faint smell of garbage flooded my senses as the door slammed behind us and I turned to face the guy.

Declan was what the royal couple had called him, right?

"Please let me explain. Declan."

That made his eyes narrow—*oops, should not have used his name*—but he didn't say anything.

"I'm not some sort of criminal, I promise. I work a few overnights for Masterkleen as a maid—I'm actually *the* maid who cleans your apartment three nights a week. So even though I was there, I didn't actually break in or anything."

Good point, Abi.

I gave him what I hoped was a sweet smile, an expression that would confirm my innocence.

He frowned.

"I had a key card," I said, "so it wasn't like—"

"You moved into my apartment for a night. Into my *bedroom*." His voice was calm, but he *definitely* wasn't interested in understanding. His scowl made that abundantly clear as he said, "I don't believe that's part of your job description. That's called trespassing. *Abi*."

Okay, the mocking way he said my name was straight up insulting and made my teeth hurt.

But I needed to keep my cool.

I tried again. "I know, but it was only because my apartment building has bedbugs. See, the property management company— who are total slumlord jackasses, by the way—said I had to find somewhere else to stay for a few days and I was low-key freaking out because I don't have another place, right?"

He stared at me like I was picking food out of my teeth, but I forged on out of desperation.

"But when I was cleaning your room last night, I thought, *Who would it hurt?* I knew that you were in London for the month—I mean, apparently you came back early, but I guess you forgot to tell Masterkleen—so I just thought I could crash for a few hours and no one would be the wiser."

His jaw flexed, but he remained quiet. I really wanted to believe he was considering my defense, but he looked like one of those über-controlled types who keep their mouths shut and wait for their adversaries to bury themselves.

Which meant RIP me, because I was the world's worst rambler.

"And I'm sure you don't care," I continued, "but I'm really

good at my job. I'm *great* at cleaning your apartment—you could eat off the bathroom floor. I mean, not that you would, because that's disgusting, but you genuinely could because I'm just that thorough."

He cleared his throat and looked down at his expensive watch, the asshole, and I realized that no matter what else happened, I was going to lose my job.

Oh, God.

This man was definitely going to fire me.

And I needed that job so badly.

I inhaled through my nose, gritted my teeth, and swallowed my pride, because what other choice did I have? "I know I have no right to ask this, but please don't tell Masterkleen. I'm begging. I really need this job and literally can't afford to get fired. Please don't tell my boss."

His dark eyebrows knit together, and he looked insulted by my request.

"Oh, I will *definitely* be telling your boss," he said without even blinking. "Because you trespassed in my home."

"Or," I countered, grabbing his right arm as I desperately tried to get him to understand. "I fell asleep at my job. That's not a crime, right?"

"I'm not interested in your justifications," he said, looking down at my hand so aggressively that I dropped it. "I just came here to see who the hell had broken into my place and had breakfast with my parents. Now I know."

"*Please.*" My voice cracked and I hated it, but I couldn't get fired. "Can't you just forget it ever happened? Like, just pretend I never stayed there."

"I wish I could," he said, shaking his head. "But you have no idea what you've done."

"Come on." God, why was he such a hard-ass? "Who did it really hurt, though?"

"Me!" He barked out a mirthless laugh and said, "Now my parents and my colleagues all think *Abi* is coming to the most important dinner of my life tonight because *Abi* told them she was."

"Why can't you just tell them Abi's not going?" I shrugged and didn't get it. "And why did they act like they knew me in the first place?"

"Because they think I have a girlfriend named Abi, for Christ's sake," he snapped, his voice full of frustration. "What are the odds my *maid* would have the same damn name?"

"So . . ." I was missing something, something that had nothing to do with my sleepover at his penthouse. "You don't actually *have* a girlfriend named Abi?"

"I do not," he said through gritted teeth, his eyes on the alley just beyond my shoulder, his thoughts no longer on me but on his apparently stressful situation.

"What did you do," I said, watching him attempt to mentally formulate a plan. "Make her up or something?"

His intense gaze snapped back to me, and I regretted the question immediately. His voice was dangerously quiet when he asked, "Have you ever been arrested, Abi Mariano?"

"Of course not!" My cheeks were hot even though I deserved the inquiry.

"So if I ran a background check, you would—"

"Call the authorities on you for stalking? *Yes*," I said in a near yell, frustrated he was treating me like a criminal after I'd explained the bedbug situation. Not everyone had piles of money for hotel stays or multiple residences, damn it, and it stung that my tiny questionable decision made him behave as if I'd stolen the family jewels.

But then he smiled at me.

He smiled, and whoa—it was *something*.

That grin packed a punch, sexy and dirty from the slide of his lips to the squint of his very green eyes. Declan's voice was silky smooth when he stepped closer, so he was towering over me, and said, "But you can't do that, because you've been trespassing, remember?"

"Stop playing with me." I swallowed hard and crossed my arms. "What are you going to do?"

"I'm still working it out," he replied as his eyes went down to my chest. "What does that mean?"

"What?"

His eyebrows lowered, and he gestured to my shirt with his chin. "Your shirt. I don't get it."

Of course you don't. The custom T-shirt shop behind my apartment had a clearance rack where all their mistakes were 80 percent off, so my wardrobe was full of tops that were off-center, riddled with misspellings, or downright stupid.

I didn't care, when I could get a shirt for two bucks, but I'm sure that wouldn't make sense to someone like him. I raised my chin and said, "What exactly don't you get?"

The shirt—my favorite shirt, actually—had a picture of a squirrel wearing underpants. The letters above it read *Hamilton Won Chip* and the letters below it read *Working for Under-*

wear. I couldn't even fathom what the attempt had been, but it made me smile every time I pulled it out of the dryer.

"Does it mean something?" he asked, seeming irritated that he didn't understand.

I made a face like he was an idiot for being confused and said, "Obviously."

"I don't have time for this today." Those green eyes moved all over my face before he said, "I'll be in touch. Answer my call."

And then he just turned and started walking away from me like a freaking king who had no more time for peasant interaction. I wanted to throw a rock at his perfect suit as he strode toward the parking lot in gorgeous leather shoes that surely cost more than my car.

"What are you going to do? What does 'I'll be in touch' mean?" I yelled, wanting to chase after him and force him to put me out of my misery. "You don't even have my number."

"I'll get it from Carl," he yelled, not even looking back at me.

"Who the hell is Carl?" I said to myself, frustration filling every molecule in my body. I didn't need this; I had enough problems, for the love of God.

"My doorman," he replied, apparently in possession of both supersonic hearing *and* privileged arrogance. "According to him, you two are thick as thieves."

I sighed and watched him disappear, my stomach sinking with dread as I wondered how long I had before the millionaire jerk destroyed my life.

Photo by Jackson Okun

LYNN PAINTER is the *USA Today* and *New York Times* best-selling author of *Better Than the Movies* and *Mr. Wrong Number*, as well as the co-creator of five obnoxious children who populate the great state of Nebraska. When she isn't reading or writing, she can be found binge-watching rom-coms and obsessing over Spotify playlists.

Ready to find
your next great read?

Let us help.

Visit prh.com/nextread

Penguin
Random
House